Jacinta Bell has bee[n]
long as she wants t[o]
Her story, *Tilting a[*]
winner of the Rhys Davies Award.
She lives near Rhayader, with her husband
and three children.

PARTHIAN BOOKS

Exiles

JACINTA BELL

PARTHIAN BOOKS

Parthian Books
53, Colum Rd. Cardiff
CF1 3EF
First published in 1988
© Jacinta Bell

ISBN 0 9521558 85

This book is published through **The Cambrensis Initiative** which is a programme of publication supported by an Arts for All Lottery Grant from the Arts Council of Wales.

Parthian would like to thank The Lottery Unit and the people who make it possible it for the direct support of The Cambrensis Initiative.

A CIP catalogue record for this book is available from the British Library.

Printed and bound by ColourBooks, Dublin 13, Ireland.

Typeset in Sabon by JW.

Cover design by Griffiths & JW.

From original work by Jessica Cooper and Gillian Griffiths. ©

For Pat

For exile hath more terror in his look,
Much more than death...

William Shakespeare

1

"Will one of you get off your big fat bum and come and help me here?" Ciaran's appeal could just be heard above the rumble of the traffic and the murmurs of friend greeting friend.

Becky and I looked at each other. She raised an eyebrow. "How can we resist an invitation like that?" she asked.

The steps we were sitting on were cold and hard, but they rested our weary bodies. Neither of us could remember the last time we'd been awake before midday on a Saturday - much less dressed and out in the streets - unless we hadn't bothered to go to bed the night before. Reluctantly we got to our feet and struggled through the crowd, treading on toes here, sliding between conversations there. "Oops...sorry...excuse me...sorry..." This refrain accompanied us along the obstacle course which divided us from Ciaran.

He surveyed us with the eyes of a jaded revolutionary. "At long last," he said. "Sure, I thought I'd be carrying the bloody thing all by myself. Has anyone else arrived?" For fear we might mislead him, his blue eyes scanned the crowd behind us. Ciaran certainly had presence. He stood solidly with legs apart, one hand clasping the folded banner, the other clenched in a fist, resting on his hip, curly red hair blowing across his face. He wore the statutory straight-legged jeans of the day, an old donkey jacket and Dr Marten boots - a veteran campaigner.

"None of my lot are here yet," I replied, "but you know what geologists are like."

He shrugged his shoulders dismissively and looked at Becky. "Well?" he asked.

"Tim was here but he's gone off to find a pub. He says he

9

needs a drink before he goes off on any 'silly, bloody march', so that's probably the last we'll see of him. Karen, Sue and Geoff have arrived with a crowd from English and Dave's here with some first-year students who don't know any better."

Ciaran glanced at his watch. "We should be moving off soon. I hope Matt makes it." He looked meaningfully at me. "He promised he'd help carry this bloody thing."

Ciaran's stumpy red fingers began to tug and fumble at the knot of string holding the banner together, whilst his eyes continued to stray across the crowd. Becky went forward to help. I was clearly redundant to the operation.

I didn't feel cold yet, but it was only a matter of time. It was one of those leaden, damp October days. Our bodies, enveloped in a gossamer shroud of chill, would gradually be penetrated to the bone as the day dragged on. I pulled my coat tighter around me and yawned. Perhaps my lazy colleagues had a point. We tough geologists liked to think we knew about the cold and the damp - we suffered it enough on field trips, so why put ourselves through it unnecessarily?

"Done it!" I heard Becky cry triumphantly.

I felt slightly apprehensive as I turned to watch them unravel the dirty material, stiffened by dry paint. It had been a last minute decision to sacrifice a sheet for the greater good of humanity. At one o'clock that morning, full of ardour and cheap red wine, we had telephoned my brother Matt, a graphic artist, and begged him to come over and design the ultimate banner for the march. By half-past-three we all agreed he'd reached the pinnacle of unilateral disarmament artistic expression, but in the sober light of day my confidence faltered.

"Wow!" I heard a shout of approval go up behind me as the vibrant artwork was revealed. At each corner flew a line drawing of a dove, Picasso-style. A deep green jungle scene of palms and ferns provided the backdrop for a centrally situated black C.N.D. symbol around which were written the words, NUCLEAR WEAPONS? OVER OUR DEAD BODIES!

I needn't have worried, Matt was good. I took the side that

Becky was struggling with and said, "I'll carry this side till Matt gets here." The glory was snatched away from me as I heard Ciaran cry, "Matt, you bastard, where the hell've you been?"

The crowd gradually started thinning out and moving off. Ciaran and Matt, after a moment's affectionate abuse, each took a side of the banner and strode off. Familiar faces from the Polytechnic seemed to congregate together under the ensign, smiling at one another amid the bustle, safe in the knowledge that we all shared a common goal.

I found myself walking with Dave, one of the English Literature lecturers. He'd been recently divorced and had spent many long evenings at our house discoursing either on the structuralist approach to Shakespeare or on the disaster which is marriage and the anguish which is divorce. He was good fun, but conversation at this stage of his life was limited. He was also very tall and the only way to hear what he was talking about, above the rumble of the crowd, was to watch his lips. I soon got a stiff neck, so I decided the best course of action was to join in with the chanting despite my English inhibitions.

"Maggie, Maggie, Maggie."

"OUT! OUT! OUT!"

Stewards in fluorescent yellow tabards ensured orderly behaviour as the police looked on stern-faced and bored. At the top of Piccadilly we could see the pointillist river of humanity flowing slowly ahead of us. It was breathtaking to be part of such a movement.

By the time we reached Park Lane cold and fatigue had usurped the early euphoria. People were grumbling about the discomfort of marching on tarmac and it was with sore toes and aching calves and ankles that we were disgorged into Hyde Park where the river swelled into an untidy lake.

Our enthusiasm was rekindled at the prospect of sitting, even though the ground was cold and muddy. The speakers had already started when we arrived. In the far distance undistinguished-looking figures stood awkwardly to the back of a massive stage. The loudspeakers carried their messages inadequately but we could pick up those words and phrases we longed to hear. "...Mutually Assured Destruction...Hiroshima and Nagasaki....Never again!...Peace, what peace?....the unacceptable price of 'defence'.....we will rid our country of all weapons of mass destruction..."

People, well-known then, but lost in the obscurity of recent history, voiced our fears and pledged support for the cause. There grew a oneness in the disparate crowd, which I'd never known before, a singularity of purpose. As the last speaker concluded her powerful rhetoric the crowd broke into song. The strains of "We Shall Overcome" filled the park - our hymn of resistance.

I abandoned myself to the crowd, which by now had a total and misplaced belief in its own power. Uncharacteristically, Becky, Ciaran, Matt and I joined together, faces wet, in a warm hug. As brothers and sisters we embraced, resisting the authority of the martial state.

As the crowd began to break up a shout went up. It was Ciaran. "So who's coming back to our place for a piss-up, then?"

* * *

Seven o'clock was way too early for a party.

By the time we reached home, depression and exhaustion had settled in. Peace was the last thing on anyone's mind. Matt had plans for the evening and couldn't come back with us. This upset Ciaran which, in turn, annoyed Becky. The resulting row between them, which took place somewhere on the Northern Line, was spectacular. The whole carriage got caught up in the fireworks.

Matt was the sort of person people wanted to be with. Older than me, he'd only recently taken an interest in my student life and I was pleased to have him around, although Ciaran's obsession with him was becoming uncomfortable.

By about half-past-nine the gloom was as oppressive as the

heady smoke haze which hung over the dimly lit sitting-room. Around the dark walls people huddled in groups, talking hesitantly and quietly under cover of the music, while others, overcome by fatigue, lay sleeping.

In one corner of the room Becky sat, aggressively reading a dull textbook, eyes constantly darting towards the open door, waiting for Ciaran to give up centre-stage in the kitchen, where an alternative, more vivacious party was under way. I could see she was hoping he would come to her with an apology and declaration of his love. I don't know why - their quarrels never ended that way. Invariably there would be a final dazzling display of fury on both sides before sleep, and in the morning an uneasy truce generally warmed up to normality by evening.

"I think I'm going to bed," I said.

Becky glanced up at me sternly, annoyed that I should invade her anger. "I mean," I went on apologetically, "there's only so much fun you can have."

Her face softened. "Claire, what can I do? What is it with all this bloody hero-worship anyway? If Matt had come tonight Ciaran would have followed him around like a lap-dog, drinking himself silly to celebrate. As it is, he's drowning his sorrows in the kitchen while I sit here on my own like a bloody lemon."

I had spent many evenings recently commiserating with Becky over the shortcomings of her relationship with Ciaran and I struggled to find new assurances of sympathy.

"Ain't life a bitch, eh?" She smiled and nodded. "Listen, instead of sitting here giving yourself an ulcer, why don't you and I grab a couple of cans and a joint and sneak up to my room to watch the telly? There's probably a film on."

"Okay. You get the cans though. If I go into the kitchen and hear Ciaran preaching on about oppression, I swear to God I'll hit him."

So we took our leave of the somnambulant guests and like two naughty children crept up the dark stairs to my cold attic bedroom, clutching our goodies to our breasts.

"Oh!" I was startled by the bright light and lone figure

sitting crumpled up at the end of my bed watching the television. He glanced over at us and hissed, "Ssshhh. It's the march."

Becky and I looked at each other, mouths open, and then looked back to this interloper. Eyes still fixed on the screen, he beckoned us in. "Can you believe that? Only two hundred and fifty thousand. Jesus, they're liars - it was nearer half a million."

"I wasn't aware that the party had extended into my bedroom," I said.

"Oh, sorry. I wanted to catch the news and someone in the kitchen said I could watch it up here."

I turned to Becky and raised my eyebrows. "Ciaran!" I said.

"And if I'm not much mistaken, " said Becky, "we have in our midst another bloody Irishman."

"Mary, mother of God and the saints preserve us from another bloody Irishman!" I exclaimed in my best Irish accent.

We laughed together and all was forgiven.

"You're one of Ciaran's Nationalists, are you?" I asked.

"What?"

"Ciaran. The red-haired Republican downstairs. You can't miss him, he's surrounded by a bunch of first-year students, proving to them just how 'right on' he is."

"Claire!" Becky sounded hurt.

"Well...sometimes he gets right up my nose, especially when he goes on about the bloody British."

"Let me know when I annoy you, won't you?" asked Becky.

"Not a chance. I'll save my feelings about you for Ciaran when you and he have another row. Here," I turned to the stranger, "have a can of lager."

"Thanks. I'm John, and no, I'm not one of his Nationalists. I don't even know the fella, though I'd not admit to it now even if I did."

He smiled hesitantly. He was not immediately good-looking but there was something about him - I think it was his eyes. Small and deep-set in his large angular face, penetrating and liquid blue, partly obscured by long dark hair and sad, always sad, even in laughter.

"You're not his friend from Dublin, then? He's expecting someone," said Becky.

"No. I'm from the North. Londonderry...Derry, but I've been in London for nearly ten years."

"Are you a student?" I asked.

"No. I'm with a friend who's at the Poly."

"What do you do?"

"Questions, questions."

"Sorry."

"It's okay. I'm a carpenter."

"How rewarding, working with wood," Becky said. I glanced sideways at her. John raised the can to his lips, stifling a smile.

"On building sites. It's mostly bloody hard work and cold, this time of year. Still, it pays the bills."

We sat together contented, television flickering in the background as the conversation meandered this way and that. Becky and I chatted about ourselves. We'd covered the same ground at school and since. Both of us had spent a couple of years as secretaries in multi-national companies. Things were going to be different when we graduated - Becky had her hopes set on becoming an editor with a literary publishing house, while I hoped my geology degree would take me to distant and exotic lands and pay me handsomely for the privilege. Oil companies paid well.

John listened attentively as the two of us carried on, laughing at our more outlandish dreams, but he said little about himself. I was intrigued and attracted by him and as time went on I grew restless and silent, willing Becky to leave, but she too was clearly enjoying his company.

It was Ciaran who finally relieved me of Becky. He put his head round the door looking red-eyed and dishevelled. He pointedly ignored John, which delighted Becky, since she recognized this as a mark of Ciaran's jealousy and affection for her.

"It's here you are, so! I've been looking for you. Come on now, Becky."

"Why?"

"There's someone I want you to meet."

"At this time of night? You must be joking!"

"Becky." There was an edge to his voice and she bowed to his authority, smiling. As she reached the door he dealt her a heavy blow. Looking at Becky, but talking to me he said, "Claire, Matt's just turned up. He's given the party a real kick-start."

I cringed inside for Becky, feeling responsible for her pain. He was my brother. "By the way, Ciaran."

"Yes?"

"Knock next time you come into my room." It was petty, but the only thing I could think of at the time.

He slammed the door and angry voices travelled down the stairs.

John and I looked at each other.

"He can be a right shit sometimes," I said.

"We all can."

I started to roll a joint, shy now that we were finally alone together.

"Are you living with somebody here?" he asked.

"No. I'm on my own. How about you?"

"Me too. I've been married, but it didn't work out."

"Are you divorced now?"

"Separated."

"What went wrong?"

"We were too young - I was only eighteen and she was sixteen. We ran away together, to London."

"How romantic."

"I suppose it might seem that way. It wasn't, though. It was back in '72, after Bloody Sunday."

"Shit! Were you there?"

"No. Siobhan - my wife - was. A friend of her brother's was killed right in front of her eyes, he was only seventeen. It was awful. We couldn't stay after that. Got married as soon as we got to London. Hard to believe it was all ten years ago." He paused. "We've been separated about a year."

"Kids?"

He shook his head. "Seems wrong bringing children into a world like this."

"I used to go out with someone who kept saying that. Now he's a father he's completely changed his tune. Twitters on about hope for the future and crap like that."

I lit the twisted end of the reefer, pulling the heavy smoke deep into my lungs, relishing the catch in my chest. As I held the smoke there I was excited by the intimacy of our conversation. I passed the joint to John, my head swimming. He drew from it in short, sharp bursts. The grey smoke curled up between and around us. We were quiet for some time.

"I should go now, it's late." John threatened to break the spell.

"Where do you live?"

"Islington. Off the Liverpool Road."

"How're you going to get there this time of night?"

"Walk. It's not far. I love walking the streets at night."

I took a deep breath. "You could always stay here."

He looked at me. "Are you sure?"

"Yes." He took my hand and moved towards me.

We looked at each other for a moment before kissing, tentatively at first, then longer and deeper. I felt his hands stroking, caressing, gently pulling off my clothes. I fumbled with the buttons on his shirt as he continued kissing me harder. His skin was so smooth, sliding against my body but his hands were rough and calloused, unfamiliar.

After we made love he fell asleep quickly, his breath deep and slow, while I lay awake unsure, wondering whether this was the start of a new affair or just a brief fling. I was ready for something more.

I was woken by the dull light of day and John's hands caressing my body again. He kissed the back of my neck and shoulders and hugged me to himself. I turned over and faced him.

We kissed and bit each other's lips over and over. His hands were between my legs, playing and stroking. I moaned with pleasure and anticipation, breath agitated by desire.

"I want you again," he whispered.

And so a new relationship was born, delicate at first but growing stronger with every story we told each other about ourselves and every time we made love. The afternoon drifted into evening and it was hunger that eventually drove us downstairs.

Becky was sitting at the kitchen table reading the paper.

"Thanks for clearing up."

"Someone had to do it," she said, looking up. "Oh John, still here? What a surprise."

"You know how it is," he shrugged, "I forgot the way home."

"We're starving. Is there anything going?" I knew I was pushing my luck.

"No. There's bugger-all in the cupboard and I'm not cooking tonight."

"Where's Ciaran?"

"Downstairs, finishing an essay."

"Are you friends again?"

"None of your business."

"John, what shall we have, then? Scrambled egg on toast? Baked beans on toast? Marmite on toast?"

"God, Claire, you're pathetic! Cook a bloody meal for once," said Becky. "If you hurry you can get some onions and tomatoes from the shop. We can do spaghetti. That is, you'll do it, I'll supervise."

John and I grabbed our coats and hurried downstairs. Outside I linked my arm through his and we walked close to one another. The air was sharp and cold, my face tingled. I couldn't stop smiling. We bought groceries and a couple of bottles of wine.

Ciaran had appeared when we got back and Becky seemed happier. I formally introduced him to John, each of us pretending that they hadn't met the night before.

"So, where're you from, John?"

"Derry, but I've been in London for years."

"Derry's a beautiful part of the country. I've an aunt lives just outside Letterkenny. I remember going up there as a kid - it was magical."

"Do you know Derry, then?"

"No. I've not been to the city and I don't think the Brits would let me in now - I'm too subversive, but sure, you must know all about that. Claire, do my eyes deceive me?"

"What do you mean?" I asked.

"Well, all this chopping onions. You look like you're seriously threatening to cook a meal. This has to be a first for you."

I picked up the dirty wet dishcloth and threw it at Ciaran. It landed over his face and we all laughed. There was a good feeling in the air - the early stages of love.

2

John and I spent all our time together over the next few days. Careless of the outside world, we were only interested in each other, taking time to get to know every inch of the other's body. Time well spent.

John was strong, working as a carpenter ensured that, and thin. I'd walk my fingers down his ribs, counting and kissing them. Sometimes I'd watch him sleep, face exposed as he lay on his back; heavy, black hair falling back in a dark halo on the pillow. His face, expressive and responsive when awake, would relax and empty in sleep, except when dreams troubled him. Then he would twist and turn, muttering, as his eyes darted about behind closed lids. He was new and unfamiliar to me, yet it felt as though we had always known each other.

Sometimes, we'd creep downstairs when the others were out and steal food from the kitchen. We'd sit huddled in blankets, sipping hot tea, like a couple of refugees. When we heard the front door open we'd jump up and run giggling to my room.

When we weren't sleeping or making love we spent long hours telling each other about ourselves. John listened well and I talked a lot, reflecting on my most recent relationship. It had been with a man whose partner was pregnant. I'd tried to assuage my guilt by arguing that Bob hadn't wanted a child and that his infidelity was the result of his partner's selfishness. It was so easy to be righteous then.

John talked a good deal too, but I was dimly aware of a secret self, a self entrenched in the past, which he couldn't yet share. Sometimes it felt as though he was measuring out parcels of information about his childhood or life in London to share with me and then quietly evaluating my reaction. Nothing he said surprised or shocked me, but still he remained guarded. He told me about his life with Siobhan and how the marriage had deteriorated over the years. He told me how communication had broken down completely between them, but not why. He still saw her from time to time, they lived close to each other, and remained friendly with her family. I was jealous of this faceless woman.

"I should go home today," he said eventually.

"Why?"

"See if there's still a world out there. Besides, I need some things."

"How do I know you'll come back?"

He laughed softly and pulled me closer to himself. "Come with me. See where I live."

"Really?"

"Why not?"

It was no big deal for John, but it was for me. With Bob I had been a secret, never allowed to step over the boundary into his home life, his real life. In that world I didn't exist. It was a relief to know John wanted me in his life as much as I wanted him in mine. By asking me to go with him, I could refuse. It would be good to be apart from one another for a bit and sharpen the edge of our desire.

"No. I'll stay here and tidy up."

As soon as I saw the back of him walking purposefully down the street, I regretted my decision. At the corner he turned and looked back, we waved to each other, and I let him go. I filled my emptiness with manic energy and started to clean the house. By the time Ciaran and Becky got back from shopping I was in a shining kitchen, drinking coffee.

"About time you did some bloody work around here. You owe us fifteen quid for groceries." Becky was in a mood.

I glanced over at Ciaran who just shrugged.

"Keep taking the charm tablets, Becky, they're sure to work one day."

"I think you should shove another tenner in for John. He's been here two weeks now. How much longer's he going to stay?"

"I don't know. He's gone home. Shall I ring him and tell him not to come back?"

"Oh, piss off!"

My happiness stung Becky now our roles were reversed. In the past she'd picked up the pieces and nurtured me when Bob came and went as he pleased. At that time I would have given anything for a relationship like she had with Ciaran. Not any more. Now I was the one falling in love while Becky and Ciaran were falling apart.

I decided to ring Matt, but he was out, so I 'phoned my friend Sarah.

"Where on earth have you been?" she asked.

"In bed."

"You poor thing. There's 'flu going round. Steve was off sick with something."

"No, Sarah. Not in bed ill."

She let out a shriek of delight and then started snorting with laughter.

"Whoever with? You're not back with Bob?"

"No, no, nothing like that. This one's single and available. Well, not any more he's not. He came back to the house after the C.N.D. march and we got together then. That reminds me, where were you?"

"Sorry. I forgot."

"You and the rest of the Geology Department."

"Are you coming tonight?"

"Where?"

"Peter's having a party."

"Oh."

"Go on, come along and bring this man of yours. What's his name?"

"John."

"I want to meet him."

"Okay. It'd be good to go out."

"We're meeting at the Royal Mail first, about ten. See you then?"

22

"Right. 'Bye".

It was dark when John got back. I'd bathed, dressed and made myself up. I wanted to please him.

"You look gorgeous," he said.

"You too." He was dressed in heavy denim jeans and a black shirt and jumper. "All dark and mysterious."

"Good. Maybe your friends won't ask me clever questions and realize what an idiot I am."

"Don't be daft. Just because they're all at college doesn't mean they're any more intelligent than you."

"Oh no?"

"No." I was surprised by his lack of confidence.

We met in the pub as arranged and arrived at the party as a student clique. Peter's flat was heaving with people - some I knew but many I didn't. Peter was a mature student with a substantial life behind him before coming to college.

I was proud of John. His fears were unfounded and he quickly became one of the crowd. He and Sarah got on very well. Anxiety growled in me. It was good.

With plastic cup of wine in hand, I took John to meet Peter, who was having a heated discussion with Ian, a technician from the Poly.

"...but they got most of their demands a couple of days later," Peter was saying, "of course they won."

"Don't be stupid. The government's proved itself. It won't cave in under pressure. They waited till the strike was called off before granting any concessions."

"Oh, come on, there must've been some sort of deal between Westminster and the IRA, agreeing to give the prisoners some sort of political status if they called off the hunger strike."

"You're suggesting this government negotiates with terrorists?"

"It was breaking down as a political weapon anyway." John joined the debate.

"How?" asked Peter. "The funerals were pretty bloody

23

political."

"Aye, but the men's families were stepping in when they fell into a coma. Thatcher used the love of their families against the strikers. Would you watch your child die?"

"So the families of the men who died didn't love them enough? Is that what you're saying?"

"No. It's just that as time went on people realized that the government wasn't going to be moved by the death of one, two or even ten men, so if their own son or husband went into a coma, they knew he'd die unless they took direct responsibility. In the early days, especially after the death of Bobby Sands - an M.P. don't forget - people believed the British government would do something to stop these men dying."

"Why should they? It wasn't up to the government. These men were terrorists. Murderers," Ian argued.

John simply shrugged; he'd said his piece so I took up the gauntlet.

"But the government has a responsibility to its citizens, even if they are prisoners. Besides, we did away with capital punishment, remember? I read the other day that eight, nine years ago the IRA prisoners had political status in all but name. It was only in '76 that their concessions were withdrawn. Why? They were the same men fighting the same cause. If one British government's prepared to see them as political prisoners then why should another say they're just criminals? Those ten men were killed by this government's arrogance."

"Those men had the choice to go on hunger strike or not. The people they murdered didn't."

"But this is war, Ian, and people get killed in wars."

"You sound very hard, Claire," said Peter. "I thought you were a pacifist?"

"I can't judge people who take up arms when our so-called democratic process fails them."

"But surely all violence, whether it comes from the British army, the paramilitaries or the RUC, is wrong? The only way forward has to be through negotiation."

24

"It's too late to talk."

"Non-violent direct action. It got the British out of India."

"Yeah, but you'd have to mobilize the whole population for it to really work. I don't know if it could be done in Northern Ireland, could it, John?"

I turned to him but he'd gone. I'm not sure when he left, but personal disappointment took over from political rhetoric. I hoped he'd heard my arguments.

I found him in the kitchen pouring himself a drink.

"Here you are!"

"I was thirsty."

"Why did you go?"

"I shouldn't have got involved. I usually keep out of arguments about home. People think because I come from Northern Ireland I have some inside knowledge. I don't know any more than you."

"But I do know about the situation over there, Ciaran's told me. Besides, I read the papers, I watch the news."

"Claire, love, it's more complicated than all that."

"Don't patronise me. You know as well as I do that reunification's got to happen sooner or later, it's just a matter of time."

He looked me in the eye. "Perhaps I do know more than you."

"And what's that supposed to mean?"

"Claire! Guess who's here?" Sarah's urgent voice made me jump. "It's Bob. Do you want to see him or what?"

"Oh shit." I wasn't ready for Bob and John to meet and my confidence in our relationship had just nose-dived.

"Will you come home with me?" John asked.

"Yes."

We walked back through the empty streets in silence. When we reached his tiny, empty flat John poured out some more wine. We snuggled close to one another on the sofa.

"How often do you go back to Derry?" I asked.

"Not much. I didn't go back at all for the first six years, until my brother was shot. I went home for the funeral. I've been back a couple of times since."

"You never told me you had a brother who'd been shot." I was stunned and a little excited to have the experience of the violence in Northern Ireland this close.

"I didn't know Billy that well. He was young when I left home."

"How old was he when he died?"

"Seventeen."

"Who did it?"

"God knows. He was involved in a lot of stuff."

Television news images flickered in my head. I saw John's young brother throwing bricks and bottles at the British troops. An idealist ready to die for the cause. I wished I'd met him.

"He didn't die in vain, John."

"He was a thug, Claire. Even my ma says so. I'm sorry he was killed - he was my brother - but he was a vicious little thug. Always had been."

My scenario crumbled.

"C'mon, let's go to bed."

It was my turn now to be John's guest. We carried on with our journey of discovery of each other. We argued our way round to the conviction that our meeting was cosmically inevitable and that we were two parts of a single whole. I think we were probably right.

3

The day was monochrome. Greasy rain fell from deep grey clouds onto dirty streets. I rushed down Parkhurst Road, chasing the rivers of rain which poured down the hill. The only thing unmoving was the traffic. Cars and buses, engines idling, pumped out noxious fumes. Heavy raindrops flickered and fell in the spotlight of headlamps. The inertness of the traffic underlined my own need to hurry. I had a progress test that morning and was late.

I arrived at college dripping, with seconds to spare. Turning over the paper, I was met by a bank of incomprehensible questions. Panic set in and I felt my breathing quickening. I searched for terms I recognised and started, half-heartedly, to bluff my way through the test. I jotted down sparse answers to questions about the Thames terraces and ancient pollen and when I finished, much too soon, I sat worrying about the previous night.

"I'm not going to be able to see you tomorrow," John had said.

"Why?" I raised my head from his chest and turned over onto my stomach to look at him.

"Siobhan's brother's over for a couple of weeks. I said I'd meet him for a drink."

"Can't I come too?" It would be our first night apart.

He paused. "It's just that Siobhan'll be there. I'd feel uneasy."

"But she knows about me."

"Aye, you're right. It's just me. I don't want you to meet yet."

I carried on arguing my point to no avail, fretting and

sulking by turns, while John stroked my arm, fussing and muttering, "Best not...Not yet.."

Eight years of history threatened my security with John and I was troubled by his gentle but determined insistence that I shouldn't meet Siobhan. The exclusion brought back the pain of my relationship with Bob.

"Hey, Dr. Stokes's bearing down on us, chaps. Who do you think he's after?" I asked the group I was sitting with. We were drinking coffee, smoking and commiserating with one another.

"Claire, have you got a moment?"

Sarah raised her eyebrows and pointed at me, "You!" she said.

Unlike Becky and Ciaran's lecturers, the Geology Department didn't fraternise with its students, except on field trips. At college a respectful distance was kept between staff and students and it was clear that today Dr. Stokes was on official business. I got up and followed him out into the corridor.

"The department's worried about you, Claire. You've been missing lectures and tutorials. I've just glanced at your progress test paper. You'll be lucky to get fifty per cent. What's going on?"

I looked at him, distracted by his luxuriant, grey beard. He was waiting for answers. I could have told him that I'd found my soulmate and was drowning in love but he didn't strike me as ready for that information, so I lied instead.

"I've had some problems this term, Dr. Stokes. Personal problems."

The shutters came down at the mention of the word 'personal'. Academic problems, financial problems, accommodation problems were within his brief; in these areas the man had power, but God protect him from female students with 'personal' problems.

"Oh, I see." There was silence. He knew he should coax out of me the cause of my distress but clearly he wasn't up to the job. In desperation he reached for his academic mantle, "I'm sorry to hear that, but think about your degree. At the end of last semester's exams you were doing quite well - you must maintain your results. We can disregard the results from this test only if you do well in the Quaternary Studies exam, but you've got a lot of catching up to do." He dropped his lecturer's tone, "You know the department's under threat. We don't stand a chance unless our results improve. At the moment your year are doing well, don't let them down." He resumed the distance of Head of Department, "If there's anything I can do to help, please let me know." He gave a brief smile and left.

"What was all that about, then?" asked Peter when I returned to the canteen.

"Oh, you know, 'could do better if she put her mind to it', that sort of thing."

"Well, turning up for lectures would help."

"Don't you start."

"I'm serious," he continued. "We've hardly seen you for the past few weeks. The Geology Society's ground to a halt since you stopped turning up for meetings - what about organising some decent lecturers or a wild field trip somewhere, Madam President? And whose notes am I supposed to rely on when I don't come to lectures, if I can't use yours, eh?"

"You never miss lectures, Peter. Anyway, I'm in love."

"I think the whole Poly's aware of that." He raised his voice, "Yes, it's official, Claire Marshall's in love."

"Shush!"

He looked me in the eye, uncharacteristically serious. "Don't blow it, Claire. You can easily be in love and get your degree. The two things aren't mutually exclusive, you know."

I was quiet. The others round the table murmured agreement with Peter's views. Peter wore his maturity with the air of one who'd already been there and done everything. He enjoyed the respect of the younger students, but the lecturers found him daunting. I was embarrassed by his concern but knew he was right.

"Come on Claire," I was jolted out of my reverie by Sarah,

"we'll be late for the tutorial."

So I stayed at college and at the end of the day went to the library where I worked until it shut. Studying occupied my mind and kept thoughts of John and Siobhan at bay.

I arrived home about nine-thirty - my spirits lifted because I felt I'd achieved a lot.

"Hi, Matt, what brings you here?" I was pleased to see him sitting at the kitchen table with Ciaran.

"You."

"Oh shit! I'm really sorry. I forgot we'd arranged a meal tonight."

"How was it, anyway?"

"The progress test? Don't ask. I'm late because I've been trying to catch up with everything I've missed. Have you eaten?"

"Becky made us an omelette." Ciaran said.

"Where is she?"

"Gone to bed."

"Already? Let's go down the pub. You look like you could do with a drink."

Ciaran looked shattered.

The bustle and noise of the pub was a welcome change from the silence of the library. The juke-box was on, bright lights around the walls lent a sense of well-being, and bursts of laughter exploded in pockets around the bar.

I got the drinks and took them to where Ciaran and Matt were huddled together at the corner of a table. I perched on the remaining stool.

"I rang Mum last night," Matt said. "She's concerned. You haven't been in touch for over a month. She wondered if everything was all right."

"God, has it really been that long? I'll ring her tomorrow, I promise. I've so much to catch up on."

"I told her you were in love and that she wouldn't get any sense out of you for another couple of weeks."

"Is that all you give it?"

Ciaran cleared his throat and spoke without looking at me.

30

"Matt and I've been talking about you. We think you're in way over your head with John. He's a great fella, sure, but you know better than anyone that you need to get a good degree if you're going to get anywhere as a geologist, being a woman and all. Besides, you're only twenty-two, you can't afford to be tied down."

"What's brought all this on? It's none of your business what I do with my life."

He glanced at Matt. "We got a letter from the housing association this morning. We have to be out after Christmas."

"You're kidding! I thought this was going to be a longer let." We lived in housing association properties which were due for renovation - short-term lets. Over the past eighteen months we'd moved around north London, living in houses and flats in various states of disrepair. We'd been led to believe that our current house wasn't due for renovation for another year. "Why so soon?"

"It seems they've money that needs spending before the end of March."

"So where are they going to rehouse us?" I hoped it wouldn't be too far from college.

"They're not."

"What?"

"They've nothing available."

"So what are we going to do?"

He took a deep breath, "Becky and I have decided to split up. It's for the best. You know we've not been getting along too well just recently." He paused, waiting for my reaction. I was speechless - it was no surprise, just a shock. I thought they'd stay together until we all finished college. "I'll be moving in with some friends over at Wood Green, and Becky's managed to get herself a place in hall. You'd get a place too. They give priority to third years."

I looked to Matt for some words of sympathy, some form of support, but this was not news to him. He'd heard it all earlier.

"Talking it over, we don't think it would be a good idea

for you to move in with John just yet - I mean not right now in your final year and everything," said Matt.

"We? You and who?"

"Ciaran was telling me how difficult he's found living with Becky and trying to study too..."

"Don't you dare compare me and John to Ciaran and Becky. And how dare you tell me how to live my life. Neither of you would know a decent relationship if it hit you in the face, so why the hell should I listen to either of you?" I rose to my feet and made for the door, muttering as I pushed people out of my way.

God, I was miserable. I lay on the bed wrapped in my coat. I hadn't dropped the blind or turned on the light or fire. The thick orange glow of London was the room's only illumination. My stomach started to churn. I wanted to move in with John, but with each passing hour I believed the love between him and Siobhan had been resurrected on that cold December night. The prospect of moving into hall filled me with gloom. I started to cry. Lovely, fat, self-indulgent tears. It wasn't fair. I was young and thought I had a right to be happy, to have all I wanted.

There was a knock at the door. I froze and said nothing, but the door opened anyway. In the shadow I could make out the familiar shape of John. Relief and self-pity overwhelmed me.

"What are you doing here?"

"I missed you."

Words I wanted to hear, but mistrusted.

"What's the matter?"

"It's just awful," I said.

I held on to my sadness a little longer, savouring the power and comfort of John's arms as he rocked me gently. Eventually I stopped and told him what had happened. Throughout my monologue he remained still and quiet. He listened with dedication. Then, at last, I finished and lay back in his arms sniffing.

It was some time before he spoke. "They're right you

know - Matt, Ciaran, your friends at college. We have to sort ourselves out. I'm having problems myself because I'm never at work." He paused. "I don't know how you feel, but I think you should move in with me, whatever the others say. I want you with me, all the time. What do you say?"

"I thought you'd never ask!"

"Mind you," he said, "I'd quite understand if you did want to move in to hall - all those eighteen-year-olds, the Rugby Club vomit-ups you told me about and sharing a kitchen with fifty other people. I can see the attraction, no, really I can..."

I turned on him, tickling and wrestling. We giggled and snorted and fell off the bed. He kissed me slowly and gently, then harder, with a fierceness I craved. I could smell beer and cigarettes - I thought of Siobhan. We grappled with each other's clothes, kissing, biting, squeezing - holding on to each other, afraid to let go. We made clumsy love on the cold, hard floor, tangled up in discarded clothes.

Shivering afterwards, we climbed into bed, still wrapped together for warmth.

"They'll think I'm doing it to spite them, you know," I whispered to John before falling asleep.

"Let them think what they like."

4

I hadn't seen Matt since that night. As far as I was concerned he was in the wrong and owed me an apology, but Becky had this sentimental last supper idea so I rang Matt to invite him.

"Claire! I've been meaning to ring you. How's tricks?"

"I'm moving in with John, after Christmas."

"Just like that, eh?"

"Yes. Just like that."

"I'm glad you didn't take any notice of me and Ciaran the other night. You're right, it is none of my business. I must have been more stoned than I thought."

"Ciaran's a bad influence on you."

"Maybe."

"The reason I'm ringing is to see if you want to come to dinner on Friday. It's the end of term and what with us all going our separate ways, Becky thought it'd be nice to have a meal together."

"Sounds good. How is she?"

"Brilliant! It's amazing, but since they decided to split up she and Ciaran have been getting on really well."

"No expectations, I suppose."

"Will you come?"

"Is it all right if I bring someone?"

"Sure. Who?"

"Don't ask. Knowing my luck it could all have finished by Friday."

"By the way, I finally rang Mum the other day. I'm taking John home for Christmas."

"If you want a lift I'm going up on Christmas Eve."

34

"Thanks. See you Friday."

Becky had taken it upon herself to prepare the feast. She'd bunked off lectures to spend the whole day cooking and decorating. When I got in, the house looked really festive. Paper chains and foil lanterns were hanging in the sitting-room. Holly and mistletoe adorned bannisters and doorways and the smell of cooking was overwhelming.

"Becky, this is tremendous!" I said, sitting down at the kitchen table.

"Oh, it's nothing really," she said, placing pastry holly leaves on top of an enormous apple pie. "Cup of tea?"

"You're going to make someone a lovely wife." I said it without thinking.

She put the teapot down and looked at me earnestly, eyes heavy with tears. "If only it could be Ciaran. I want him to see what he's giving up."

"Oh Becky, I thought you'd both agreed about splitting up. You seemed okay about it."

"It's Ciaran who wants to go, not me. I can't bear the thought of life without him. We've been getting on so well the past couple of weeks. I've been trying really hard."

"So all this, the meal and everything, is for him."

She nodded.

I'm not usually a demonstrative person but she looked so powerless standing there, fighting back the tears, that I went over and hugged her.

The evening got off to a shaky start. Ciaran arrived home later than expected, drunk.

He was oblivious to Becky's hard work.

"You're looking good, girls," he said.

"Women, Ciaran. Get it right."

"Oops, sorry. Ideologically unsound. Forgive the man and get him a drink."

"Get it yourself." I wanted everything to be right for Becky and was afraid he'd ruin it. Becky hurried into the kitchen to get him a beer.

"Ciaran!" I hissed as Becky left the room. I gestured at the decorations, the beautiful table she'd arranged. His eyes swivelled round the room. "She's spent all bloody day on this."

He smiled and winked. "Becky!" he called. She came into the room, beer in hand. "You've done a grand job. Really it's marvellous." She glowed. "Seems a shame to have to take it all down before Christmas, doesn't it?"

The doorbell rang and I went to answer it.

Sarah and Dave arrived together, having bumped into each other at the tube station. They'd met a couple of times and Sarah had told me she quite fancied Dave. The meal was a good opportunity for them to get together, especially since Dave seemed to be in a bit of a decline. Having spent months boring everyone about his divorce, he'd stopped going out altogether, except to work. I was pleased he'd come tonight. When I opened the door to them, Sarah was regaling him with stories of sheep ticks burrowing into her thighs during our last field trip to Aran. They were both laughing.

"Come in, come in. John's still not here. Matt'll be along later."

"What a lovely smell," Dave said as soon as he walked in through the door.

"And look at the decorations!" said Sarah.

"It's Becky. She's done everything."

"That explains why she missed my lecture today. Clearly her time was better spent here."

As I was getting everyone a drink Becky came into the kitchen, eyes shining.

"He's suggested that we spend Christmas here. Just the two of us. Then we'll move out on the 30th," she said.

"Oh Becky, that's great. What will you do then?"

"Still move into hall, but we'll probably see each other after that and Christmas gives me more time with him."

The six of us huddled round the small, decrepit gas-fire

which was turned up full. I was rubbing John's hands which were raw from working outside.

"Thank God the building trade closes down for two weeks over Christmas. You'll be able to spend some time in the warm anyway," I said.

"I don't ever remember it being as cold as this for so long and it's only December."

"You're a braver man than I," said Dave. "I couldn't work outside, not in this country, it's much too cold."

"Sure it's a good job that one of us is man enough to leave this room for the icy wastes of the hall and landing out there," said Ciaran, getting up to answer the doorbell.

We laughed as he left the room and chatted on about the chances of the snow staying until Christmas.

It seemed a long time before Matt came bursting through the door, tinsel wrapped round his neck, arm linked through that of a very striking looking young man. They were singing "Jingle Bells" at the tops of their voices.

"Oh no, Ciaran!" I shouted. "I told you not to let in any carol singers. They'll be demanding food next."

"Hi everyone, meet Dominic," said Matt. "It's his fault we're so late."

"Sorry. I got some overtime packing hampers. I hope I've not held you up too much."

"No," said Becky. "I'll go and dish up now. What've you done with Ciaran?" He hadn't reappeared.

"I think we've shocked him, but we couldn't resist the mistletoe, could we, Dom?" They caught each other's eye and smiled.

"It's the first we've seen this year," said Dominic.

"That we could make use of."

Becky and John went to bring things in from the kitchen. I heard raised voices so started talking loudly to shut out the conflict.

"Think of this meal as an adventure. The food's bound to be brilliant - I didn't cook it - but we're short of plates and cutlery so you'll have to improvise. There's probably not enough room for us all to sit round the table either."

We started helping ourselves from the dishes being put on the table. Becky came in and sat down at the table. Her cheeks were flushed and her hands trembled. I looked at John, who raised his eyebrows.

"Where's Ciaran got to?" I asked, halfway through the meal. "He seemed pretty drunk earlier, do you think he's all right?"

Becky, calm now, shrugged and carried on talking to Dave.

"He'll probably be up in a minute," said John.

But he wasn't, so after I'd finished eating I went to look for him.

I knocked on the bedroom door. "Ciaran?" There was no reply. I turned the handle and pushed the door open. A shaft of cold air hit me. Ciaran was staring out of the open window. I could see his red hair blowing in the draught and outside heavy flakes of snow rushed earthwards.

"Must be awful for the down and outs, this weather," he said without turning around.

I closed the door behind me and made my way through the clothes and books scattered over the floor. The bed was unmade and there was no shade to soften the glare of the single bulb hanging in the middle of the room. There was a feeling of dereliction - of a place where once there'd been love but which had long since gone.

I sat on the bundle of duvet at the foot of the bed and spoke to his back.

"What is it, Ciaran?"

"I don't know."

"Becky?"

He shook his head.

"Christmas?"

He turned around and looked at me.

"Why did you never tell me Matt was gay?"

I hesitated. "There was no reason to. It wasn't relevant.

He's my brother, the fact he's gay is incidental. Anyway I'd have thought he would have told you if he felt it mattered."

"He didn't"

"And does it? Sorry, stupid question, obviously it does."

"I feel so betrayed. For him to have kept it from me. And now with this Dominic, he doesn't need me. I wonder if our friendship counted for anything. We were so close. Now, to think of him with Dominic..."

I said nothing. This was a conversation he should have been having with Matt, not me.

"Come on back upstairs. Have a drink, you'll feel better."

He took a deep breath and turned back to look out of the window.

"I'd just spoil it for everyone."

I got up to leave, shivering with cold.

"Do you want me to get Matt to come and see you?"

He swept round and looked at me. Fear in his eyes.

"Dear God, no. I'm not ready for that."

In the sitting-room conversation had been subdued by full stomachs, warmth and exhaustion. I got myself some apple-pie and made coffee for everyone. Becky had ceased to join in and answered questions in monosyllables. At last she went to bed.

"What do you do, Dominic?" I asked.

"I'm working in town over Christmas. I'm still at school, studying for 'A' levels."

"How old are you?"

"Eighteen."

"Oh God, Matt. You're going to get yourself arrested."

"You wouldn't think twice if Dom was a girl."

"I know, I know, the law sucks, but be careful, please."

"Do you still live at home?" John asked Dominic.

"Yeah, but Matt wants me to move in with him."

"Oh does he? That's rich. What about Dom's studies, Matt?"

He ignored me.

"My Mum'd probably be quite glad to get rid of me. I've

got five younger brothers at home."

"Any sisters?"

"Two, but they're married. One of them's just had a baby. I'm Uncle Dominic!" We all laughed. He really was very young.

"That's quite a family," I said.

"We're Catholic."

"Ah, say no more. I suppose your parents don't know about Matt then?"

Dominic shook his head and looked down. There was a shadow over his happiness.

Sarah and Dave left together amid much nodding and winking and Matt took Dom home soon afterwards. They'd only managed to spend one whole night together during their short relationship, but Matt was plotting to change that. I was nervous that Dom was too young for the sort of commitment Matt needed. He'd been hurt so often, I didn't want to see it happen again.

John and I cleared the dishes and started to wash up. It was lovely to be alone together, reflecting on the evening.

"Did you see Ciaran?" John asked, plunging his hands into the hot soapy water.

"Yes. He's in quite a state about Matt."

"I thought that was it. When we went in to get the food, he and Becky really went for each other. So sudden. I've never seen them like that."

"We heard it in here. Only minutes before, they'd been planning to spend Christmas together."

"She was so aggressive. Made it clear Matt wasn't a threat to her any more. Like she was sniping from a position of power."

"They're such a mess, those two. Really bad news."

"Sarah and Dave seemed to be getting on though."

"Didn't they? All the undercurrents seemed to pass them by."

I was woken by a knocking on my bedroom door. I looked

at the clock. It was midday. As I struggled out of bed I glanced at John and admired his ability to sleep through anything. Becky was outside the door, red-eyed and pale.

"He's gone," she said.

"What do you mean?"

"He's left. Taken all his stuff and gone."

"But...I don't know...Maybe he's just taken his stuff over to Wood Green so he doesn't have to do it later."

"No, he's gone, I know. We had a huge row last night. It was awful. I said some terrible things and when I woke up he'd taken all his stuff and gone."

"Let's go and make some tea."

She sat at the kitchen table quiet and still, as I busied myself with kettles and teabags. I placed the mug of mud-coloured liquid in front of her, she cupped her hands around it for warmth.

"I'll ring round some friends, see if he's there," she said.

"Is that wise?"

"What else can I do?"

"But what are you going to do if you do find him?"

"Apologise. Ask him to come back."

"But Becky, you and Ciaran have lurched from crisis to crisis over the past few months. I know it sounds hard but it'd be best if you just put it all behind you."

She made no reply. The effort of talking seemed too much for her. She reached for a cigarette and lit it. She inhaled deeply and started coughing, thick, relentless rasps which tangled up with tears. Her thin frame shook rhythmically and she stamped her foot over and over, shouting, as she gasped for air, "It's not fair. It's not bloody fair!"

I let her be and watched her distress helplessly. John came into the kitchen looking worried. He looked to me for explanation.

"Ciaran's gone."

Unafraid, he went over to Becky and knelt by her chair. He took her cigarette from her and stubbed it out. He held both her hands in his and looked up at her. His effect on her was dramatic. Hysteria left her and she relaxed, sobbing gently. Watching John I felt so sorry for Becky - she had no one now.

"You've not slept, have you?" John asked.

She shook her head.

"You should get some rest then you'll know what to do."

I put the kettle on and filled a hot water bottle while Becky lit another cigarette.

"Come on then," John said when she'd finished.

We took her down to her room and settled her in bed, like worried parents fussing over a sick child.

"We'll be in the sitting-room if you need anything," I said.

"You've got a good man there," Becky said, echoing my earlier thoughts. "Take care of him."

As we walked back upstairs John put his arm around me, "I love you," he said.

I turned to look at him. Words I vowed I'd never say again came spilling out, "Don't ever leave me like that."

5

"So what time was this?" I asked Matt.

"I don't know, about five or six."

We were facing west on the M4, trapped in a traffic jam. Matt was telling us about the visit he'd had from Ciaran the morning after the dinner-party.

"How did he look?" asked John.

"Awful. I don't know who'd upset him most, me or Becky. He felt we'd both turned on him. Said he hoped Dom wouldn't come between us and that we could still be friends."

"What did you say?"

"What could I say? We both know it'll be different, but I had to go through the motions. I admit I'm a coward letting him know the way I did, but it seemed the only way. It'd got to the point where I couldn't actually tell him."

"So he went home?" asked John.

"Yes. Said he wanted to go back to Dublin for Christmas but didn't have the fare. I gave him some money and took him to the station."

"That got him out of your hair, then," I said, leaning back in the seat and sulking on Ciaran's behalf all the way to the Severn Bridge, where we got stuck in another traffic jam.

I was glad to be sitting doing nothing. My arms and shoulders ached from helping Becky move her stuff into hall the day before. It had been a grim, laborious task, made even more tedious by the fact that her room was on the second floor and the lifts weren't working. Her room was tiny - scarcely big enough to contain all her belongings.

"It'll be okay when I've unpacked," she'd said. "Dad's picking me up tomorrow anyway, so I can take some stuff home."

Uneasily, John and I had left her to her dreary task. On the way out we passed a couple of foreign students - outsiders abandoned in a remote land at the turn of the year.

As we slowly edged our way north, up the Wye valley, my excitement grew. I was really looking forward to my parents meeting John. I knew they'd like him. I'd made all sorts of plans - long walks by the river and up on the hills, overlooking frozen reservoirs. I'd take him to my favourite pubs and promenade through the town so that everyone could see him.

The snow wasn't as heavy in Wales as it had been in London, but it was freezing, promising a white Christmas. As we drove over the bridge into Cwmdauddwr I caught sight of the cottage across the park. Bright lights shone through the windows and thick, grey smoke swirled out of the chimney.

"Hello everyone!" My mother greeted us. "I wondered if you'd be able to get through with all the snow at your end and Christmas traffic at the Bridge. You must be John. I'm so pleased to meet you. Claire's told me such a lot about you. Go on into the warm. Matthew, push the dogs out the way, they'll never let you in. Betsy, Gelert - basket!" They took no notice.

As we fought our way past the dogs into the cottage I was relieved to see that the place hadn't changed. The huge kitchen, centre of our family's life, had recently been whitewashed, but all the old furniture had been returned to its rightful place. Even the cooking area still housed the utilitarian fridge and cooker which I remembered from childhood.

The smell of woodsmoke and cooking filled the air. Paper chains, tinsel and familiar seasonal greenery gathered from the hedges along the back road, hung in the usual places. In my personal world of flux, here was stability.

"Where's Dad?" I asked. Even his absence was routine.

"Where do you think? He's got a surgery this evening and I'm afraid he's on call tomorrow and Boxing Day. He's got himself a new Land Rover - he's like a child with a new toy, but at least he'll be able to reach virtually all the farms now, whatever the weather."

We sat around the fire drinking tea and eating mince pies, catching up on local gossip. My mother asked John about himself and seemed satisfied with what she heard, although the fact that he wasn't actually divorced troubled her.

Matt tried to tell her about Dominic, but she grew distant, she didn't want to know. She'd known for some time that Matt was gay and had tried, unsuccessfully, to accept it. When my father returned she fled to the safety of her cooker and prepared the meal.

"Claire, Matthew - and you must be John, how do you do?"

After dinner we went to the little pub at the top of the road and had a couple of drinks. My mother had dug out a battered old game of Cluedo to play when we came in, in spite of the fact some of the pieces and most of the lists were missing. When we finished that we played charades until my parents gave up on our childish giggles and went to bed. Matt rolled a joint and I looked across at John. I'd never seen him so relaxed as he was that evening, away from life in London.

"What were your Christmases like when you were a kid?" Matt asked him.

"Different. This is better." That was all he said and in the absence of any further explanation I embellished my picture of his family - numerous, poor and discriminated against.

I squeezed John's hand and whispered, "This is going to be your best Christmas ever. Wait and see."

Before we struggled off to bed we hung socks from the mantelpiece.

"You have to be kidding," said John. "Father Christmas still visits?"

"You bet. When I come back home I'm a kid again and don't you tell my Mum and Dad any different."

I woke early on Christmas morning and watched John as he lay sleeping - my mother had been liberal-minded enough to put us in the same room. He slept deeply, breathing in before a second's pause, a beat in time, and a smooth breath out again. Just over two months previously I hadn't known this man who shared my bed, in my family home. I wanted him to wake up so that we could start Christmas Day together but knew I should let him sleep on; he usually had to get up so early for work.

I kissed his cheek and eyes and whispered, "Happy Christmas!" His eyes opened a little, unfocussed. "Happy Christmas, John."

His eyelids closed and he pulled me to lie with him.

"I love you," he murmured but was dreaming again within seconds.

I dressed clumsily and, when I was done, kissed him again, still hopeful that he might wake up. He didn't and compassion got the better of me. I let him sleep on.

When I got downstairs Matt was putting his coat on.

"Look at all those," he pointed to a stack of presents under the tree, which stood in the alcove near the fire.

"And the stockings. When did they do all that?"

"It was Father Christmas, stupid! I'm going to take the dogs out. Want to come?"

"Where to?"

"I don't know. The junction pool?"

"I want to be back before John gets up."

"You'll have to bloody run then, won't you?"

Night was only just giving way to a watery grey daylight. There'd been another frost overnight and the new fall of snow had frozen over. Even the dogs had trouble getting up the steep slope of the road at the back of the cottage. Now firmly entrenched in our childhood roles, we slid over the ice and threw snowballs at each other, breathless with cold and laughter.

"If only it could always be like this," Matt said.

"It'd be bloody cold!"

"No. This easy."

"What do you mean?"

"Sometimes I just wish I could conform. It'd make my life

so much easier, but I am what I am, that's all there is to it."

I didn't know what to say.

"Mum and Dad still don't accept it. It's been three and a half years since I told them and they were great then. Told me they'd always love me, no matter what - well, Mum did anyway. But things have cooled off. They never ask about my friends or if I've got a partner and you saw what Mum was like yesterday when I started telling her about Dom. I'm jealous of you, you know, Claire. Jealous that they like John so much and make it obvious."

"Why don't you bring Dom home some time? It would do them good to see you and him together. They'd realise how happy you were and how natural it all is."

"No."

"Honestly, you should give it a try."

"Maybe."

"There is one thing though."

"What's that?"

"Make sure he's not wearing his school shorts when you bring him, won't you? You dirty old cradle-snatcher, you!"

He pushed me into a bank of snow and tried piling snow on top of me. We giggled and fought. Eventually we arrived home chilled to the bone and soaking wet.

"Let's spy on them," I suggested. "Like we used to, remember?"

Holding our breath and trying not to laugh we crept round to the back of the cottage. We peered in through the window. My mother was cooking, moving quickly from fridge to cooker to sink and back again in a domestic dance. Her activity created a draught which set the tinsel and Christmas cards fluttering. I was disappointed to see John already dressed. He was kneeling on the hearth rug making up the fire. Smiling, sometimes looking over to my mother, I saw his mouth moving - responding to her conversation. As she came back to the cooker to turn the bacon she was smiling to herself. Matt glanced at me. She could never be so comfortable with Dom.

47

She looked up from the frying pan and pointed the fish slice at us. We were discovered and, released from our silence, tripped over each other, helpless with laughter. The dogs leapt on top of us, licking and barking, joining in the excitement.

The hours of daylight were magical - eating, drinking and tearing paper from carefully wrapped parcels. John gave me so many presents - the leather briefcase he insisted I'd need when I became a top oil company executive and I loved the jewellery, earrings, a bracelet and a brooch in the shape of a peacock, but most of all I loved the small, tear-shaped geode, sliced in two, revealing shining crystals inside. He told me he'd made a special trip to the Geology Museum to buy it. It was beautiful. I gave him back one of the halves so that he could carry it around with him while I put the other half in my coat pocket so it would always be with me.

My father came and went throughout the day, but Christmas wasn't spoilt. Only when it grew dark and John disappeared into Dad's study to make some 'phone calls did everything fall to pieces.

"I'm going back to London tomorrow, Mum," said Matt.

"Oh! I thought you were going to stay a few days?"

"Work's really piling up and if I can get stuck in this week I shouldn't be disturbed by too many calls. Most people are off all week."

"It seems a shame to come all this way, and in this weather too, for such a short time."

"I'm missing Dom too."

She avoided his eye.

"I think I'll bring him up next time I come, okay?"

"If it means you'll stay longer."

"That'll depend on how you and Dad treat him, won't it?"

"Don't start, Matthew, not today."

"You'd like Dominic, Mum. He's great," I said.

"I'm sure he is, and he's probably breaking his mother's heart too. I'm sorry Matthew, I can't help the way I feel, so there it is."

John came in.

"I'm going back home tomorrow, John."

My mother winced. This was his home.

"To London?"

"Yes."

John was flustered. He looked from Matt to me and back again.

"Can you give me a lift?" he asked.

"What?" I was horrified.

"Something's come up. I have to go back."

"No! I've been looking forward to this for weeks. What's happened?"

"I'm really sorry, my love. It's Siobhan. Steve's just left her. She sounds awful." He kept his voice low, inhibited by the presence of Matt and my mother. I was loud, confident in my own house, among my family. My mother was washing up noisily while Matt, I knew, listened.

"So? Why do you have to be the one to go to her?"

"She hasn't anyone in London just now. They've all gone back for Christmas."

"Jesus, it's like being with Bob again. What about me? I need you here. What power's she got over you?"

"It's not like that. Trust me. You know you mean everything to me, but I still have an obligation to her."

"What if I asked you not to go?"

"Please don't."

"But if I did?"

"I'm worried she might do something to herself. It wouldn't be the first time. If I do go back tomorrow I could start moving your stuff into my place and you could always stay on longer here, if you wanted to."

"I don't want to be here without you."

"So come back with me tomorrow."

"I can't. It's not fair on Mum. All the trouble she's gone to and then everyone buggers off!"

"I know. I'm sorry. I don't want to go back."

"I'm going to miss you."

He put his arms around me and held me very tight.

"I'm going to miss you too."

I hardly slept that night, nursing my disappointment and jealousy. We got up early and after breakfast went for our only walk together of the holiday. The roads up to the dams were almost impassable so we followed the same route I'd taken with Matt the day before. We walked in silence until we reached the junction pool. I watched the frozen turmoil of the two waters meeting, remembering warm summers as a child swimming among the deadly currents.

"Why did he go?" I asked.

"Steve?"

"Yes. I thought he was a grand chap ?"

"Me too. Turns out he has a wife and kids back home. Siobhan'd planned to go back to Belfast with him on Christmas Eve and then travel on to see her own family in Derry. She wanted to surprise him. He didn't know she was going until she took her suitcase out to the car. Then the shit hit the fan."

"I thought they'd been together a while though?"

"Just over a year."

"How on earth has he managed to carry on like that for so long?"

"He'd go back to Belfast every three or four months, for a week or so. He told Siobhan his mother was ill. He must've been going back to his wife and kids - his youngest is only six weeks old."

"Oh my God, the poor woman."

"Which one?"

"Either. Both. You've not got another wife stashed away over there, have you?"

"Jesus, Mary and Joseph! I've a woman too many to worry about as it is."

We walked back arm in arm; the tension between us lifted. Having heard the details of Siobhan's abandonment, I was a little more relaxed about him going back, although I resented the hold she had over him and knew that the next few days would be dull and empty without him.

6

It's almost impossible to get to London from Llandrindod Wells by train. On a good day it takes over four hours, when the country is paralysed by snow it takes twice as long. We were more than three and a half hours late and, as we pulled into Paddington, I hoped John had waited for me.

I shouldn't have doubted him. There he was, scanning the faces of weary travellers struggling up the platform with their luggage.

"John!" I shouted, dropping my heavy rucksack. "Over here!" I ran towards him and when he saw me he started running too. We crashed together in an orgy of kissing and hugging. We alternated between examining each other's face and squashing our bodies together until we could hardly breathe.

I nuzzled his ear and whispered, "You waited!"

"A whole week. I wasn't going home without you. I've missed you."

"Me too."

"Let's get home."

We got a cab and snuggled in together on the back seat, touching and talking, happy to be together again.

Back at the flat, we fell on each other. Outside, the afternoon darkened to night while inside we made love, making up for the nights spent apart. Daylight came quickly, but it didn't matter; we had each other for a week before the old routine was re-established.

We spent the first few days living off nothing but toast, satsumas and wine. Morning was marked not by a regular time of day, but by a cup of tea which John dutifully went off to make once a day. Towards the end of the week, I padded out to the kitchen in search of something different to eat. I hadn't noticed the chaos in the sitting-room the night I'd arrived. Previously barren, it was now crammed with boxes and tatty furniture.

"Shit! Is all this stuff mine?"

John came in from the bedroom. "It is. I was nervous of throwing anything away, so just packed the lot into boxes and brought it round."

"I hadn't realized it was such a huge job. Thanks for doing it all for me."

"Matt helped out too and Becky dropped by once when I was there, so she could tell me which of the kitchen stuff was yours."

"What kitchen stuff?"

"None of it!" he said. "Seems you don't even own a frying pan."

"I wouldn't know what to do with it."

"That's roughly what Becky said, only not so politely."

"Do you mind?"

"What?"

"That I'm such a cretin in the kitchen?"

"Why should I?"

"I love you. You make me feel I'm perfect even though I know I'm rubbish." It was too easy fishing for compliments.

"You're not rubbish. Well, not all the time."

We went out that night for a pizza. The snow had thawed and London was wet and dirty. It felt strange to be out after spending so long tucked away inside. We walked towards Upper Street, arms linked. I could hear the murmur of the traffic and feel the light spray of rain on my face. In the distance I heard a siren wail - someone, somewhere needed help. Out on the night street there was a sense of urgency, of busyness, in contrast to the peace of the last few days.

We found a table at the back of the Pizza Hut, in the corner. A little candle danced wildly in greeting as we took off our heavy coats and sat down.

"How was Becky?" I asked John. We'd talked of nothing but each other since I'd come back but now, outside, I grew curious about the rest of my world.

"She looked pretty bad, but brightened up a bit when I told her Ciaran had gone home for Christmas. She thought he'd done something to himself because she'd not heard a word from him."

"She's going to find it really hard going back to college without him. Especially in that bloody awful hall of residence."

The food was delicious, all mozzarella cheese and salt. It was the first proper food I'd had since leaving Wales.

"I ought to ring Matt. Maybe we could meet him for a drink."

"Now, there's another unhappy soul."

"What's happened?"

"Dom's mother won't let him move out till he's finished school. I think she has wind of what's really going on. She's told Matt not to come to the house again."

"I tried to talk to Mum about it but she just wouldn't. It's weird. She's so open-minded about lots of things, but not this, not when Matt's involved."

"She may get used to the idea."

"I doubt it."

"Did you talk about me at all?"

"Your name did crop up once or twice."

"What did she say? Am I suitable for her daughter?"

"What do you think?"

"Aye, I think so."

"She does too, but she'd rather you weren't married."

"I'm not."

"You're not divorced."

He went quiet for a moment. "Why does it matter?"

"I don't know. After all she told me not to settle down yet, until I'd established myself as a geologist. It's her problem, not mine." I wasn't being honest. "Did you speak to your mum over New Year?"

"Yes."

"Is she well?"

"She's okay."

"Did she have a good Christmas?"

John nodded. It was like trying to get blood from a stone.

"Will you go and see her this year?"

"If you'll come with me."

"Only if you'll protect me."

"From what?"

"All those bombs."

He smiled and shook his head. "Derry's safer than London."

"How do you know? You haven't been there for ages."

"Trust me. Maybe she could come over here."

"That's a good idea."

He laughed. "You really are frightened, aren't you?"

"The only things I know about Northern Ireland are what Ciaran's told me or what I hear on the news. I get the impression from them that it's bloody dangerous."

"Ciaran's never even been to the North. He doesn't know what it's like. I was there when the troubles started. I admit things were pretty hairy then, but when I was growing up things were no worse than in your little Welsh town. People weren't too sectarian-minded where I grew up, although I suppose the seeds of hatred were sown even then. Separate schools divided us kids. If you don't meet kids different from yourself, you'll believe all sorts of lies told you about them."

"We haven't got a clue over here, have we? We're totally uninterested. If we hear of a bomb or killing in Northern Ireland it means nothing. If people think about it at all, I'm sure they see the reunification of Ireland as logical, but they hate the IRA so much they can't admit it."

"It doesn't look that logical from where the Unionists stand."

"But it's inevitable. They'll have to come round to the idea."

"Inevitability doesn't come into it. You should go there. See for yourself."

"I'll send off the order for my bullet-proof vest today."

When John went back to work I started the long haul to catch up on all the work I'd missed or neglected. I had exams in February. I found revising about glacial moraines, boulder clays and palynology so tedious that at every opportunity I'd spread my map out on the floor and, using special pastel crayons, colour the different rock types I'd identified in the field. I'd neglected my mapping project and since it made up twenty per cent of my degree, felt justified in spending time on it. I loved having a large area of, perhaps, oolitic limestone, which I'd identified, to colour in. I could use long, swooping strokes. Where the rocks were convoluted and twisted, as they so often were in the foothills of the Alps, the work was more painstaking, but the final combination of different colours brought its own satisfaction.

Working on the map brought back the simplicity of the previous summer which I'd spent in France. I stayed with a family near Geneva and took the Annecy bus every morning to my mapping site. Fieldwork was the main reason I loved geology. Piecing together a picture of the forming earth from fragments of knowledge gleaned from outcropping rocks and land formations. I spent the evenings consolidating the work I'd done during the day and after supper I'd fall exhausted into bed. The work was fulfilling but the social life dull, which is what I needed at the time. An oasis of calm in the turbulence of my relationship with Bob.

As I shaded in the different colours I remembered details of particular localities. That spot where I climbed out of the shadow of the trees and was confronted by the raw power of the jagged, grey mountains reaching up high into the crisp, clear sky. There were the dappled ruins of the spa baths I found in the little wooded valley. The year 1937 was carved into the lintel over the door. I remembered the abattoir whose putrid smell hit me long before I came across the building, and that tiny quarry I found, tucked away behind the site where an Englishman was building a new home for himself. Echoes of all these places and experiences I fixed into the colours of my map.

I had almost finished when there was a knock at the door. I didn't want to answer it, engrossed as I was in colours and memories. There was a second knock and I gave in to its insistence.

I knew immediately it was her. Siobhan. She stood there small, pale-skinned, dark hair falling round her face. I felt large and clumsy, dressed in John's old jumper and paint-splattered jeans. She couldn't have planned it better.

"Hello, Claire. I'm Siobhan."

"John's not here. He's back at work."

"I thought he might be, but it's you I've come to see. May I come in?"

My heart sank. I wasn't ready for this. I wanted John to be with me when I met Siobhan. I led her into the kitchen, quickly closing the sitting room door on the way. I wanted to keep my life with John private from her.

"I'm actually in the middle of some work."

"You're a student, aren't you?" She had a gentle accent, softer than John's.

"Yes. I'm revising at the moment and I'm a bit pushed for time. What was it you wanted to see me about?"

"John," she said and paused, shifting her weight from one foot to another. There was nowhere to sit in the dingy kitchen. We stood facing each other. I leaned back on the sink and folded my arms, staring her full in the face, hoping my stance would intimidate her.

"What about him?"

"He's a good man. But you already know that."

I nodded.

"Don't worry about me, Claire. It's just that John and I are like brother and sister, we've known each other so long, and sometimes we need each other like at Christmas. I thought you should know that."

I didn't want to hear how close she and John were. She couldn't know him as well as I did. The John she knew belonged to Northern Ireland and childhood. He was different now.

"Is that it?"

"I'm no threat to you."

"So you said."

"The only other thing - but I'm sure John's already told you - is that we won't get divorced. We can't."

In that instant my happiness became focused on a single point - the need for John to be free. It was only then that I recognized just how much his marriage nagged at me. I caught my breath as the balance of power shifted. She felt the change and looked straight at me.

"You seem surprised. Surely John's told you?"

I couldn't speak. Rage and hurt stripped me of my voice. She studied her feet briefly and then looked me in the eye again.

"Being Catholic, you see. I couldn't do it."

"But you've been sleeping with another woman's husband for the last two years!" I said, finding my voice at last.

"I didn't know he was married."

"No, but you were! How does your Church judge that?"

"You don't understand."

"Too bloody right I don't. I don't go in much for theological acrobatics."

"I didn't want it to be like this," she said quietly.

"What did you expect? 'Hello, I'm John's wife. Send him back when you've finished with him.' "

We stood in silence. I didn't need this.

"I shouldn't have come," she said eventually.

"Why not? You can see you've shocked and hurt me. Made me doubt John. All in all, a job well done!"

My hatred for her filled the kitchen. The hint of a smile flickered in her eyes.

"Maybe you're right," she said. "Maybe I have got what I wanted. I still miss him, you know. I'd have him back tomorrow if I could."

"What about Steve?"

"A diversion."

"But John left because of him."

"Is that what he told you?"

I was bewildered by the fact that she still wanted John. I'd worked so hard to believe in the irretrievable breakdown of their marriage.

"Did you sleep with John over Christmas?" Weakening my position still further, I regretted asking the question.

She hesitated, aware that she had the power of knowledge. She shook her head. "He's a loyal bastard, that one. That's why he'll never divorce me."

"We'll see."

I was shattered when she left. Hurt, angry, unsure - she'd done well - and yet I felt strangely triumphant. John did love me and his love was all the more valuable because another woman wanted it.

I couldn't settle back to my map, so I sat on the sofa with a carbonate sedimentology text-book. I hoped the words might transfer themselves from the page to my brain by osmosis. They didn't.

A couple of hours, half a bottle of wine and nearly a packet of cigarettes later, I heard the key turn in the lock. John whistled to let me know he was home. I didn't rush to greet him. He came in to the sitting-room, pulling off his jacket.

"What's the matter?" He came over and squatted down in front of me.

"Siobhan's been here."

He touched my cheek and stroked it gently with the palm of his hand.

"What did she say?"

"That you promised her you'd never get divorced. It gave her a lot of pleasure to know you hadn't told me. Is it true?"

He nodded slowly. "I thought as time went on she'd change her mind. If she meets someone else, she might want a divorce."

"Is it religion?"

"No. No, that's just an excuse."

"I thought so."

John was quiet and I felt too exhausted to speak. I was overwhelmed by the reassurance of his presence. He knelt down in front of me and reached for my glass. He drank from it.

"She says she still loves you and she'll have you back any time."

"That's what she says."

"What do you mean?"

"It's not me she loves. She sees in me her past and a chance for security. She's very mixed up and this business with Steve's confused her even more."

"A diversion."

"What?"

"Her relationship with Steve. That's what she called it - a diversion. She didn't strike me as someone confused. She knew just what she wanted - you."

"She was seeing Steve before I left."

"Is that why you went?"

"No. Partly. We're two people who shouldn't be together. Things are so good between you and me. It was never like this with Siobhan. She's very angry. Angry and hurt. She had a breakdown once, you know. Tried to commit suicide." He hesitated and looked at me before looking sharply away. "She blamed me. I know she was ill, but I couldn't handle all the guilt."

"Why's she so messed up?"

"God knows. We're none of us all that sane though," he said looking up at me. "She had a hard time, saw some terrible things and carries them with her. Her suffering is the one thing that's constant in her life."

"Where does that leave us?"

"What do you mean?"

"What do we do about Siobhan? About the future?"

He drained my glass and shrugged. "I'm not sure. What I do know though, is that I love you and won't let anything threaten our happiness."

He reached up and cupped my face in the palms of his hands. I responded by sliding onto the floor with him and hiding in his arms. I felt happier and didn't press him further on the matter. If need be, I would demand grand gestures and great sacrifices another time. For now this was enough.

7

Ciaran didn't come back. Becky's letters to him poured into a bottomless pit from which there was no reply. She finally stopped writing after attempting to contact him by telephone, in March. She spoke to his mother who, she told me, sounded charming but vague. Yes, he'd been home for Christmas. Lovely to see him after so long. Then he'd popped up to stay with his cousins in Donegal. He'd be back in London now, she assured Becky, at college. It was his last year.

Becky didn't feel able to set her straight and tell her that he'd disappeared. It would be too cruel.

"I wouldn't mind so much, if I just knew where he was, what he was doing," she told me when we met for a drink at the end of the spring term. "I'm over him now, really. I just need to know where he is and if he's all right. I walk down the street sometimes and catch sight of someone who looks like him and follow them, just to make sure it's not him."

I stared into my empty glass.

"I don't suppose Matt's heard from him?" she asked.

"No. You've asked me already. I promised I'd let you know if he does."

"It's such a tragedy that he's dropped out right at the end. He was doing ever so well. Dave reckoned he could have got a two one, you know. Maybe even a first."

"You said."

"And the Poly haven't heard a word, although I suppose they wouldn't tell me anyway. But Dave would let me know if he heard anything. Those friends he was going to move in with over at Wood Green have let his room to someone else. I think he's still in Ireland. I can feel it in my bones."

"Do you want another drink?"

She nodded, drained her glass and handed it to me.

The pub was almost empty. It was still early and the rumble of the evening rush hour could be heard crawling along the Holloway Road outside. Most of the people inside were from the Poly - students, a couple of lecturers and technicians. I was overcome by the tedium of my life. Hemmed in by the inward-looking world of the Poly, I was fed up with being a student. The lack of money, constant pressure to study and lack of any promise of a job at the end of it all was too much. The companies had already done the milk round and left virtually empty-handed.

I paid for the drinks and wandered back to Becky.

"I thought I might go over there," she said.

"Where?"

"To Ireland. Dublin. Up to Donegal if he's still there."

"He could be anywhere by now. Just because he's not in London doesn't mean he's still in Ireland. He could be in Timbuctu for all you know." I wished she'd change the subject.

"I could follow his route, though. Don't you see? I'd know where he went, I'm sure I would."

"Give it a rest, Becky."

"Well, what else can I do?" She sounded injured.

"Listen, you and Ciaran split up before he actually left. What you had was over. You need to start looking forward, not back. You've got your own finals in a couple of months, you should concentrate on those."

"It's all right for you, you've got John."

"I know, I know. But don't forget I watched you and Ciaran tearing each other apart. It was time to move on then and that was three months ago."

"I just need to know where he is," she insisted, her voice small now. "For my own peace of mind. Then I can put it aside. Just think, if I did find him during the Easter holidays I might be able to persuade him to come back and take his exams. That's what I really want to do."

I lit a cigarette and glanced at the door. I wished John

would hurry up, I couldn't stand much more.

"How's life in hall?" I tried to change the subject.

"Okay." She shrugged. "I'd look for somewhere else but I know that as long as I'm there Ciaran knows where to find me."

"Do you go to any of the discos?"

"No."

"How about the bar?"

"Occasionally, but everyone seems so young. They're all straight from school. The only people my age are all foreign."

"Tall, dark and handsome?"

"Small and swarthy mostly, with accents so strong you can't understand a word they're saying."

"They can't all be that bad." I wanted to hear something positive from her.

"Come down and see for yourself. It's all very well for you in your nice, quiet little flat with John, who cares about you. You want to try living on a floor with a bunch of people who leave pans of smelly old curry in the kitchen for days, or be woken late at night by the sounds of partying and God knows what else and then to be woken again early next morning by the Muslim students calling one another to prayer."

"And you're putting up with all that just in case Ciaran wants to find you?"

"Well, what would you do?" she asked.

I thought for a moment, but couldn't imagine myself in that position again. A year ago I'd abandoned my self-respect over a man, but with John I'd grown in confidence so much, that I couldn't see myself ever being in such a pitiful position again. "I don't know. I really don't know."

I fumbled in my purse and went over to the juke-box. I needed to escape from Becky. Her misery was contagious. I hadn't seen her for a few weeks and had been looking forward to getting together that evening but it was all turning sour. I was horrified to see her purse-lipped and middle-aged, muttering about the idiosyncrasies of the foreign students and the frivolity of the young.

I pored over the juke box, examining every record title. I wanted John to come, so that I could go home. As I started to press in my selection I felt a hand on my shoulder. He'd arrived. I turned around and hugged him.

"Can we go now?" I asked, like a small child bored by adult company.

"I was just going to get us all a drink. Matt said he'd be along later."

"Shit!" The evening yawned before me.

The music punched into the quiet bar and the atmosphere lightened. I followed John over to the bar and stood with him, leaving Becky alone at the table. He'd just had a shower and his hair was wet.

"You smell of shampoo," I said, standing on tiptoe, trying to nuzzle his ear. "Smells good."

"It should do - it's yours."

"Thief! I'm glad you finally got here. Becky won't shut up about Ciaran."

"You want me to change the subject?"

"Bet you can't," I challenged.

"Bet I can."

We took the drinks over to the table and sat down.

"I've an announcement to make," John said.

"What?" My heart thumped. Divorce?

"I'm going to be a student too in September."

"Oh." It was such an anticlimax.

"Are you not pleased?" He looked at me, disappointed by my reaction.

"Yes. Yes. Of course. I'm just surprised, that's all. What are you going to study?"

"Cabinet-making. It's only for a year, but it could be my ticket off the building sites. It's not all practical, there are modules on the history of furniture-making and stuff. I didn't think they'd take me with no qualifications, but they did. I must have dazzled them with my sparkling wit and personality."

"Why didn't you tell me you'd applied?"

"In case I didn't get in. I didn't want to disappoint you."

"Haven't you any qualifications at all?" Becky asked. It was this piece of information that seemed to interest her.

"No."

"Not even a C.S.E.?"

"When I was sixteen there was more excitement on the streets than in the classroom. Exams didn't come into it."

"Well done," I said, kissing him lightly on the cheek. I felt guilty about my reaction, and tried to make amends.

Matt turned up soon afterwards, unshaven and pale. He seemed distracted.

"Where's Dom?" asked John.

"Safe at home with his mum. He's confessed all to her."

"Why?"

"Guilt. Now she won't let him out of his sight. She's threatened to go to the police if we keep seeing each other."

"If there's anything we can do," I offered inadequately.

"I know. Thanks." He looked down at his drink, rubbing the condensation off the glass with his fingers.

"What will you do?" John asked.

Matt cleared his throat. "I don't know. I've told him I'll wait till he's taken his exams. We'll see what happens then."

The four of us sat in an uncomfortable but respectful silence for a while, until Becky could stand it no more.

"Have you heard from Ciaran at all, Matt?" she asked.

"What?"

"Ciaran. Have you heard from him?"

Matt shook his head.

Becky looked at her watch. "I'd better get going. I'm not keen on wandering around Market Way on my own when it's dark."

"Stay a bit longer. We'll see you home," John said.

Becky looked at Matt and then back to John. "No," she said. "I've work to do, anyhow."

She blamed Matt for losing Ciaran and couldn't bear to be

in his company.

"I miss him, you know," said Matt after Becky had left the pub.

"Who?" I asked.

"Ciaran. I didn't realize how close we were. Dom's so young. There's such a lot he doesn't understand. You underestimated Ciaran, Claire. He knew it too."

"What do you mean?"

"He always said you wrote him off as no more than an armchair revolutionary."

"Well he was!"

"No. He was more than that."

It wasn't the evening any of us wanted. John wanted to celebrate his news but was mindful of Matt's unhappiness and, although I was pleased for John, I was weary with studying and lack of money, and the prospect of being on the dole while John's only source of income was a student grant didn't fill me with joy.

We did have a couple of drinks to celebrate John's achievement - Matt said all the right things when John finally told him, but I could tell his heart wasn't in it.

We left the pub early. The night was dark and cool. Matt dropped us back at the flat on his way home and that's when John started to show his disappointment at the evening's turn of events. He was sullen and quiet and slammed the bedroom door behind him, so I didn't follow him in. Instead, I put the television on in the sitting room.

"Do you want a coffee?" I called. The newsreader was informing the camera that a group of Argentinian salvage workers had landed on the British island of South Georgia in order to dismantle an old whaling station and had hoisted the Argentinian flag above it. Britain was affronted, murmuring threats of sending in a gunboat. It all seemed so Victorian and I vaguely wondered where South Georgia was.

"No." He came into the sitting room. He'd changed his jumper.

"Where is South Georgia, anyway?"

"I'm off out. A couple of Siobhan's brothers are over. I said I'd go and see them."

"God! How many brothers has that woman got?"

"Are you coming or not?" he asked, shortly.

"Didn't know I was invited."

"You always are, every time I go. You know that. I want you to come with me tonight. After all, it's a bit special."

Irritated by the way the evening had gone, I refused. "I've had a really long day and want to got to bed. I'm not up to it."

He sighed heavily. "Will you not make the effort, for once."

I stared at the television. Wherever South Georgia was, it looked pretty cold.

"Why are you not pleased for me?"

"I am."

"You've a funny way of showing it. I thought you'd be thrilled with my news. I'm trying to improve things for both of us, you know."

"I'm tired, that's all."

"So go to bed," he said walking away from me, the front door swinging shut behind him.

I was sorry immediately. I'd acted badly, messed everything up. I turned the television off and went to the front door to find John. His figure had vanished from the alleyway. He must have arrived at Siobhan's already - I hoped her reaction to his news wouldn't be spectacular.

I waited until nearly midnight, with no sign of John, before brushing my hair and putting on my coat. I would go to Siobhan's flat. I would make it up to him. It was silent outside, broken only the clack of my heels on the pavement. With each step closer to the flat my stomach churned more, then I was there, looking up at her kitchen window, blind pulled down tight, but the light on inside. I thought I heard laughter inside and what little confidence I had evaporated. I turned round and went home.

John didn't come back until after four o'clock. I'd been

lying awake in bed, the duvet wrapped round me for warmth. I could smell the whiskey on his breath as soon as he walked into the bedroom. He tripped over the bed. Instantly all my remorse and good intentions were transformed into anger because he was drunk, because he'd been out enjoying himself, while I'd spent the night alone and miserable, waiting for him to come back.

"You've come home then."

"Ssh. Yes. It's all right, I'm home now. Go to sleep. Jesus, my head. I've a hangover already, Sean kept filling my glass. You'll like him, he's great fun."

I didn't deign to answer him, just turned over emphatically, grateful though that he'd come home to me.

8

When I woke up the following day my mood had changed again, back to remorse. I decided I'd make it up to him, by taking him out somewhere special for breakfast. I didn't want anything to spoil my plans and wouldn't have opened the door when I heard a knocking, if John hadn't insisted. I opened the door to an enormous bunch of daffodils.

"Peace offering," a man's voice behind the daffodils entreated. A face looked round the glowing yellow heads. "I didn't steal them, I promise," he said. "I wouldn't let your man go last night. It's my fault, hope you didn't give him too hard a time."

I looked round to see John smiling through his thick headache and giving Sean the thumbs up sign.

"Is this some kind of conspiracy?" I asked, wishing I could raise one eyebrow for greater effect.

The two men began to laugh, nodding at each other.

It was only then I realized I'd never seen John with any of his own friends. He didn't mix much socially with the men he worked with and although he said there was a lot of male bonding on site, he never brought any friends home. But here was someone he clearly shared a friendship with, one that long preceded me. I was intrigued by this new side to him, even though his friend was Siobhan's brother.

"Come on in," I said, taking the flowers from him. "They're lovely. I expect you'll be wanting a cup of strong, black coffee if you feel as ill as John."

"The fella's no whiskey-drinker and that's for sure. No, you go and sit down. I'll put the daffs in water and the man himself can get me a coffee." He was irresistible.

I went back to my desk in the sitting room. Listening to them in the kitchen, I couldn't make out what they were saying but the affection in their voices was unmistakable. They came in carrying mugs of coffee and an unopened packet of biscuits. I left my books and went to join them.

"Now," said Sean, sitting himself carefully in our only armchair, "Siobhan's cooking us all a meal tonight and she'd like you both to come. I know what you're going to say Claire, that you've assignments and essays to finish but they'll keep, so they will. But now Siobhan's spaghetti carbonara - that won't keep. Make me a happy man, say you'll come."

I looked across at John and wondered whether all this had been planned between them the previous night. I felt I was being manipulated - Sean already knew my usual excuses.

"I was going to see my brother tonight."

"Let him come too," said Sean.

"Maybe," I said, knowing that Matt had other plans.

Sean stayed and finished his coffee, chatting comfortably about himself. His conversation was easy and general and he swept me into it at every opportunity.

"I'm an electrician, Claire, but I've spent more time over the last two years out of work than in it. There's very little work at all at home any more. You had riots over here yourself last year, didn't you? Strange to think of people over here taking to the streets."

"They're so angry. They feel the government doesn't give a damn about anyone and there's no hope of improvement unless we get the buggers out."

"It's been like that at home for years, eh, John? I'm over with my brother Eamon. There's nothing for him back home. I'm trying to persuade him to go to college. He's the bright one of the family. What's your college like?"

"Okay. Depends what he wants to study."

"I'm thinking of coming to London myself, but I'd miss home, I know I would."

"I can't see you surviving far from Derry, Sean," said John.

"London's so unfriendly."

"Still, it might be better than unemployment."

At last he got up to leave. "See you at eight then."

I nodded, committing myself to an evening at Siobhan's.

We arrived at Siobhan's laden down with cans of beer and bottles of wine. I'd spent a lot of time deciding what to wear. I wanted to look good this time and was glad I'd made the effort. She opened the door to us dressed in a heavy white blouse which tumbled over tight blue jeans. Her hair was loose. She looked small, vulnerable.

"Hello, Claire." Her greeting was forced and cool. "John," she said smiling, before kissing him on the cheek.

The success of the evening would almost certainly depend upon Siobhan and I behaving. I looked at John. I would if she did. She left us to busy herself in the kitchen while Sean took our coats and got drinks.

"This is Eamon, Claire," John said as we entered the sitting-room.

"Hi."

He nodded in greeting; the shadow of a smile never crossed his face. Another pea from the same pod, small and dark, but this one was wrapped in an aura of gloom. The very opposite of Sean.

"He's not been well," John said quietly as we sank into big cushions propped up by the wall.

Siobhan's flat seemed larger than ours although it, too, only had one bedroom. Rooms led off a narrow central corridor. Her sitting-room overlooked a small, walled patio which housed numerous containers, overflowing with plants bursting into new life with the advent of spring. The sitting-room also dripped with foliage. The walls of the room were painted a deep, dark red. It was like sitting in a drop of blood.

John had lived here with Siobhan, for five of the eight years they were together. I wanted to sense something of those years they'd shared here but felt nothing. The only evidence of John was the plentiful shelves on every wall. Our own sitting room was the same. Siobhan's shelves held plants; the ones in our flat held my books.

A large pine table sat at the window end of the room, where cutlery and glasses were scattered for the evening's meal.

Sean came in with drinks and I relaxed, listening to the banter between Sean and John - it was light and entertaining. I glanced over occasionally at Eamon whose eyes were always fixed on a plant by the door. It was an abundant maidenhair fern; its soft, flat leaves floating continually in the draught coming from the passageway.

By the time Siobhan was ready to serve dinner I'd already had a couple of glasses of wine and was feeling warmer towards her.

She presided over the meal with skill and poise. It was as if she'd practised the order of events so that everything should proceed perfectly. She was flanked by her two brothers - one loquacious, the other mute. Eamon's presence lent a sense of the bizarre to the meal.

She talked constantly about the past. A shared past when she, John and Sean had been teenagers together. I told myself that if she had to go back that far to remember the good times, she was no real threat to my happiness.

I managed to steer the conversation around to myself at one point, telling them about my field trip to the Peak District, during the Easter holidays. It seemed so long since I'd been away, I was really looking forward to getting out in the field again.

By half-past-eleven Eamon had taken himself off to bed, having said scarcely more than a dozen words all night. I wondered how his sharp intellect, which Sean had mentioned earlier, manifested itself. Sean went out to the kitchen to make some coffee and a couple of minutes later John collected up the remaining dirty plates and followed him.

I was paralysed. Should I go after him or stay alone with Siobhan? I swallowed a mouthful of wine. To leave might be construed as weakness. I'd stay. Perhaps she would leave. She didn't. We sat in silence for a while, avoiding each other's eye.

"So, how's it going then?" I broke the silence.

"Okay." She nodded slowly. "You?"

"Looking forward to going away."

We were silent again.

"John tells me you're looking for a permanent job," I said, giving conversation one last try.

"Yes. I've had enough of temping. A permanent job this time. Maybe something different altogether."

"I was a secretary before I went to college. I really hated the last job I had. My boss thought I was his slave and the woman I shared an office with was off her trolley. She lived alone with her mother. The job was everything to her."

"Sounds familiar," she said warming to the conversation. "There's one of those in every office. They specially hate temps and give them all the crap jobs."

"Why don't you go to college?" I asked, my vision narrowed by three years of student life.

"What would I do? I've no qualifications."

"Neither's John but he's got a place."

"But he has a skill. I've nothing."

"What are you interested in?"

In a few short minutes the relationship between Siobhan and I leapt forward, separate now from the events that had brought us together. A combination of wine and the lateness of the evening fuelled my desire to help her find a fulfilling career. That and the thought that my best chance of her becoming independent of John was in the easy social life of college.

"Plants," she said, gesturing to the abundance of them about the room.

"Why don't you go to the library or the careers office at the Poly. They'd have information about horticulture courses or whatever."

"Maybe I'll pop down there when the boys have gone back."

"You should go as soon as you can," I insisted. "You never know, you might get something for September."

"We can't leave Eamon on his own just now. I promised I'd watch him so Sean could look for work."

"What's the matter with him?"

She looked away. "He's not been well."

"John mentioned something about it. What's the problem?" I knew I was treading on dangerous ground and half-expected her to tell me to mind my own business.

"Depression."

Mental illness stalked her family.

"I've had a breakdown, you know. I go to see someone now. A psychotherapist. It helps. I want Eamon to see him too, but Sean says it's all bollocks and that he shouldn't go."

"What does Eamon say?" I asked.

"He's so drugged up at the moment, he can't think straight. But I watch him sometimes. They don't blank it out, those drugs. They didn't with me and they don't with him. They just make the pain further away."

"Pain?"

"Living with what we've seen. I was there at Bloody Sunday. Sean's best friend was with us too. He was gunned down in cold blood when we were running away. Shot in the back."

"Was Eamon there too?"

"No, he's too young. I don't really know why he feels the way he does. He left school when he could, but there's no work so he stayed home. Sure, it'd be enough to depress anybody." She looked at me. "We're not a happy family. My father drinks and Sean's the same. I've two other brothers in hiding. They've been mixed up with the Republicans for years, which leaves Eamon at home, unemployed. John can't see it - the hopelessness. But then of course he wouldn't, would he?" She looked down, her voice bitter.

"I'm sorry." I didn't know what else to say.

She looked up. "Why? It's not your fault." Then she smiled. "At least, not that bit anyway."

I smiled back at her. A gulf had been bridged. Perhaps we could be friends.

9

We left for Buxton on Sunday morning and John's letter arrived the following Thursday. The only letter he'd ever written to me. I kept it.

Dear Claire,

I know I was in a right mood when you went and I'm sorry for it but it frightens me when you go away because I think you'll find somebody else and I couldn't bear being without you. I've been thinking about the future and you leaving college and went to see Siobhan on Tuesday night. Sean and Eamon are still there so it seemed like the best time to talk to her. I know you won't like me saying it but I felt bad asking her for a divorce but she seemed okay about it and Sean's there for her if she needs someone. In August we'll have been separated two years and you could marry me if you want. I've never met anyone quite like you. I feel stupid sometimes because you know so much but perhaps when I'm a student you'll be proud of me too. Even Siobhan's talking about going to college you're making students of us all. I'm lonely without you and have being doing overtime this week now the clocks have changed. Matt came round last night and we both felt so miserable we drowned our sorrows in too much wine. I nearly didn't get up for work this morning. Dom says he's got a girlfriend so Matt's fed up even though he doesn't believe him. I'll be okay when you get home but it's been a long week. You can see I'm no good with words and won't read this back otherwise I won't send it but I wanted you to know about Siobhan and how much I miss you. I love you and wish it was Saturday now.

All my love always,
John

Thursday was transformed by the letter. I didn't give in to the sense of loss I'd carried around with me all week because this was our group's last field trip together, and even the chill, damp weather didn't bother me. I was excited by the thought of him being free of Siobhan, although talk of marriage made me nervous. I shouldn't have rung him that evening.

"Thanks for the letter. It was lovely," I said.

"Well?"

"Well what?"

"Will we get married in August?"

"I'm not sure. Depends really, what's happening. But I am really pleased about you getting divorced."

I couldn't read the silence that followed.

"How is Siobhan?" I asked.

"I haven't seen her since Tuesday."

More silence followed, so I filled it with tales about incidents that had happened during the trip. He didn't respond to what I said.

"What time'll you be back Saturday?" he asked.

"About four. Will you meet me?"

"I will."

Friday was the last day of the trip and the weather ensured we made a solemn vow never to do fieldwork in this country again except for huge amounts of money. The wind was furious and a mixture of rain and sleet whipped our faces as we made our way from the minibus to the site at Ribblesdale. We were looking at reef knolls. I wanted to be alone and wandered off from the others before scrambling my way up the hill, pulling myself up with cold and muddy fingers by the tough grass. There was no view. Battered by wind and nearly blinded by rain, I could see only a heavy grey mist hanging in the valley. It was impossible to imagine this place three hundred million years ago - an azure sea, slowly rising and creating new life in the warmth of the sun. Paradise lost.

Disappointed by my solitary expedition, I found the others at the selected outcrop struggling to control pencils which slid over wet field notebooks. Recording our findings was hopeless. The rock, like the sky, was a deep grey and so heavily weathered that we could break off pieces with our hands. To get a clearer picture of the depositional features we tapped away at the rock with our hammers, the sound of muffled clinking not carrying beyond the ancient quarry.

At last Dr Stokes called out that it was time to go. I lost Sarah on the long, muddy walk back to the minibus. She and Peter had fallen behind arguing over the specimens they'd found. I caught up with Dr Stokes who was striding off ahead. He always liked to be first back at the minibus, thus avoiding criticism from his cold, tired students.

"Not a bad locality. Shame it's so weathered, though," I said.

"Yes." His parka hood was pulled tightly round his head and secured by a drawstring which was hidden in his beard. "In Tunisia there are whole horizons made up of brachiopods, so much better preserved than here."

"Is there much Carboniferous in Tunisia, then?"

"Not really. Mostly Cretaceous and Tertiary."

"Sounds like my mapping area."

"Near Geneva, wasn't it?"

"Yes." I was flattered that he remembered.

"Do you speak French, Claire?"

"Yes. I wouldn't have done my mapping there otherwise."

He went quiet for a while. I thought he was concentrating on the route back. I still couldn't see the familiar red minibus and wondered whether we'd lost our way.

"Fieldwork's so different over there," he said. "Too hot to work in the summer. Not like here. You wouldn't dream of going out without taking plenty to drink. I got bogged down in sand a couple of times last year, way out in the middle of nowhere. I'd have been stumped without my water."

"There's the minibus," I said. "I was beginning to think we

were lost."

"Claire! Have I ever got you lost in the three years you've been at the Poly?"

"No, but in this weather anything's possible."

"You know I've got a second year's contract in Tunisia this summer?"

"You said."

"I'm looking for a field assistant to come with me. One that can speak French. Would you be interested?"

I looked across at him, my mouth open. His face was screwed up against the weather and set straight ahead.

"Me?"

"You've specialized in sedimentology and you speak French. Think about it."

"I don't need to think about it. I'd love to come."

"The money's not brilliant, but all your expenses would be paid-"

"Yes. I've said yes. You don't need to persuade me."

"Good. I've had you in mind since I was offered the contract but didn't know what your plans were." He turned to look at me. "We'd work well together."

We reached the minibus. He turned and shouted to the others, "Come on, you lot! Last one to the minibus buys the first round tonight." His voice was carried away by the wind.

We were drying ourselves after a hot bath when I told Sarah my news.

"You jammy bugger! One day John asks you to marry him and the next Dr Stokes offers you a job. Some people have all the luck."

"It's amazing. I never dreamed anything like this would happen. It's too good to be true."

"Will you go out there for the whole summer?"

"I'm not sure. I think so. He hasn't gone into any detail yet. I hope he'll tell me more tonight. Just think, fieldwork in a hot country."

"Sounds to me like a contradiction in terms," Sarah said rubbing her feet dry. "Even that bath hasn't warmed me up. How do you think John will feel about you going away?"

I'd put John out of my mind, especially after our strained telephone call the previous evening. His reaction was something I'd have to deal with later. For now I just wanted to concentrate on my good fortune.

"He won't mind. He'll be really pleased for me," I said, deciding not to ring him that evening. "The only thing that worries me is if I can put up with Dr Stokes for a whole summer. We get on okay but..."

"A bit too well, according to Peter," said Sarah.

"You're just jealous," I said, throwing my wet towel at her.

Travelling home wasn't the melancholy journey I'd anticipated. Instead of dwelling on the passing of three happy years, I concentrated on the details Dr Stokes - Richard, he told me to call him Richard - had told me the previous evening. The summer abroad was just the beginning. It would be followed by lab work, examining thin sections of the specimens we'd taken, probably at the Poly. Then there would be other trips to Tunisia until we had a clear picture of the porosity out there. He estimated the contract could take about a year in all and mentioned the possibility of putting some of the research towards a further degree, as long as the oil company employing us didn't object.

As we reached the outskirts of London I began to grow concerned about John's reaction. I pulled out his letter and read it again. An August wedding was out of the question. I wondered how much he'd miss me when I went away in the summer, how he'd cope, how I'd cope without him. Events seemed to be beyond my control but in my favour. I hoped John would be happy for me, that he'd understand.

He was already there when the minibus pulled into the car park. After a week without seeing him he looked slightly unfamiliar, different, standing there waiting. We hugged each other amid much whistling and name-calling from the others. I was pleased and a little embarrassed by their attention.

It was on the way home that I told him my news.

"Tunisia?"

"Yes. It's fantastic, isn't it? Sarah's so jealous."

"And you said you'd go, without talking it over first?"

He stopped walking and turned to face me. I could feel my heart thumping. This was the reaction I hadn't wanted to think about, hadn't prepared for.

"I had to make a decision then and there. It's such a fantastic chance, I couldn't let it go."

"We should have talked about it first."

"What difference would it have made? I couldn't turn down an offer like that, no matter what. Besides, you never discussed going to college with me."

"That was different."

"Why? Because you're a man?"

"That's not fair. I'll still be here."

"Oh John it's only a couple of months, for God's sake. I thought you'd be pleased for me."

We walked the rest of the way home in silence.

He'd gone to a lot of trouble cleaning and tidying the flat - it had been a real mess when I left. Bunches of flowers around the room welcomed me home with a brightness neither of us felt. He'd been expecting a lot in my homecoming.

"I'm sorry," I said, dropping into a chair.

"What about my letter?" he asked.

"What about it?"

"Getting married in August, getting married at all. I shouldn't have said anything to Siobhan, not yet."

"Not without talking to me first." I threw his argument back at him.

"I wanted to make you happy." His voice was low and hard. "You've kept on about me getting divorced, I thought it's what you wanted."

"It doesn't mean I want to marry you. Not yet. We've only

known each other six months. I'm only twenty-two, I don't know about getting married. I've got my career to think about too."

John stared at the carpet; his knuckles were white where he clasped the arms of the chair. His face was red. I wanted him to say something.

"John?"

"Jesus!" he shouted, standing up. "You fucking women! I can do nothing right for you. Ever! What would make you happy? Tell me, what?"

I sat transfixed by his fury. I had never seen him so angry.

"These..." he said walking over to my desk. "Fuck them!" He swept all my books onto the floor with his arm. He picked up a vase of flowers from the table and threw it at the wall. It smashed. Flowers and splinters of pottery ricocheted off the wall as the water from the vase wept onto the carpet.

"Stop!"

"See what you do to me?" he shouted. "See?" And then he was gone, doors banging behind him.

I sat very still, unable to move. The strength of his passion unnerved me. Of all the awkward scenarios I'd pushed out of my mind I had never imagined the violence of the reality. As I sat there, trembling, I could hear the children running up and down, shouting at one another, playing "Tin, Tan, Tommy" in the alleyway. In the flat above the occasional footfall or distant laugh contrasted with the electric silence of the flat. I wanted John to come back, calm and apologetic, aware of his mistake. The John I knew and trusted.

When I realized he wasn't coming back, at least not immediately, I went into the kitchen. He'd laid out a little tea for us. The kettle was full and the teapot emptied of its dregs. I was still shaking and leaned on the work surface to steady myself. I took deep breaths in an effort to relax.

I put the kettle on and went into the bedroom to unpack. On the bed lay a parcel, gift-wrapped. I couldn't touch it. It was a present bought for a happy occasion, not the disaster my return had turned out to be.

As the evening wore on I tidied up the mess - I was going to leave it for John to do, but couldn't bear watching the flowers die. I finished unpacking and had a bath, jumping at every click which sounded like John's key in the door.

I needed support and tried to ring Matt but there was no reply. The evening dwindled into night and still he didn't come home. I opened a bottle of wine and tried to concentrate on the television.

At midnight I tried Matt again, but there was still no reply. Perhaps he and John were out together. In desperation I rang Siobhan to see if he was there.

"Siobhan?"

"Yes." She didn't recognize my voice.

"It's Claire. I'm sorry ringing you so late and everything but I just wondered if John was there?"

"No. Why?"

"Oh. He's gone out without his keys and I want to go to bed. He's not out with Sean is he?"

"No. We've not seen him since Tuesday." Her voice had changed. I thought I detected a smugness, reassured that John had walked out on me. "If he turns up I'll tell him you were looking for him."

"Thanks. 'Bye."

I didn't know who else to contact. It was too humiliating to let people know I was looking for him. I gave up and went to bed.

I didn't sleep and John didn't come home. I was left alone again waiting for him to come back. I hoped it wasn't a new pattern in our relationship. We'd argue, he'd walk out. I wanted to know if he often did this, but since the only person who'd know was Siobhan I'd never find out. I couldn't bear the thought that there might be any similarities between her relationship with John and mine.

I hated him that night, hated him for hurting and frightening me, for spoiling my excitement about going to Tunisia. And I was angry that he should make me worry so much about him and where he was.

In the morning there was still no sign of him so I threw some clothes and books into a bag. I could go and stay with Sarah, or Matt, or maybe go home for a couple of days. I hadn't been to Wales since Christmas. I wasn't going to sit waiting for him to come back. On my way out I wondered whether to leave a note, but since I hadn't decided where I was going there didn't seem much point. Besides, I wanted him to suffer like I'd done during the long night.

I'd make the decision about where to go when I got to the tube station. Wales was the most inviting option although the thought of my mother's questions put me off. I walked slowly down the brick-rich alleyway, flats on either side, above, behind and ahead, enclosed and imprisoning. Behind drawn curtains were other lives, each different from my own. I would have swapped places with any one of them.

I glanced across as I passed Siobhan's flat. The blind was still down. Sunday hadn't started for her yet. And then he turned the corner, dark and gaunt. I stopped, frightened still, but waiting. He walked towards me without hurrying, his eyes pained and fixed on me. We held on to each other in silence for a long time. I buried my face inside his jacket, all anger and resentment gone. He smelt of stale tobacco and beer but I didn't care. I wanted to burrow my way inside his chest and sit there within him, protected from the world.

"You're going?" he asked in a broken voice.

I shook my head as best I could, trapped as it was between his arm and body.

"Shall we go home, then?"

He released me and I nodded, overcome by exhaustion and relief.

Back at the flat I followed him into the bedroom where he pulled off his coat and shoes before falling on the bed. I did the same, still without words, and lay close to him staring at the ceiling. I didn't know how to begin.

"I'm ashamed of how I was yesterday," he said eventually.

"I want to say I'm sorry and make everything right between us, but I can't. It's not there. I'd probably do the same again. I hurt Siobhan and didn't need to with you leaving me anyway."

"I'm not leaving you, John."

I turned over onto my side and pulled his arm under my head.

"I need time. I need to know it can work with you being away. We can't afford to make a mistake, Claire. Things have been so good between us."

"Nothing's going to change. Trust me."

10

There was a tension between us in the weeks that followed. We were each a little nervous of the other. I never wanted to see John so angry again, especially not with me and I know he thought I was going to leave him, if not before the summer, then certainly when I went out to Tunisia. I had the added pressure of my final exams looming at the end of June and had to do well in order to justify my position as field assistant to the others. In poring over my books day after day it seemed the more I revised the less I knew. They were a grim few weeks.

When Sarah rang and invited us to Dave's party at the beginning of June I jumped at the chance. It would be a welcome break from all the dreary revision and an opportunity to catch up with everyone's news. I also hoped I'd see Becky there. We hadn't been in touch since the evening in the pub just before the Easter holidays.

Dave's flat was on the top floor of a huge, deep-grey, Victorian house, which sat in a large square parallel to the Camden Road. John and I were breathless by the time we'd climbed the innumerable flights of stairs towards the sound of revelling. Inside the flat, the rooms bulged with people. Some I knew, others were strangers. In the dusk-lit sitting room UB40 pounded out their rhythm and those who were already a bit drunk bounced to the beat. In the kitchen a small group of young men had taken it upon themselves to be the keepers of the drink. They laughed and chatted, taking cans and bottles from new guests before moving away reluctantly when those same guests wanted to fill their own glasses. But there was goodwill in the air and besides, the off-licence didn't shut for another hour.

As time wore on, the small attic rooms grew hot and stuffy

and we wandered higher up onto the roof. The strains of the music competed with squeals of taxi brakes and the distant roar of engines pulling away from traffic-lights. We sat watching the tired old sky, slowly become a thicker blue. In the square, the leaves of the horse-chestnuts and London plane-trees were out. Rooftops and aerials created a jagged horizon, with the landmark of the Post Office Tower standing tall above the rest.

Even away from my books I couldn't really forget the pressure of the exams and grumbled about the arts students, who'd already finished theirs.

"Don't worry," Sarah said. "We'll have another party when we finish ours. Dave will want to celebrate the end of all his marking, anyway. I don't know what you're moaning about, at least you've got a bloody job."

"I think Dr Stokes might change his mind if I fail," I said.

"That's hardly likely. How's John about you going away. Any better?"

I grimaced and looked around for him. He'd gone to fetch some drinks.

"I don't know." I lowered my voice in case he came back. "He still won't discuss it. I'm frightened to mention it, but we're going to have to talk about it some time."

"You must be worried about losing him," she said.

That idea hadn't crossed my mind. "He's afraid he's losing me."

"And is he?"

"Course not. Honestly, if it was him going away to work for a couple of months instead, nobody would think anything of it. I'd just be expected to wait for him."

"You're probably right. Two months is a long time though."

"I know."

"What's happening downstairs? Are we missing anything?" she asked when John came back, having negotiated his way across the roof, stepping over groups of people who, like us, were up there wallowing in the thick evening air.

He smiled and shook his head, handing her a drink. "Some happy soul's just turned the telly on down there. Must be something of a patriot. He wanted to watch the news - see how many Argies the Brits killed today."

"It's sick, it really is. What does that bloody woman think she's doing in the South Atlantic? She was all ready to sell the islanders down the Swanney, until Galtieri showed an interest," I said.

"Don't. What's really sickening is the way her popularity's increased since this war or conflict - whatever it is - started."

"When my Dad was taking his finals Britain was at war. Now I'm doing mine and we're at war again. Strange, that."

"Maybe it goes in forty-year cycles?" suggested Sarah.

"This is the best type of war," John joined the discussion. "Not like Northern Ireland. With this one you can watch from eight thousand miles away without feeling threatened. Unless you've someone in the forces."

"The other thing is, you know exactly who the baddies are," I said. "In Northern Ireland you're never sure. Loyalist or Republican, they're all suspect."

"I wonder what's happened to Dave," said Sarah, scanning the figures on the roof.

"He was being mobbed by a group of students when I was down there," said John.

"They're probably hoping that if they're nice to him, he'll be kind when he's marking their exam papers. They're wrong. He can be a right bastard when it comes to marking. I think he over-compensates for socialising so much with his students. I'm glad he's not one of my lecturers."

"Have you started revising yet?" I asked Sarah, knowing revision was low on her list of priorities.

"A bit, but I'm still trying to finish my project."

"That should've been handed in today!"

"I'm going to hand it in first thing Monday. It'll be okay."

"I've all these joys to look forward to," said John.

"It'll be nice to see you under pressure for a change," I

said. "Just think - this time next month it'll all be over."

"Forever, as far as I'm concerned. I never want to take another exam as long as I live."

I went off in search of the bathroom, leaving John and Sarah on the roof. I was able to by-pass the stuffiness of the rooms where the party was now seriously under way. Alcohol was still flowing freely, the music seemed louder than before and the sweet smell of dope meandered out onto the landing, where people who'd spent the last three years together, were just finding out how much they'd miss each other now that college was over. It made negotiation of the stairs difficult.

"Excuse me. Oops! Sorry." I trod on toes, hair and fingers and was still sober enough to find this obstacle course mildly embarrassing. It was with relief that I turned the cold, white porcelain handle of the bathroom door. Inside I found a woman pulling up her dungarees.

"Oh God, sorry," I said.

"Not at all. My own fault. I never lock the bathroom door. Come in, I've nearly finished."

As she flushed the toilet, I saw that she was older than the other guests, without make-up and dressed in tatty old clothes. She didn't look like a party-goer and I wondered if she'd wandered in off the street. She walked over to the wash-basin and filled it with water. She cupped her hands to collect some water and then buried her face in it. She repeated this action again and again, muttering something about London being so dirty.

"Could you pass me a towel?" she asked.

I looked around and found a huge, green bath-towel, stuffed into a rail attached to the bathroom door.

"I won't be a minute. If you're desperate, go ahead. Doesn't bother me," she said gesturing towards the toilet. I stood there rooted to the spot. It did bother me.

She dropped the towel on the side of the bath and, to my dismay, pulled a brush out of her bag. She started to tug at her thick, wavy black hair. I started tapping my foot in time to the music upstairs and hoped she'd get the message and leave.

"I suppose you're one of Dave's students," she said to my reflection in the mirror above the basin.

So she was a legitimate guest. "No," I said.

"My subject's history. I lecture a bit. Part-time. I've two children, boys. They're twins. What a handful! My mother's living with me too. She's got Alzheimer's - more of a liability than the children."

And so she went on, staccato-fashion yet scarcely pausing for breath, brushing the right side of her head over and over. Eventually, she turned around, still brushing, still talking. There was a wild look in her eyes as she pinned me down with her life-story. She'd known Dave at university, a good friend of his first wife. They'd both divorced around the same time and the romance which she hoped would bloom between them had withered in the bud. It was inevitable with Hull being so far from London. Then came the struggles with the children. They wanted to live with their father now. Perhaps the time was right, she could do with a bit of freedom. If only there wasn't mother.

On and on she went, hypnotising me with her flood of words.

All of a sudden she stopped talking, put her hairbrush back in the bag and leaned over to tear off some toilet paper to blow her nose on. The left side of her hair remained untouched.

"I'm sorry. I didn't mean to go on. Getting away from it all makes me realize how much I don't want to go back." She paused and then sat, balanced on the heap of towel which she had discarded on the bath. After a moment's silence she pulled her bag over her shoulder, smiled wanly and left. I locked the door after her, afraid that she might come back and start on me again.

I sat on the side of the bath, next to where she had been sitting, and replayed her words. A life burdened by disappointment and responsibility, chained to the generations above and below her, she didn't stand a chance. I shuddered at her imprisonment and knew I was right to forge ahead with my career in spite of John's unease. I didn't want a career only glimpsed at, before being weighed down by the convention of marriage and kids, but I didn't want to be lonely either.

"Where on earth have you been?" Sarah asked, when I eventually returned to the roof.

"I got trapped in the toilet with some friend of Dave's."

"Are you okay?" John was concerned.

"Yes. It was some woman. I thought she'd come in off the street but she was at university with Dave."

"Jill," said Sarah. "She's been under a lot of pressure lately."

"You're telling me. She's not in the mood for a party."

"Maybe I should go and find her," said Sarah.

"I don't want to stay any more," I said to John as Sarah walked away. "That woman's given me the creeps. You don't have to come. Stay and enjoy yourself."

"No, I'd rather come with you."

As I opened the flat door to leave, two people stumbled in.

"Becky! How are you?"

"Okay now my exams have finished."

"It's all right for some."

"I know. Ali's still got his coming up."

I smiled at the man Becky was with. He held out his hand.

"Ali, this is Claire."

He took my hand and shook it firmly. "I'm pleased to meet you. Becky has told me about you." He looked stern. I felt a little afraid.

"All good I hope."

The flash of a smile, showing arctic white teeth, beneath a thick black moustache, and then it was gone.

"And this is John," said Becky.

"How do you do?" Ali held out his hand.

I caught John's eye as Ali shook his hand, bowing his head slightly. We were not used to such social correctness.

"Pleased to meet you," John said, finding the right words.

"I hoped we'd see you here but we're off now. Why don't we meet up for a drink some time? Give me a ring. My exams finish on the third."

"Good luck!" she said.

I turned to say goodbye and caught Ali's eye. He smiled faintly at me. I shivered. There was something about him.

"He looked a bit fierce," I said to John as we made our way down the uncarpeted communal staircase.

"I wonder if they're together."

"Looked like it. He must be one of the foreign students she was so scathing about at Easter."

"So she's finally over Ciaran."

"I wouldn't bank on it."

Out on the street the night was even more sultry. Gone was any hint of breeze which we'd felt on the roof. The hub of the city was distant but constant, accompanying us on our walk home through hazy backstreets, empty of people.

11

Sarah was the only one in our year to get an unclassified degree. It was no surprise. She'd done hardly any work in her final year because of all the problems she'd had going out with Dave. She joined in the celebrations though, snuggling up to him on the hard wooden benches of the wine-bar while Peter and I tactlessly discussed our success and argued about which of us had got the highest overall mark. We had spent three years in competition with each other and although we both got the same degree, the challenge continued.

I was already a little drunk by the time we reached the wine-bar. John had taken the afternoon off work and come with me to get my results. On the way home we picked up a bottle of champagne and back at the flat made languid love in the airless heat of the late afternoon. My ego was sated by his obvious pride at my success and that night my confidence was impregnable. I was bad company.

We sat at the same table as Sarah, Dave, Peter, Dr Stokes and his wife, Hilary. A table in the middle of the dark room, from where we could see everyone as they squeezed their way to the bar. The atmosphere was rich with delight - the students who did well were happy, the lecturers were happy, the department was safe for another year or so, and even those who hadn't done well were glad it was all over. The juke-box thumped out Police and Madness and we had to shout over the music and one another to make ourselves heard. In a corner behind the bar a television flickered silently, displaying images of the day's carnage in the parks. It was the picture of the horses' blood washing over the tarmac in Hyde Park which brought a hush to the bar, rather than the more familiar footage of ambulances, broken bodies and twisted metal.

"So you're Richard's star pupil, are you?" Hilary Stokes shouted to me.

"Peter might disagree with you," I said.

"But you're going with him to Tunisia."

"That's because I'm prettier than Peter."

Her smile wavered a little and I glanced across at Dr Stokes, who was discussing the Polytechnic adminstration with Dave.

"Just kidding. Peter's already got a job and I've got more experience in sedimentology than him. Are you a geologist?"

She shook her head. "I used to teach. Maths. I'm a full-time mother now."

"You must miss adult company. Isn't it boring being stuck at home all day?"

"Most of the kids I used to teach weren't intellectually challenging and, besides, when you have your first baby they remove your brain. They've found women adapt better that way."

I laughed nervously. I wasn't sure what to make of her, but knew she was making fun of me. She wasn't the little woman I'd written her off to be. I was grateful to see Becky walk in at that moment and was able to leave the table to greet her.

"You made it," I said, giving her an uncharacteristic peck on the cheek. "No Ali?"

"He's gone back for the summer. Well done, by the way. You must be pleased."

"I wanted a First really, but you can't have everything and I didn't work hard enough anyway. My love life kept getting in the way."

We squashed our way into a tiny gap at the bar and I ordered a carafe of red wine.

"Had any luck getting a job yet?" I asked.

"Yes. I heard today. I've got a job in a publishing company."

"That's great. It's what you wanted."

"Not working as the receptionist."

"Still, it's a start. Which company?"

"A new one, quite small. Specializing in travel books. The bloke who interviewed me said that if they took off there might be a chance for me to get into the editorial side of things."

We looked at each other and smiled. Neither of us voiced the thoughts I knew we shared. However well-educated a woman is, if she's presentable and can type the chances of her becoming anything more than a secretary are pretty slim. Becky and I had gone over this a thousand times but I thought I was more at risk than she was. There were few women in geology and most oil companies refused to employ them on the rigs. In my darkest moments I saw myself back behind a typewriter rather than out in the field using my newly learnt skills.

"We're over there." I pointed to the table with one hand, holding the carafe and glass in the other.

"Wait a minute." She grabbed my free hand. She was flushed, her eyes glittered.

"What?"

"I've got to tell you. I was going to tell you later but I can't."

"Tell me what?"

"I saw Ciaran today. Here, in London. He's come back. I knew he would."

"How is he?"

"I don't know. I didn't talk to him, but it was him, I know it was. I was changing trains at Oxford Circus. We must have been on the same train. I saw him in the carriage when I was walking down the platform."

"Did he see you?"

"No. I knocked on the window, but the train was already moving. He didn't hear me."

"Wow!" I didn't know what else to say. Her relationship with Ali hadn't displaced her obsession with Ciaran. She was trembling with excitement.

"Does Matt know he's here?" she asked.

"Not as far as I know, but I haven't been in touch with him for ages."

"I had to tell you. Let me know if he hears from him, won't you? Give him my new address."

"But he might not contact Matt."

"He will," she said confidently. "I know he will."

When we finally got to our table the Stokes were leaving - they had a babysitter to get back for. Richard promised to contact me before we left in a couple of weeks in order to finalise details. Hilary's smile in my direction was minimal. I knew she didn't like me. I wasn't sure if it was jealousy that I was going off with Richard or simply a cold personal judgement; either way I didn't care.

We spent the rest of the evening, drinking, arguing and slapping one another on the back. Too soon, time was called and Peter suggested that we continue the party at his place. I was anxious to go although I could see John was tired, but when I got outside the wine hit me.

"Tell Peter we can't go," I whispered to John, struggling to stay upright.

"They're on their way now. They'll not notice if we don't go."

"Where's Becky?"

"Jesus, you are drunk. She left ages ago with Sarah and Dave."

He put his arm around me as I stumbled along the pavement. I relaxed into his hold, grateful for his support.

"Hope I enjoy college as much as you lot have done," said John, as we edged our way up Islington Park Street.

"Sarah's not enjoyed it that much."

"No? I thought she did. I thought that's why she did badly."

"No. Having to work did that."

"You didn't tell me she was working."

I was rapidly losing interest in the conversation. The traffic-lights at the top of the road were too bright and changed too often.

"I did. She had to work at that hotel in Bayswater after her mum stopped her grant. Her parental contribution." I said the last words carefully, testing myself to see how drunk I was.

"Why did she stop her money?"

"I told you," I insisted again. "After Christmas. When she started going out with Dave. Because he's black and divorced. She told Sarah she'd have to stop seeing him or she wouldn't get her money."

"She could have lied."

"Very honest, our Sarah. Besides, she loves to aggravate her mum."

"Why didn't Dave help out?"

"He did. He let her move in with him to save on rent, but he couldn't give her any money. He's hard up himself, what with all his maintenance payments."

"You never told me any of this."

"I'm sure I did."

By the time we reached the traffic-lights I couldn't be bothered to talk any more. As we turned to go down the Liverpool Road the dark shape of a cat jumped out in front of us. In the background I could hear John talking but wasn't listening. Further in the distance the mumble of engines grew close. The cat sank back and then, for no obvious reason, leapt out under the wheels of van. I stopped, frozen by the horror of what I was witnessing. As the van passed over it unnoticing, I could see its head and neck stuck to the road as its body writhed wildly in the air, defying gravity, and then its body squashed by two more cars hurrying to get home. Its entrails burst out onto the hard tarmac. I sank to my knees watching its life escape.

If we'd left the wine bar five minutes later we would simply have seen another dead cat in the road, but in witnessing its death I felt I could have prevented it. Within seconds a living creature had been wiped out. Sitting there it seemed possible to flip the clock back, change the order of events - frighten the cat back to the pavement, change the traffic lights so it would have crossed safely, whisked it away from the wheels of that van - but the longer I sat, time passing, its death became bearable and playing with time impossible.

As in a dream I watched John walk out into the road and gently push the animal, bit by bit, towards the gutter with his foot. I don't know why he did it. Perhaps it was the thought of all those wheels grinding the creature's body into the road.

"It was killed instantly," he said to comfort me.

"But it was fighting."

"No. Just reflex."

He lifted me to my feet and I saw blood on his boot. I glanced into the gutter but could only make out a bundled shadow.

"If I'd just seen a person run over, I don't think I'd feel nearly as bad as I do about that cat," I said.

"You would, believe me. You'd feel a hundred times worse."

12

The nearest we got to discussing me going away was John telling me on the morning I left that he wouldn't come to the airport with me.

It was a cool farewell. We hugged and kissed each other as if I was going away only for a couple of days. He left for work as usual and I pulled out the suitcases I'd packed surreptitiously when he wasn't around. It was a crazy situation, carrying on as if I wasn't going away when we both knew I was, so neither of us comforted and reassured the other, and when I left I was unsure of how John really felt. I was unsettled by Sarah's remarks, and increasingly nervous that he might not be there for me when I came back.

The journey to the airport was frantic. All tubes westbound were halted by an "incident on the line", so I got out at South Kensington and searched for a cab. The roads were impenetrable. Cars, buses and taxis were trapped by one another, each locked into routes they were programmed to follow, but they could move neither forward nor back with only inches between vehicles. A summer morning, bright and yellow, warming smug pedestrians who hurried to get to work, while I stood on the pavement gripped by desperation. My flight was in forty-five minutes - I'd already kissed the check-in time goodbye. I caught sight of a cab, its orange hire light glowed encouragingly, and climbed into it. I sat in the metal prison for a full ten minutes before it inched forward at all. At the first sign of movement I lit a cigarette. I might just make it. I knew that if I missed this plane I'd lose my chance of making it as a geologist - there was no way I could afford to pay for a flight to Tunisia myself. If only I'd broken our self-imposed taboo and left the flat when John had left for work. Slowly, the taxi budged forward, bit by bit, a little further each time space was created until, at last, the driver escaped by swinging off down a side-street lined with red-brick mansions, taking a secret, tortuous route to the M4 and Heathrow.

I made it with ten minutes to spare. As I ran through the barrier I caught sight of Hilary Stokes walking slowly in the opposite direction. She held a baby in one arm and clung on to the wrist of a fighting toddler with her other hand. Richard was pacing backwards and forwards in the Departure Lounge.

"Where've you been?" He was angry. "They called the flight fifteen minutes ago."

"The tubes..."

"Come on."

We ran along miles of corridors to the right gate. The stewardess reprimanded me for holding up the other passengers and I crept to my seat hot, sweaty and flushed with embarrassment. It was a million light years away from the capable, self-assured young woman I'd imagined myself to be, moving effortlessly from one new situation to another.

Africa. A new continent. I wanted to feel the essence of alien soil, the absence of Europe, but the heat overpowered my senses. It was like walking into a furnace. My tee-shirt was wet with perspiration before I stepped onto the soft tarmac and I struggled to catch my breath in the scorching air as claustrophobia closed in. I looked at the flat, dried ground of the airport and then beyond, to see where the real Africa started. Way off in the distance, cream-coloured mountains rose out of a shimmering heat haze. It was in mountains like those that we were to do most of our work.

"It's so hot," I said to Richard as we made our way to passport control.

"This is nothing. Wait till we get further south, further inland. That's hot. You'll get used to it."

Guns. Police and customs officials were all armed, strutting around safely defended from the public by their positions of power. Men in uniform were in the ascendancy and I felt threatened.

My French was pressed into serious service at the car rental counter, hiding in a cool, shadowy corner of the terminal building. Richard had made arrangements in London for the hire of a four-wheel-drive vehicle, but in Tunis there was no record of his reservation and no suitable car available. The only car not currently in use was a tiny Fiat Autobianci - which was totally unsuitable for the sort of terrain we'd be driving over. Richard's anger overflowed. I tried to convey his exasperation to the young woman behind the desk in the least threatening way I could, but even I was intimidated by Richard's irritation.

Half an hour later we wandered out into the airport car park, clutching the keys to the Autobianci. The woman, feeling cornered by arrogant Europeans, had sent for reinforcements. A tall dark Tunisian, with aggression that matched Richard's, told us that even the offer of the Autobianci would be withdrawn if Richard didn't calm down, and since tomorrow was Friday and everywhere would be closed, there was no chance of his finding a suitable car anywhere else. At this point my translation skills disintegrated, Richard grudgingly accepted defeat and we all shook hands.

In the rental parking lot the air quivered and I believed in mirages. The smell of effluence from the Lac de Tunis hung heavily in the air, pervading everything. Burning ourselves on the plastic seats, we squeezed into the tiny car and roared off to air-conditioning and other western luxuries in our hotel, which overlooked the sea near Sidi bou Said. We were due at the Tunis office of Austin Exploration Inc. the following morning, to pick up some of the geological references we'd need and our work permits. That gave us the rest of the day to recover from the stress of travelling.

We slept in our air-conditioned rooms in the afternoon and met in the evening for dinner. We walked down to the beach along dusty, unlit roads and sat there for a while enjoying the cool stillness of the dark. Single white lights littered the stretches of land on either side of us but offered no real illumination. Richard talked about his young daughter and the love he felt for his baby son. I was bored by the conversation but felt reassured by his devoted father-and-husband image.

Austin's offices were housed in an old, narrow, labyrinthine building near the centre of Tunis. The only people in the office that day were expatriates, since Friday was the Muslim Sabbath. Richard was in his element among American colleagues, discussing features and places already familiar to him, recalling incidents from the previous summer and talking about people I'd never heard of. I wilted into the background, being of no interest to the company men who didn't realise that Richard had taken on a woman as his field assistant.

It turned out that a couple of days previously they'd had a significant oil strike in one of the wells drilled in our study area. That was the good news. The bad news was that no one had bothered to get the references Richard had requested and we were without work permits. If we were stopped by the police we would have to pretend to be tourists.

It was good to get away from the frenzied chaos of the capital's roads that afternoon and drive down to the ancient and holy city of Kairouan. Out in the countryside things were very different. We travelled down straight black roads, through strange landscapes. Miles of flat plains out of which rose the sheer mountains, djebels, I'd seen from the runway, many of them almost pure outcrop. There were people everywhere, some in western clothes, others in more traditional robes. We were of great interest to them, speeding along in the tiny white Autobianci, especially to the children who smiled and waved as we passed.

I was anxious to get out in the field and prove myself as a geologist, but even this desire was submerged by an unfamiliar aching for John. The strength of my feeling for him took me by surprise. The experience of travelling through this unfamiliar land only distracted the edges of my mind while most of my thoughts were concerned with him. I thought about the last few months we'd spent together. There had been a distance between us caused in part by the pressure of my exams, but mostly because I was going away. Secrets, small meaningless secrets, had grown between us. I'd bought things for the trip - sun-tan lotion, maps of Tunisia, a compass-clinometer - and hidden them from him, afraid of upsetting the uneasy equilibrium that developed between us since our argument in April. In the silence of the journey into Tunisia I promised him that I would make things right between us again when I got back.

But there was always the danger that he might find someone else while I was away, a fear I had not properly confronted in London, but one that sent me into a panic so many miles and weeks away from home. If only I could 'phone him to tell him how I felt, to talk to each other about the things we'd ignored over the past few weeks. I wanted to hear his voice, soft and reassuring, but couldn't afford the phone call, not yet. That night in the small stone-floored hotel room I tried to capture my feelings in a letter; suffering that would be out of date by the time it reached him. I cursed myself for not bringing a photo of him, already I couldn't picture his face. I picked out his features in my mind but fitting them together didn't result in John's likeness and the harder I tried, the more the image disintegrated.

We were on our way to the first locality by seven o'clock the next morning. The air was cool and clear, the plains and mountains dun-coloured, speckled with green. People were busy before the heat of the day burned too strong.

Richard had been to the east side of Djebel Mrhila before and knew where the outcrops were that he wanted to look at. We tapped away collecting samples, sketching and writing in our field notebooks.

"Is this a collapse breccia?" I asked pointing at the outcrop.

"You tell me," he said.

"What?"

"I'm not your lecturer any more. You work it out."

I could see all the brecciated fragments and the matrix but didn't know how to tell whether it was Quaternary or part of the Cretaceous stratigraphy.

I opened my mouth to ask for guidance, but Richard had moved off and was scribbling in his field notebook. Confidence abandoned me. I'd never make a geologist if I couldn't sort out a simple problem like this and felt more than ever the need to prove to him that he hadn't made a mistake in asking me to be his field assistant. I stared helplessly at the outcrop, searching for any small clues that might help me.

"Come on. There are two more localities I want to look at before lunch," he said at last.

I nodded, silenced by my own inadequacy.

"How did you get on?"

"I...er...Well, I'm still not sure if it's a collapse breccia or more recent."

He winked at me, "Neither am I," he said.

"Thank God for that."

Relieved by Richard's honesty, I realised that geology wasn't the precise science I'd been taught it was.

After lunch of bread, tomatoes and cheese, we dozed under the shade of a huge rock, until the worst of the midday sun eased a little. Two hot hours spent dipping in and out of memories and dreams about life in London enhanced my sense of loss.

We visited three localities that afternoon, before returning exhausted to the hotel. I was disappointed by the tediousness of the day and the magnitude of the task ahead.

The long days afterwards followed the same pattern as that first day, although as time went on I grew more confident in my interpretation of what I was seeing. Every day an early start, squeezing in as many localities as possible before it became too hot to work and then lunch and rest. In the afternoon when the land simmered, we'd start again, driving to one locality after another, doing as much as we could before darkness or exhaustion overtook us.

The constant pressure to achieve as much as possible every day was wearing. Richard said we would be able to leave for England as soon as we completed the fieldwork so it was in both our interests to get the work done quickly. We spoke less and less to each other as time went on, except on geological topics. We would come in at the end of the day and collapse in our rooms, grateful at last for privacy. We'd meet again at dinner, when we discussed the day's work and, very occasionally, the people we were missing back in England. Richard always maintained a certain distance. I was glad of it.

We slowly worked our way round the outcrops of central Tunisia. Maktar, Sidi bou Zid, Sbeitla, Kasserine - exotic names, monotonous outcrop. We spent a couple of days in Austin's grubby office in Sfax, which is where we eventually got our work-permits, having already been stopped by the police on several occasions. As it turned out, it was quicker and easier to plead tourism than to baffle the police with the lengthy documentation associated with the permits. They soon got stuffed into our suitcases and forgotten.

Each place was different, the landscape altering from miles and miles of plains fractured only by ripples of mountains, to acres of regimented olive groves rooted in russet soil, and then to wooded hills, like the foothills of the Alps, but these smelling of rosemary, then back to the flat, rocky desert, parched and unyielding. It rained on a couple of occasions, after which the countryside was transformed, the arid ground airbrushed by a rich but fragile green. Seeds which had lain dormant for months leapt into life before the sun came out and relentlessly dried up any moisture they may have thrived on. One rainstorm washed away part of a road we were travelling on. The dry river-bed was filled with a torrent of thick brown water pulling along anything that lay in its path. We never got to that locality.

And everywhere we went they watched us, the people whose land we investigated. They watched and smiled and communicated with us as best they could, fascinated by the presence of ghostly Europeans. The further south we went, away from tourists, the less use my French became. Here they spoke Arabic. We quickly learned the most valuable phrases - *aslem, bislem, choukran.*

These people who had nothing, gave willingly what little they had. Our basic lunch was usually enhanced by gifts of almonds, eggs, dates and, from the very poorest, prickly pears. I was unused to such generosity and was shamed by it. We carried sweets around with us for the children, but the adults only wanted to give. The one thing they would accept were lifts in the car. The destination didn't matter but being in the car, able to stare at Richard so closely, seemed to give the old men, in particular, great pleasure.

It was at the end of August, halfway through the trip, that I decided to ring John. Although I'd sent him several letters I'd heard nothing back, but then he'd said he wouldn't write - my punishment for going away. His silence preyed on my worst fears.

I had to go through the international operator to telephone London so he knew before I spoke to him that it was me.

"Claire! Where are you?"

The sound of his voice, so close, made me want to cry out.

"Gafsa. It's in the middle of the country. There're date palms in the car-park. I wish you could see them. Are you missing me?"

"Yes."

"Honestly? You haven't gone off me? I wish you'd write."

"You know I'm no good at letters but I love getting yours. You're right, we've got some real catching up to do when you get home. I'm sorry for the way I was, it was stupid. Will you still be back on the 26th?"

"At the latest. We're trying to get through the field work as quickly as possible, so we can come home sooner."

In the distance pips beeped.

"What's that?" asked John. "You still there?"

"Yes. I think it means I've been on a minute. I can't stay long, but I had to hear your voice. Make sure everything's all right. It is, isn't it?"

"It is now you've rung. I wish you were home. There's so much to say, to put right."

"I'm so lonely. Richard and I are getting really sick of each other - all we've got in common are the bloody rocks."

"What about the people in the offices?"

"In Tunis it's only the office manager, Amor, who believes I'm a geologist, the others think I'm Richard's bit of stuff. And in Sfax they don't take me seriously because I've only just graduated. What's going on with you?"

"Work. Sean's over here now, staying with Siobhan till he gets a place. I've seen a lot of Matt. You should send him a card. And your ma. She only knows you arrived safely because she rang here to find out."

"It's not easy..." The pips interrupted me. "Next pips I'm going to have to go."

"We'll do something special when you get back."

"Maybe we could go away for a couple of days, just the two of us. Cornwall or somewhere."

"I'll see what I can do."

"God, I miss you. We're about half-way through now, so it can only get better."

"Time goes so bloody slowly, just waiting."

"I know. Mind you, there aren't enough hours in the day to get in all the localities we're supposed to visit. When will you finish work?"

"Not until I start the course. There's no point finishing before, I'm going to need every penny for next year."

"Give my love to Matt, and Mum if you speak to her again. I'll try and send them a card."

"Keep writing to me. Your letters keep me going. Jesus, it's so good to hear you."

The pips went again.

"I'm going to have to go. I love you and miss you."

"You too. Take care."

I pushed the tiny black buttons on the receiver's cradle down with the tips of my fingers. Disconnected. I lay back on my bed and put the receiver back to my ear.

"John?" Silence. He was gone. I saw his face fleetingly before it fragmented in my memory.

"Oui, madame?" The receptionist's voice crackled through the receiver. Her voice sounded more distant that John's.

"Oh - Rien, merci," I said and dropped the receiver back onto its cradle. She'd broken the spell.

13

We arrived back in Tunis the day the news broke about the massacres in Sabra and Shatila. We learned about it from Amor who was waiting for us at the hotel. He arranged for our bags to be taken to our rooms while we went out on the terrace overlooking the sea. We sat in the sun drinking mint tea from tall glasses.

"I didn't expect anyone to meet us," Richard said. "We're coming into the office tomorrow anyway. The car boot's full of rocks that we need to sort out and ship over to London."

"No problem." Amor's eyes were hidden by dark glasses.

"It's much cooler here, by the sea. I might go for a swim later," I said, feeling a gentle breeze on my skin.

"Not today. I came to warn you not to leave the hotel until tomorrow morning. Perhaps I'm being over-cautious, but I think it's best."

"Whatever's going on? Don't tell me the masses are finally rising up against Bourguiba," Richard said, but Amor didn't smile. You didn't make jokes like that about the President.

"It's the Palestinians. The police think there might be some trouble after the business in Sabra and Shatila."

"Sabra?"

"The massacres. You don't know?"

"We haven't seen a newspaper for weeks."

Amor pulled off his sunglasses and rubbed his eyes. "All this business in Lebanon. The PLO had to leave Beirut, they're here in Tunis, a couple of kilometres up the road from here. There've been massacres in two refugee camps in Lebanon. The police here are worried their anger will spill onto our streets. Many of the men have had their families killed."

It wasn't until I turned on the television that evening that the horror behind Amor's words hit me. I couldn't understand the newsreader's foreign words, but watched the story unfold as pictures of stiffened bodies, piled up in narrow streets, filled the screen. Bodies of old men and young women splayed out in the shadows of empty buildings. Dead children lay close to mothers shielding infants in lifeless arms. They'd looked for protection and found none. Toothless women howled, tearing at their hair, over bodies long dead, while others, screaming rage and grief pushed black and white photographs of their dead into the camera's eye.

"Did you see the news?" I asked Richard over dinner.

He nodded. "Terrible. How can people do it?"

"If I was Palestinian I'd take to the streets tonight."

"Amor seems sure we'll be okay as long as we stay in."

Over coffee he asked me if I'd enjoyed the fieldwork. Images swirled around my mind; digging the car out of sand that was too hot to touch, eating lunch at the very top of Djebel Semama, watching the flat land laid out hundreds of metres below us and the deep pink and turquoise channels filled with thick salt water by the side of the road that crossed Chott el Djerid.

"It's certainly been an experience."

"Would you feel confident coming back on your own?"

"Probably."

"We're going to come across gaps when we sort out the rocks and go through our notebooks. There's a chance you might have to come back without me, to clarify some of the data."

"Maybe I could persuade John to come with me." I liked the idea of that.

"If not, I'm sure Amor would look after you. He seems to know what he's doing."

At the end of the evening we went to our rooms. I didn't turn the light on and went out onto the little balcony of my room and stood for a while just listening. I was expecting to hear a lot of noise - shouts, car-engines revving in low gears and horns blaring out the anger of a wronged people, but all was still. It was cool out there, looking over the top of the dark trees which grew below the hotel. I waited for something to happen, wanting to be able to say, back in London, "I was there when it happened. I heard it," but nothing did.

Just as I was getting ready for bed I realised that I'd run out of water. Room service wasn't answering the telephone, so I pulled my dress back on and went to fetch a bottle. It was late, Reception was deserted, but the wall lights were still on in the lounge. I went down the steps and saw the waiter drying glasses at the bar. He had a drink in front of him and was talking quietly with someone.

"Excuse me," I walked towards the bar. "I wanted some water. There's no one at Reception."

"Certainly, mademoiselle. Safia or Ain Garci?"

"Safia."

"One moment. I must go to the kitchen."

I folded my arms and looked out of the window but all I could see was my own reflection in the glass. I felt the man sitting at the bar turn to look at me. I hoped the waiter would hurry back.

"I know you," the man said.

I turned away and pretended to look for the waiter.

"We met in London. At a party. I was with a friend of yours. Becky."

At the sound of her name I turned and looked. He was familiar.

"Come, sit. Ali, remember?"

Yes, I remembered. I walked slowly towards him. He wore a crumpled white shirt, open at the neck, and jeans. His hair, coarse and black, stood up where he'd been raking his fingers through it and the whites of his eyes were moist and red. He'd clearly had too much to drink.

"Sit down." He patted the stool next to him. "What brings you here?"

"Work. I'm over here with a colleague. We're looking for oil." I tried to sound formal.

He laughed heavily. "Oil, here? Were you lucky?"

"We're not sure yet. We've got more work to do." I could see the curve of his chest through his shirt, smooth and muscular. I looked back into his face. "I didn't know you were Tunisian."

"I'm not. I have an uncle here. I'm Palestinian. I've been trying to visit my cousin, but the police aren't letting anyone through. They're frightened of trouble."

"At PLO headquarters?" My heart thumped at being so close to the news.

"My cousin's family were living in Shatila. We don't know if they're alive."

He rubbed his eye with the heel of his hand and reached for a cigarette. He offered me one. Disque Blue. I shook my head. I didn't like foreign cigarettes.

"How will he find out?"

"News will get through eventually."

I watched his hand move towards his mouth as he drew on the cigarette. His fingers touched his lips, then his hand fell back to the bar. His knuckles were sharp, dark hairs covered the back of his hand.

"Where is he?" I twisted round in my seat.

"Stay. Have a drink with us. We have the rest of the night."

At that moment the waiter came back carrying half a dozen bottles of water.

"Here." He handed me a bottle.

"Thanks." I turned to Ali. "I've got to work tomorrow. I can't stay."

"Another time."

"When are you going back to London?"

He looked at me for a long time, frowning. Then he shook his head. "No. I don't know. If you see Becky, say hello for me."

Then, as I stepped down from the stool he leant forwards and kissed me on both cheeks. At the touch of his moustache on my face, I shivered.

"I will."

I felt his eyes on me as I walked back slowly through the lounge. He unnerved me.

14

I didn't recognize John immediately. He looked taller, his hair was longer and his face was turned towards a little girl he carried in his arms. She was playing with his nose. When he turned and saw us, his face lit up and he turned the child to face us.

"Daddy!" she squealed, wriggling in John's arms and leaning towards the returning passengers. Richard hurried to the barrier to cuddle her.

"Hello." John looked at me a moment, then, reaching out, kissed me across the barrier.

"I can't believe I'm finally home," I said, hugging him as I got out into the arrivals lounge. "I've been looking forward to it for so long."

We followed Richard and Hilary out into the grey afternoon, separating from them at the car park.

"See you next week," Richard called to me as I hurried off with John, anxious to be alone with him at last.

We drove straight to the Cotswolds from the airport. It was raining; fat drops of English rain welcoming me home. I savoured the heavy clouds and dark green trees, so different from North Africa. At the cutting through the Chilterns on the M40 I made John stop the car on the hard shoulder, so I could look at the patchwork of fields and woods below. I got out into the falling rain, cold under the dark sky. John walked round to my side of the car and we both watched a while until he pulled me to him and we kissed again and again, wet kisses in the falling rain. We'd been apart for too long.

"I love you," he shouted above the noise of the cars and lorries swishing by.

"It's going to be all right now, isn't it?" I asked.

He nodded and pulled me close to him.

In the hotel at Swinbrook we made love tentatively, more nervous than we'd been with each other the first time.

"I feel as though I've lost sight of you over the last few months. I'm frightened you're still angry with me," I said, as we lay together afterwards.

He lifted his head and rested it in his hand, watching me. He said nothing.

"I'm sorry," I said.

"No, not you, me," he said. "I'm the one who's sorry. I was so stupid, trying to tie you down, keep you here with me. I always knew you'd leave when you finished your course."

"I didn't though."

"You did, but you've come back. I wasn't sure you would. It's done me good. I've learnt that I can live without you. It's fucking hard, though."

"And I've learnt I can't live without you!"

"You could, if you had to."

In the peace of our time in Swinbrook I reflected on the past and came to the conclusion that over the last three or four months I'd learnt a lot about relationships and taking people for granted. Those two days laid the foundations of the relationship that followed. In some way it felt as if we had finally found each other.

We spent our time wandering through Cotswold streets, built hundreds of years ago with honeyed limestone. In the mornings we stopped at tea-shops to eat warm, sticky Danish pastries and in the afternoons, after walks along dry river valleys or up footpaths that climbed to the top of the wide, flat hills, we'd reward ourselves with huge cream teas. We spent the evenings in pubs. I told him all about my time in Tunisia and he filled me in on things that had happened in London while I'd been away. Sitting by a log fire, alight again now the evenings had grown dark and chilly, John spoke more freely about his childhood than he'd ever done. He told me of his friends, Kenny, Ian, Douglas, and others whose names he'd forgotten. Children playing on the street, bound to one another by childhood and poverty.

"I don't ever want my kids to be poor," he said one night.

"Kids?"

He looked at me and smiled.

"Maybe," he said and I didn't mind.

I was apprehensive travelling back to London, nervous that we'd slip back into the old routine.

The proportions of the flat seemed different, not quite as I remembered them. My desk had John's stuff on it now. A red ring-file lay open at a page where John had been writing just before coming to pick me up from the airport. I wondered if he'd been lost in his studying and then realised he was going to be late. Time that had stretched out interminably for most of the summer had suddenly become too short. I pictured him throwing down his pen and running from the flat, anxious and hopeful. He couldn't know then just how good our reconciliation would be. And that sentence sitting there, waiting for the next words, would never be the sentence John intended it to be.

I spent my first day back in London in the launderette - all day washing and drying my clothes. John had gone into college. That night we went over to Matt's for a meal and to take his car back.

"Claire!" He hugged me and kissed me on both cheeks. I hadn't expected such a warm welcome. He'd been so withdrawn before I left.

"Remember me?" Dominic appeared in the hall.

"What's going on?" I looked from Matt to Dominic to John. John had obviously known all along and hadn't said anything.

Inside the flat Dominic handed me a glass heavy with dark red wine, while Matt explained that he'd moved in. He was studying biochemistry at Imperial College.

116

"My mum thinks I'm in hall somewhere," he said.

"What if she wants to come and see you?"

"She won't. She's too busy. Besides, I've promised to go home for the holidays, for the first year at least."

"And what about this girlfriend you had?"

"There wasn't one," said Matt. "I knew all along. Silly sod, I'd have been much happier if I thought I just had a few months to wait rather than think he didn't want to see me any more."

It was lovely to watch them together, smiling and touching, sharing private jokes. Their relationship seemed especially valuable because it had nearly been lost. Alone together in the kitchen after the meal, Matt and I chatted.

"You know, I've never felt this way about anybody before. This is for real," he said.

I'd heard him say it all before, but this time I believed him.

"We're going home tomorrow, to Wales. Do you want to come?"

"With Dom? Does mum know?"

He nodded. "She didn't say much, but it's only till Sunday. She should manage two days. I'd like you to come."

"I don't want to. I want to spend time with John. I haven't been to the cinema or a club for months. I want to see friends, not mum and dad."

"Please?" He didn't beg.

"I'll see."

We arrived late on Friday night. Dom insisted on leaving after his lectures - fresh, dedicated student that he was. The air in Wales was chill and damp, heavy with autumn. Betsy waddled out, tail wagging. Gelert had died in the summer and Betsy was slower now, sadder. Home wasn't quite the same without him.

Dad was out at a meeting and Mum was very hesitant, contrasting sharply with her enthusiasm of the previous Christmas.

"John! Good to see you," she said, pecking him lightly on the cheek. "Claire. Two postcards in as many months. I thought you'd been sold off as a white slave."

"No such luck." I kissed her.

"You must be Dominic." She held out her hand cautiously. Dom took it and instead of shaking it, put it to his mouth and kissed it.

"I am, madam," he said, "your humble servant."

My mother's cheeks coloured and she pulled her hand away, unsure of what her reaction should be.

"You daft bugger," said Matt smiling.

"Come in, all of you. There's soup on and I'll put some rolls in the oven."

"I'll put the bags upstairs," said Matt as he entered the kitchen. "Who's sleeping where?"

She stopped pulling bread from a plastic bag and looked helplessly at him. I could see she was nervous. There was a silence.

"Well?" he insisted.

"You and Claire in your own rooms and Dominic's in the front. It's such a lovely view from there."

"And John?"

"Where he slept before." She spoke with a false brightness.

"How come?"

"It doesn't matter," Dom whispered to the air, looking as if he wanted to melt into the wall. All he wanted was to be liked, not to be the cause of a scene like the one Matt was warming up to.

John walked up behind Matt and took the bags from his hands. "Here, I'll take them up. I don't care where I sleep," he said. "I'll go in with Dom. We can share the front bedroom."

"But..." My mother stopped short, her mind trying to disentangle this new muddle of sleeping arrangements. There was a second's silence, the atmosphere poised to jump either way but at last she smiled and then laughed a little as she recognised the absurdity of it all. John, Dom and I joined in with her laughter - more out of relief than humour. Conflict had been averted and we could relax.

118

"Oh sod it!" she said uncharacteristically. "Sleep where you like."

This set her attitude for the weekend. She dropped her prejudices and allowed herself to get to know Dom, which meant that Matt could abandon his offensive. My father, on the other hand, found the situation much more difficult and stayed out of the house as much as possible, avoiding mealtimes altogether. When he came across Dom he was polite but distant. He would have liked Dom if he'd been anyone other than his son's lover.

We spent Saturday on the hills above Craig Goch, taking a picnic to eat alongside the mountain stream which we'd swum in as kids. Afterwards we walked on to the end of the track where the longhouse lay, wrecked by decades of harsh weather and neglect.

"I'd like to live here," said Dom, looking back towards the slate grey water of the reservoir, just visible between the slope of the hills.

"Oh no," said Matt. "Not here."

"Why not? It's perfect. You two are so lucky to have grown up here. When I was a kid I thought Hampstead Heath was the countryside."

"Maybe, but you wouldn't want to live here. This is suicide valley. People come from all over to poison themselves with carbon monoxide up this road," I told him.

"Why here?" asked John.

"Who knows? They never live to tell the tale, but I suppose because it's beautiful and deserted. I wouldn't mind my last view of the world being this one, would you?"

John shook his head.

"I don't care," said Dom. "I'd rebuild the house, turn it into a Retreat. Everyone who came would be really happy. They'd find peace and people would come to think of this as a good place."

On the way back we had to stop off at the Catholic Church to find out the times of mass for Dom.

"He never misses a Sunday," Matt told me the next morning as we stood on the pebble beach, skimming stones across the river.

"Seven that time, beat that!"

"Does John ever go?"

"To mass? No. He never talks about it. I suppose he's seen first-hand all the damage that crap can do," I said.

"Dom keeps on at me to go with him."

"Why?"

"Church means a lot to him. He wants me to share it."

"Have you been?"

"Once," he said dropping his disc-like pebbles back onto the beach, "but it's all so alien, so judgemental. He's still riddled with guilt about us. It worries me sometimes."

I thought back to my first meeting with Siobhan. Same religion, different sin, all linked to sexuality.

"Surely if he believes in God and believes God made him, then it must be God who made him gay?"

"That's what I said, but Dom argues that just because God made him gay doesn't mean he should give in to his feelings. He says that perhaps he's supposed to deny his sexuality - that it's all part of God's plan for him. He talks a lot about sacrifice and crosses to bear."

"I couldn't deal with a God like that."

15

John and I spent that Christmas in Tunisia. Richard was right, there were gaps in our notes. I had more fieldwork to do.

The months between the two trips had glided by effortlessly. Life was easy and we both felt content with one another after the unrest of the previous months. A lot of my friends from college had gone away, for work if they were lucky, or back to the suburbs and provincial home-towns if they weren't. By October most of the men from the course had found work on oil rigs in the North Sea, the Middle East and parts of Africa. Peter was working as a mud-logger for a Norwegian company in the North Sea - two weeks on, one week off. It was a dislocated life - his time away spent working without a break, and his time back home total freedom. The rigs he worked on were dry so he spent a good deal of his time back in London in the pub. He'd drop in from time to time, but we had little in common now that we'd lost the need to compete.

I saw quite a lot of Sarah. She was still living with Dave and working as a management trainee for Marks and Spencer. She seemed cheerful enough in her new career. I also met Becky a couple of times during those autumn months. She hadn't seemed interested when I told her I'd seen Ali in Tunis.

"I don't think he ever came back," she said.

"He looked like he'd got other things on his mind. Mind you, it was around the time of those massacres in Lebanon."

It was her lunch-hour. We were sitting on a bench set back from the pavement in Tottenham Court Road, chewing our way through French sticks dripping with mayonnaise.

"Were you and he actually a couple?" I asked. "I was never quite sure."

"Briefly. We got on well to start with. He was really quite something." She smiled to herself, remembering. "He turned really weird after Israel invaded Lebanon. He was so angry. Much worse that Ciaran."

"Did you ever see Ciaran again after that time in the summer?"

"No. I keep hoping, though. I know I'm stupid but I still miss him. I sometimes wonder if I'll ever really get over him. I don't suppose Matt ever heard anything?"

"No, I'd tell you if he did. Not that I see a lot of Matt these days. He's another one up to his eyeballs in work and he and Dom don't seem to go out much, at least not with us."

We scattered our leftovers to the pigeons which were strutting manically to and fro, through the dried up yellow leaves.

"You're still busy then?" I asked.

"We've given everyone a publication date of January and haven't even written all the text yet. I hope to God it's done by Christmas or I'll be spending the festive season banging all the information into the computer."

"Still, has to be better than last year, eh?"

She looked at me. "Anything would be better than that. How's your work going?"

"Slides, slides and more bloody slides. If I'm not looking down a microscope I'm watching the clock. I never dreamt it would be so boring."

"At least you're doing what you wanted."

I nodded and felt guilty about grumbling while Becky was still stuck behind a keyboard.

"Any more about moving on to the editorial side?"

"Not yet. Everything's been put on hold until this book gets published, if it ever does."

We chatted on easily until it was time for her to get back to the office. It was the first time in a year that I'd felt close again to Becky. The acute pain of losing Ciaran was gone and the distant ache she carried with her made her a softer person to be with.

John and I spent Christmas Day at the hotel in Sidi bou Said, where I'd spent the last few days of the summer. The atmosphere was different now, only a handful of tourists and the weather so much cooler.

On Christmas morning we wandered along the beach barefooted, paddling occasionally in the cold, blue sea. John was quiet.

"This time last year we were in Wales, practically snowbound," I said as we sat on the sand, watching the gentle waves lick the shore.

He smiled in agreement but said nothing.

"Doesn't feel like Christmas - no snow, no carols, no Christmas trees and, most of all, no telly. Just think of all the films we're missing."

He still didn't reply.

"You okay?" I asked.

"I'm not going back to college in January," he said.

"Why not? I thought you were enjoying it."

He shook his head and looked down at his hands which were playing with the sand. "Not really. So far they've taught me nothing I didn't already know."

"But it's only the first term."

"It's so basic. I'm not the only one who's unhappy. It may be okay for those who've come up from evening classes in woodwork, but for those of us who are carpenters, joiners, it's all kid's stuff."

I wasn't sure what to say. I was disappointed for him; he'd been looking forward to college so much.

"What are you going to do?"

"I'm thinking of getting myself a workshop. Making and selling my own stuff."

"Where?"

"I don't know. Market stalls maybe. If I advertised I could make bespoke stuff for people."

"Wouldn't you need capital?"

"Not much," he said. "I've been looking into it. I think I

could get a loan to start up. Even if it worked out, it'd be some time before it started paying." He paused and turned to look at me. "How do you feel about that?"

"If that's what you want to do, we'll manage somehow." My own pay was pretty erratic and only slightly more than my student grant had been. I wanted more.

The following day we headed south in the same little Autobianci that Richard and I had rented in the summer. I was surprised it was still running; we'd given it quite a hammering. Perhaps it was the only car they had to rent.

Unlike the summer, the days were warm and pleasant. Often, the first couple of localities of the day were actually cold, and it would be ice as well as rock that we'd be chipping away at with our hammers. By midday the sun had heated the land and it felt like a spring day in England. To the north of our area the vegetation was greener than it had been in the summer but further south, near Metlaoui, the thin soil scattered over bare rock still craved water. Its sparse scrubby vegetation clung tenaciously to whatever moisture it could find, but even here, in this desert, people managed to scratch out a meagre survival.

I enjoyed taking John to all the places I'd told him about and loved his curiosity and enthusiasm about the land and her people. We visited all the localities I planned to and yet the whole trip felt more like a touring holiday than real work. I saw it as due compensation for all the days I'd spent staring down the microscope.

During our first week, we were joined by Amor and a couple of Americans from Austin. The younger one, Jeff, had been in Tunisia for about a year, shuttling backwards and forwards between Sfax and the company's off-shore exploration rigs. Earl was just visiting the country, having a look at the company's North African operation. He was a large, silver-haired man, more anxious to taste the local wines than to study the local rocks. Using the company's four-wheel drive, he'd drive as close as possible to a locality and, without getting out of the vehicle, suggest that the terrain looked too difficult to climb and we'd all be better off going for a drink.

We spent the New Year together in a tiny hotel in Sidi bou Zid. We were the only guests in an area off the tourist trail and quiet over the holiday period without the business trade that kept the hotel ticking over.

They laid on a seven-course banquet for us - a strange but delicious mixture of French and Tunisian cuisine, accompanied by a steady flow of Tunisian red wine. I sat next to Earl who dominated the party with his stories of the different places he'd been during his long career as a petroleum geologist. He'd been to various parts of Africa, the Middle and Far East as well as South America. In most of the places he'd been posted he'd lived on compounds, away from the indigenous population, so he'd never really got to know the countries. He talked scathingly about colleagues 'going native', leaving their job and their family for a different lifestyle altogether.

"Want to be careful it doesn't happen to you, Jeff. Living here, right next door to the Tunisians, don't you miss your own kind?"

I glanced across at Amor who was concentrating particularly closely on the piece of lamb in front of him.

"No. I like it here," said Jeff.

"You just can't trust them. Once you get that through your head it's okay. Ain't that right, Amor? We can't trust you and you don't trust us - quits."

Amor looked from Earl to Jeff. Both these men were his superiors, there wasn't a lot he could say.

"Why can't you trust them?" John asked.

"'Cos they're damn foreigners, that's why!" And Earl gave a huge belly laugh, unaware that he laughed alone. "No, seriously. We're rich, the richest country in the world and they want some of that. Can't blame them, but can't trust 'em either. Besides, they've all got such goddamn unstable governments - look at Iran. It ain't personal, just practical. I don't hate foreigners. Hell, the States is full of them, immigrants, you just need to watch them."

"Where's your family from, originally?"

Earl smiled and pointed his finger at John. "I can see what you're getting at, but I'm an American, through and through. My mom's family date right back to the first settlers. Had to leave Wales, Claire, because of religious persecution. My pa's family came over from Ireland more than a hundred years ago."

"You're a Celt!" I said.

"Honey, I'm an American."

John followed Earl up to the table where a variety of desserts were laid out. Jeff put his hand on Amor's arm.

"Sorry. He doesn't mean anything by it."

"It's okay. I've met lots of people like him," said Amor.

"We're not all like that."

We sat in an uncomfortable silence until Earl returned to the table with a flourish. "So, your man tells me he's from Londonderry in Ireland."

"Derry," I corrected him.

"Galway's where my pa's folks came from. Ever been there?"

"I've not crossed the border," said John.

"Border?"

"The north of Ireland's still controlled by the British," I explained.

"Ah, yeah. There's a war going on there, right?"

John and I answered simultaneously. As I said, "Yes", he said, "No."

"It's just two groups of thugs fighting to get their own way. The ordinary people are caught in the crossfire."

"It's a bit more than that," I said. "The north wants to be reunited with the south but the British won't let them."

John moved his chair closer to mine and put his arm around my shoulders. He looked at Earl and smiled. "That's one version," he said.

Halfway through the second week they left us. Amor took

Earl back to Tunis and Jeff returned to Sfax. We were sorry to say goodbye to them and their expense accounts. We spent the next two weeks much more frugally. After the day's fieldwork we'd have dinner and then sit in our hotel room talking about John's plans. He'd already looked at a workshop not far from the flat and hoped it would still be available when we got back.

"Why didn't you take it when you went to look at it?" I asked.

"I wanted to talk to you first. I wasn't sure what you'd think."

We scribbled various cash flow projections onto scraps of hotel writing paper, predictions which varied from the business taking fifty thousand pounds in its first three years to the most pessimistic, which put us in debt to the tune of thirty-seven thousand by the end of the first year. It was a game we played. Time would tell.

16

Thin, yellow January sunlight filtered through a mesh of grey clouds as we descended over Heathrow. It was late afternoon and darkness would soon take over. We'd traded spring for midwinter.

Our cases were heavy with rock samples so we took a cab home. The flat was cold and dismal. In the hall we tripped over a heap of Christmas cards, too late to be of any interest, and several dull manilla envelopes.

"That's strange," said John. "Sean said he'd look in. Water the plants and that."

Sean had moved to London in September and was staying with Siobhan. He missed Derry and had already been back three times in as many months.

"But they were going back to Ireland for Christmas," I said.

"Aye, but they should've been back by now."

I turned on the central heating and started to unpack. John went to buy some bread and milk.

When he came back he said, "The flat's empty and there's post piling up inside their door. I'll go and clear it for them. I have a key."

When he'd gone again I put the kettle on and on my way back to the unpacking stopped to open some of the cards. Most of them were without a message, just the signature of the sender. It made the task boring, although each new unopened card had potential. Becky hadn't sent a card, just a slip of paper with the message, "Great news! Give me a ring when you get back." I picked up the 'phone and started to dial her number but John came in just then, so I put the receiver down.

"Well?" I asked.

"Nothing. They've obviously not been there since before Christmas but I know they didn't plan to stay away so long. There's butter and eggs in the fridge."

"Hope everything's all right."

"I'm going to have to ring them." He hesitated. "You don't mind, do you?"

I shook my head and left him to it. I went into the kitchen to finish making the tea. He was still on the 'phone ten minutes later when I brought the mugs in, talking in a low voice.

"Right...Yes...Okay, Saturday then unless the situation changes....I've watered them already, they're okay.....Love to you all. Bye."

He put the receiver down and looked up at me. His face was flushed.

"It's Eamon," he said. "Took an overdose. He's in a coma."

"Shit! When?"

"Christmas Day."

"What a time to pick."

He sat down. "Sean's ma said he'd been getting worse, more and more depressed. He'd stopped taking his tablets. Hadn't been out of bed for three weeks and then actually stopped talking the week leading up to Christmas. On Christmas morning they couldn't wake him. Had his stomach pumped at the hospital, but they think he'd taken the pills hours before they found him."

I passed him the mug of tea. "When are they coming back?"

"At the weekend if there's no change. It's been three and a half weeks now. They say he'll probably survive but he's shown no sign of coming round."

"How are they?"

"Sean blames himself. Says it wouldn't have happened if he'd not come to London or if he'd brought Eamon with him. Siobhan sounded upset but it didn't surprise her. Their ma's taking it badly. That's why they've stayed so long."

"Christmas is a bloody awful time of the year for Siobhan, isn't it?" I said.

I woke up in the middle of the night to find John sitting on the side of the bed, his back to me.

"What's the matter?" I asked. He'd been quiet all evening. In the darkness I reached out to touch his bare shoulder. "Jesus, you're cold. Come back to bed."

Like a small child, he obeyed. He lay on his back, the duvet across his stomach. I could see his chest rising and falling unevenly. I put my arm across him and felt his body tense, rigid.

"Whatever's the matter?"

He lay still, silent.

"John?"

"Sorry. It's brought it all back. This business with Eamon, I thought I'd put it behind me but it's come back."

"What?"

"Siobhan. Her breakdown and everything." He paused, remembering details. "I'd come in from work early that day. She was out of hospital, but still off sick, seeing a psychiatrist every week or so. On that many tablets. Anti-depressants for the day, sleeping tablets at night. She hated me then, she really hated me."

"Why?"

"I walked in and saw her at the end of the hall with a knife in her hand. The vegetable knife. She was sawing at her wrist. There was blood smeared over the walls. I made a grab for the knife and pulled her to the floor. Then she started screaming, like she'd just seen the blood and realised what was happening. She fainted. I thought she was dead, but turned out she'd not touched the artery, hardly opened a vein. In the hospital she wouldn't see me. Said the blood on the walls was her own dirty protest. Said I was trying to kill her, that all Protestants were trying to kill her. None of that had mattered till she became ill, then she tormented me with it."

"Protestant? You, a Protestant?"

"I was wrong when I thought we'd left it all behind. It

came back to haunt us."

"You mean you're a Protestant?" I was stunned. "You always said you were a Catholic. You told me - a Catholic from Derry." I turned on the bedside light. He didn't look at me.

"No. My family are Protestant. I'm neither Protestant nor Catholic. I never said I was. I know you thought I was Catholic, a nationalist even, but I'm not. I'm sorry, Claire. I suppose I should have put you right. But I don't see why it matters, not to us." He threw back the duvet and got up. Pulling his bath robe round him he said, "I'm going to make some tea. Want some?"

I couldn't answer him, struggling as I was to reconstruct this person I thought I knew. I'd created a family for him, a childhood and home life from scraps of information I'd picked up from conversations overheard between him and Sean. An underprivileged background, a child discriminated against. One who had suffered and fled from the injustices of the majority population and a foreign army. A composite picture of someone who didn't exist. I felt betrayed.

I got out of bed and followed him into the kitchen.

"So you're not really Irish then."

"I'm British, like you. I come from Northern Ireland, that's all."

"But it's not your country. You've no right to be there."

"And Wales belongs to you, does it?"

"I've never pretended to be Welsh. I just grew up there."

There was a silence.

"Until I met Siobhan, I thought we'd always been in Ulster. It's what I was taught. We've been there nearly four hundred years. How long does it take to belong? To become part of a country?"

"But your lot dominated the Irish people and they still do, even now. How can you condone that?"

"I left, remember. I had to, to marry a Catholic. Don't you tell me where I do and don't belong. You have no idea what it feels like to leave your home because of ignorance. You have no right to be prejudiced."

"Me prejudiced? That's rich coming from you." I turned and left him, and went back to bed alone, confused by all that had been said. I was dazed by John's admission that he came from the side of the oppressors. I knew it shouldn't matter. It should be the person I loved, not some romantic version of his background.

Around half past six he came back to bed. I lay on the far side feigning sleep. I didn't know what to say to him. He wasn't the same person I'd gone to bed with the night before. I wasn't sure who he was.

I left for the Poly before he was awake, needing to sort my thoughts out. In the afternoon I rang Becky.

"You got my note then?" she said brightly.

"Oh, right." I'd forgotten about her message.

"He's back!"

"Ciaran?"

"Well back and forth, and when he's in London he stays with me."

"How come?"

"It's a long story. I'll meet you for a drink and tell you everything."

"Tonight?" I asked hopefully, not wanting to go home.

"Okay. About nine-thirty in the King's Head."

"Will Ciaran be there?"

"No. He's away at the moment."

I tried to ring John to tell him I'd be late but there was no reply. His absence cleared my conscience and I found myself better able to concentrate on my work. I was startled when Richard came in.

"Sorry I haven't got in to see you sooner, you know what Thursdays are like. I gather it all went very well."

"Yes. I've brought a load of samples home. I'll either bring them in bit by bit or borrow my brother's car."

"I can pick them up for you. I've just been speaking to Amor. They seem to like you over there, they're offering you a contract. Six to eight weeks in Tunisia, working on some of the cores from the rigs."

"Oh."

"I'm sorry it's not fieldwork. You don't sound very enthusiastic."

"No. I am. It's just... When do they want me? I can't drop everything here, can I?"

"I've been thinking about that. The cores are all related to our area and we're probably ahead of schedule anyway. I know you could do with the extra money. It's up to you."

"Money?"

"You'd be paid directly by Austin. A hundred dollars a day, plus expenses."

It sounded too good to be true. "When do I have to let them know?"

"As soon as possible. They really want you back out there for the start of next week. He's ringing me back about six. He'd like to know then."

"I ought to speak to John," I said, thinking out loud.

"They don't like to be left waiting."

Rather than talk to John about it over the telephone I left the lab and caught a bus back to the flat. It was empty. I had no idea where he was or how long he'd be. To cover myself, I left a note explaining everything. There would be no recriminations this time.

I came home to talk to you because I've been offered a contract in Tunisia for the next six weeks. Richard says he can let me go but I wanted to talk to you about it. I have to give my answer by six o'clock and you're not here, so I'm going to have to accept without seeing you first. I've done my best. Hope you don't mind too much.

Love, Claire.

P.S. I'll be back late tonight, I'm going for a drink with Becky. See you later.

All the time I was scribbling the note I hoped John wouldn't turn up. I also hoped I'd captured the right balance of concern and light-heartedness in the note which I couldn't have managed if I'd met him face to face.

17

When I arrived, Becky was already sitting at a table with two glasses of lager in front of her. "God, you look awful!" she said. "Here, get that down you. What's the matter?"

"Thanks. I'll tell you later. First I want to hear about Ciaran."

She beamed. "Christmas Eve, right? I'm sitting there watching the telly and about ten o'clock the bell goes and there he is, on the doorstep. I thought I was dreaming. He'd not changed a bit. It was like this past year never happened. I didn't know whether to hit him or hug him. He just put his arms out and said, "I'm sorry." That was it, how could I resist?"

"How did he find you?"

"Went to hall first and the porter gave him Ellen's address. She told him where I was. It was the best Christmas present I could have had. I was supposed to go in to work on Christmas Day, but didn't. We were just together. It was great. He's mellowed, you know. Much more mature now."

"What's he been doing?"

"You know he went back to Dublin. Well, after Christmas he went to visit some cousins up north. Then they all went on to stay with friends in Belfast and while he was there he got involved in some sort of youth project."

"I thought he wouldn't be allowed into Northern Ireland?"

"Me too. He says he gave the police state more credit than it deserves. They don't care. They know he's just mouthy and not a real security risk. He seems really into this youth work, though. They provide activities for unemployed young men. He's backwards and forwards to England looking at outdoor pursuits centres and stuff. When they've got enough money they bring a group of lads over to stay in one of these places. They've even taken them abroad to north Africa - somewhere near where you went. He says that when he's in England he wants to be with me."

I had to fight my cynicism. It seemed so out of character for Ciaran to come back to Becky on bended knee. Perhaps it was just jealousy, my own relationship being in shreds.

"He said he'd put me out of his mind at first. Our splitting up was too painful for him to think about, but then he saw me in the summer - remember I told you about seeing him at Oxford Circus? - well, he said that was it. Couldn't put me out of his mind."

"Took him long enough to find you," I said, wishing I hadn't.

"He was afraid I wouldn't want him back."

"Where's he been staying when he's been in London before?"

"A flat in Kilburn somewhere."

"On his own?"

"No. With two other youth-workers. Both men. I know what you're thinking, but honestly, I believe him now when he says it's me he wants. Imagine him still wanting me after all this time."

I tried, but failing miserably, got up to buy some more drinks. Up at the bar I was overwhelmed by exhaustion. I wanted to find a quiet corner somewhere and slump into it.

"Does he have to watch what he says over there?" I asked, handing her a drink. "Ciaran never could keep his mouth shut."

"Don't be silly. He's safe in the bosom of Belfast's nationalist community. He's not changed that much."

"You'd better not bring him round when John's home then," I said, trying to bring the subject round to me.

"They always got on all right."

"Oh Becky, John and I have just had the most bloody awful row. Well, not a row exactly, more a misunderstanding. A huge misunderstanding. I found out last night that he's Protestant."

"And?"

"A Protestant from Northern Ireland."

"So?"

"What do you mean? I thought he was a Catholic, a nationalist."

"You've lost me. I don't see what the problem is. You're not Catholic or Irish, so why the wobbly?"

"Jesus, Becky! I thought you of all people would understand. All that oppression by the Protestants. Ciaran's gone on about it often enough."

Becky sighed. "I don't know what it is with you, Claire. You're never bloody satisfied. You've found someone who really loves you and just because he doesn't fit in exactly with your picture of a romantic hero you want to dump him. So what if he's a Protestant? He married a Catholic and lives in London, what more do you want him to do? Plant some bombs for the IRA?"

"But I thought he was Catholic."

"So bloody what? Either you love him for himself, or you don't."

"I just feel so confused," I said, making a last attempt at Becky's sympathy.

"So, sort yourself out. You don't appreciate him, you know, never have. If you really love him you should work harder at the relationship, make things right. If not, cut loose now, before wasting any more time - yours and his."

"God, you're hard."

"The tables are turned, aren't they? The truth hurts - I should know, you told me often enough. Make a positive decision to stay because you love him or go."

"You've really changed."

"No, I haven't. I'm just stronger, that's all. I've learnt how to stand up for myself." She left the table to go to the toilet. My head was reeling. I'd been convinced that Becky would give me her unconditional sympathy and support and the fact that she hadn't shocked me. Perhaps she was right.

When she came back the conversation turned to more

mundane matters. I told her about my contract in Tunisia. She raised her eyebrows, but made no comment. She was still busy at work. The publication date for the book had come and gone and still the text remained unfinished. As she discussed office wrangles my mind wandered back over what she'd said earlier. Did I love John? If not, did I have the strength to leave him? The John I had loved was a nationalist, a refugee forced out of his homeland by violence. This new man could take some adjusting to.

In spite of the icy weather I decided to walk home, leaving Becky shivering at the bus-stop. I hoped it would give me time to think. The pavements glittered with frost and before long my toes ached with the cold. Smoke from my breath exploded into the air and hung there. At least I would leave all this behind by going back to North Africa.

By the time I got home my face and thoughts were numb. I rang the bell and watched as the sitting-room door opened and John's tall, thin form came into focus.

"Hi. You came back then," he said quietly. "You're freezing. Get your jacket off and go inside. I'll put the kettle on."

In the sitting-room, the light glowed a dull yellow and the two radiators pumped out heat. The television was on and its sound and colour lent a sense of homeliness to the flat. I didn't want to leave.

"Where were you this afternoon?" I asked when he came in with the coffee.

"College. I went to tell them I wasn't coming back."

"Were they okay about it?"

"Yes. Glad I'd come to tell them in person."

I took a sip from my mug. The liquid burned my lips.

"Claire, we've got to talk. Sort this out."

"Aren't you going to ask how Becky is?"

"How is she?"

"Ciaran's back. It's amazing, he says jump and she jumps."

"I thought she'd seen the last of him. I hope they're happy this time."

"She's had her hair done. Looks really good."

"Claire, listen, I'm sorry if you think I lied to you. I didn't mean to, but I still don't know why it makes any difference, me being Protestant."

I didn't know what to say, but could feel him looking at me, willing me to answer. We sat in silence for some time.

"Looks like I'll be flying out on Sunday or Monday," I said at last. "Amor said he'll book the seat and I can pick up the ticket at the desk."

John put his head in his hands.

"I'm sorry I didn't get to talk to you about it first," I said.

He shrugged his shoulders and pulled his hands from his face, inhaling deeply. He looked tired.

"Still Sean and Siobhan'll be back by then. Keep you company."

"Jesus Christ! Why will you not talk to me?"

I stared at the carpet. "Because I don't know what to say, because I'm not sure how I feel and because I know it shouldn't make any difference but it does."

"Things aren't that great over there for the Protestants either, you know."

"I don't want to talk about it."

"But you should. We always used to get the jobs over and above the Catholics. We believed it was our right and it didn't strike me as wrong until I got to know Siobhan and the others. But now there's no jobs anyway, for Protestants or Catholics. And housing. That's the another thing we did better at. We always got our slums before the Catholics, but they were slums just the same, not decent houses. And then I lost my family because I married Siobhan. My father said I was no son of his. When Billy was shot, ma wrote and asked me to come home for the funeral. When I got there I found out my father had died two years earlier and they hadn't told me. Do you know how that feels?" He paused. I avoided his eyes. "I've spent my whole life confused. And now this - you upset that I'm not Catholic. I thought it wouldn't be a problem over here, but it is to you.

Where is my home, Claire?"

"Does it matter? You're in London now."

"London's not my home."

As we sat in silence, I could hear John's breath sharp and shallow and allowed myself to wonder, just for a moment, how it would feel to be denied a homeland and rejected by your family - displaced and dispossessed.

18

On Saturday afternoon we went over to borrow Matt's car. John was going to pick up Sean and Siobhan from the airport. I decided to stay with Matt. I hadn't seen him since before Christmas.

"Where's Dom?" I asked, moving some papers off the sofa so I could sit down. The flat was unusually messy.

"Gone home for the weekend. His sister's had another baby. It's being baptised tomorrow and he's the godfather."

"I take it you're not invited."

"Not unless I want his mother to hold me down while the parish priest cuts off my balls."

"And that doesn't appeal?"

He threw a cushion at me.

"What's the priest got to do with it?" I asked.

"Dom's only gone and told him about us. I think he wanted support, but all he got was hellfire and damnation. Since he came back after Christmas he's been talking about moving into hall."

"Shit."

"He's got other problems too. He's under a lot of pressure at college. Once this weekend's over, hopefully things'll be okay again."

"Hope so. Let's go for a walk. I could do with some air."

We walked down the long straight street towards the park, bordered by the River Lea. Wrapped in thick jackets I put my arm through Matt's for greater warmth. Early Saturday evening, dusk falling and half the people of Stamford Hill hurrying to get the last of their shopping before most of the shops shut, while the other half had been tucked away since the previous evening observing their Sabbath. In those houses lights shone out, beacons celebrating family, food and religion.

The park was poorly lit and the bare trees stood sentry, heavy and dark on either side of the path, threatening.

"I wouldn't fancy walking down here on my own at night," I said.

"Nor me. The number of my friends that have got beaten up in places like this. I wouldn't come down here this time of day with Dom, I'm much safer with a woman."

I smiled at the irony. We walked over to the river, thick and dark, moving onwards. Canalized and domesticated, it was a different creature from the wild, shifting rivers and streams of home. We stopped and leaned on the railings, staring into the deep, black fluid.

"Funny you should be having trouble with the Catholic Church. I am too, in a way," I said to Matt.

"Siobhan again?"

"No, not this time. I always thought John was a Catholic. He told me the other night he's not."

"Lucky you."

"But I thought he was."

"So?"

I recognized the signs. I could see I'd get the same response from Matt as I'd got from Becky. I changed the subject.

"Ciaran's back, you know."

Matt's head twisted round sharply to meet my eyes.

"Really?" There was an eagerness in his voice.

"Not permanently. I think he's based in Belfast but comes over from time to time. He's back with Becky."

"Oh." There was a long pause. "Will you ask him to get in touch, if you see him?"

"Is that a good idea? You know what a shock it was for him finding out you were gay. Why should he have come to terms with it now?"

Matt didn't reply but continued staring at me, beyond me. He wasn't listening to what I was saying.

142

"He knows where you are if he wants to get in touch," I reminded him.

"I miss him. If you get the chance, mention it, please. He was a good friend."

I thought it sounded like absence making the heart grow fonder but said nothing.

When we got back, the telephone was ringing. Matt went to answer it while I turned on the electric fire in his sitting-room.

"That was John," he said, coming in from the hall. "He's taking them straight back to the flat, so can you get the bus back?"

"What about your car?"

"I've said he can use it tomorrow to take you to the airport."

"Did he say how they were?"

"Not good. He said if he's not home when you get back, he'll be over at their place. He said we could go round if we wanted."

"Stuff that for a game of soldiers! I'm not going round there to be miserable the night before I go away."

"Claire!"

"Sorry. I didn't mean it to come out like that, but I've only met Eamon once. It doesn't mean a lot to me. Anyway I still get jealous of Siobhan sometimes. I wish she'd find herself a boyfriend."

Matt and I spent the evening together and when I got back John was out. I had a bit more packing to do and as he still wasn't back went to bed as soon as I'd finished. I heard the front door slam after I'd been asleep for some time. I glanced at the clock. Two fifty-three. He must have undressed in the bathroom before getting into bed naked, his body icy cold. I could smell whiskey and turned away from him, annoyed that he'd spent my last night in England comforting his ex-wife.

"Are you awake?" he whispered, but I didn't reply. I didn't have the energy for an argument.

There were butterflies in my stomach when I woke the following morning and remembered I was off to Tunisia on my own. I had a bath and got dressed. John was still asleep when I'd finished and I wasn't sure whether or not to wake him. I decided to have breakfast on my own.

Sitting in the silence of that Sunday morning I tried to sort out exactly how I felt about him. I thought back to those first few weeks we spent together and then to the unsettled months before I went out to Tunisia the first time. Things had been so good between us recently, until this. Half of me felt betrayed that he'd let me believe he was Catholic and the other half knew it wasn't important. It was a bad time to go away; we should be together over the next few weeks, to heal the misunderstanding.

John came into the kitchen, his hair ruffled, looking pale and ill.

"What's the matter?"

"Too much whiskey. Do we have any aspirin?"

"You bastard! I'm going away and all you can do is get pissed with Siobhan the night before I go."

"I didn't get pissed with Siobhan, she'd gone to bed. Sean was in a terrible state, I couldn't leave him. What was I supposed to do? I invited you and Matt to the flat but you never turned up."

"I thought you might want to spend the night alone with me. God knows when I'll be back."

He sat down and put his face in his hands. "I don't know what to say to you." He looked up at me. "One day you avoid me like I'm some kind of leper and the next you say all you want to do is spend time with me. I can't keep up with you, Claire. Sean needed someone with him last night. I had no choice. You could have come but you didn't. Don't blame me."

"Three o'clock! Three o'clock this morning. That's the time you got in and here you are now, stinking of whiskey, looking like death..."

"This has nothing to do with last night, does it?"

"I don't know what you mean."

"I think you do."

He got up and left the kitchen. I heard him go into the bathroom and run a bath. I didn't want to leave like this, but didn't know how to put things right. He came into the sitting-room half an hour later dressed and looking a little better. I was rolling a joint. I needed to relax.

"I don't want to fight before you go away," he said. "I'm sorry we weren't together last night, there wasn't a lot I could do. They say if Eamon regains consciousness he'll be a vegetable for the rest of his life. How would you feel if it was Matt?"

I shook my head. "I don't know." He'd put things into perspective.

"Smoke much more of that and you'll turn into a vegetable!"

I looked up at him. There was a sad smile on his face.

"Come here," I said. He came and sat close. "I'm sorry for the way I've been the last few days." I could hear Becky's voice telling me how I'd never really appreciated John. "It's just that it was such a shock. I'm still reeling. I know it's stupid of me, give me time."

"You've plenty of that just now."

"Everything'll be okay when I get back."

19

Amor picked me up from the hotel on the first day. We drove past the place where the PLO still languished in exile. An endless line of metal railings surrounded acres of flat land, which separated the soldiers from the world outside. Across the compound, roads going nowhere sliced through the grass. There was no sign of the buildings housing Yasser Arafat and his men but Amor assured me they were there.

Austin's lab was situated to the north of Tunis. From outside, it was difficult to tell whether the building was being constructed or demolished, but Amor told me that a further storey was planned which accounted for its unfinished look. The view from inside the lab, in contrast, was breathtaking. The building overlooked a beach, where sand of the palest yellow was lapped by aquamarine water deepening to dark blue further out, where the sea touched the horizon.

Amor introduced me to the two technicians - Mohammed and Hussein. Mohammed's English was weak and his French not much better but Hussein, whose mother was French, spoke the language fluently although he had no English. Between us, we were able to communicate quite effectively on a business level, but ordinary everyday chat wasn't possible. The two of them spent the day talking to each other in Arabic, excluding me totally and facing me with a loneliness I'd never known before. I knew they were unaware of my isolation and vowed I'd learn some Arabic for next time.

After the first day I was picked up in the morning by taxi and dropped off again at the hotel in the evening; the lab was only four miles from the hotel so there was no justification for hiring a car. The hotel provided me with a packed lunch which I ate sitting on the beach watching the sea and thinking about John. I was glad we'd made our peace with each other before I left but still felt unsettled that he wasn't the nationalist I'd believed him to be. That was probably the main reason why I didn't 'phone him in those first weeks - I could have afforded to that time - but I didn't want to talk to him until we could be together and go through it all, face to face. I sent him a couple of postcards so he'd know I was thinking about him.

The only thing I had to look forward to during those first three weeks was Amor's daily visit. It was the highlight of my day. I hated it when he popped in during the morning because it meant the rest of the day was flat, empty of expectation. I usually made him coffee and tried to keep him talking for at least half an hour. I used any means I could to delay his return to the Tunis office; the microscope seemed faulty, I needed more information about the site where this core came from, could he help me translate a reference? With each visit I grew more inventive. He must have sensed my desperation and, at the end of the third week, with the prospect of two solitary days stretching out in front of me, he suggested I might like to join him and his friends at a nightclub that evening.

"Fantastic! What time? Can you pick me up? I can always get a taxi if that's difficult."

"No problem. Nine, nine-thirty I'll come to the hotel. I will have my sisters in the car also. It might be tight."

"I don't mind."

As I sat in front of the mirror at half-past-eight that night, applying colours to lips, eyes, cheeks, I realised the evening could make me feel even more isolated. He was taking his sisters, meeting up with friends - their common language was Arabic, I would be unable to share the evening with them. I tried to push these thoughts away and recapture the thrill that had carried me through the afternoon. It was no good. I decided to go for a couple of hours. I could always get a taxi back.

Amor's sisters were friendly. Habiba, the older of the two,

spoke excellent English. She was training to be a nurse at the city's main hospital and wanted to go to England when she was trained.

"Why?" I asked. "I thought America was the place for a trained nurse to go."

"I've always wanted to go to London. I want to go to Great Ormond Street. Train to nurse children. At the moment I'm in Emergency. I wouldn't want to do that for long."

Nadia spoke very little English but smiled and laughed with us anyway. Habiba told me she was meeting Pierre, her French boyfriend, at the club. They'd only recently met and her mother was unhappy because he was foreign and not Muslim.

Amor was able to park outside the hotel and we tumbled out of his car into the darkness of the night. Inside the hotel the reception area was bright and cool, floored with polished cream limestone. I stopped and gazed for a moment at the wonderful oolites locked into the rock creating a beautifully intricate pattern.

Amor took my elbow."You have been too long behind that microscope," he said.

A narrow stone staircase wound its way down to a large basement area where red, blue and yellow lights flashed with the rhythm of the music. Tables surrounded the recessed dance floor which was already busy. Waiters brought drinks to the table where we sat with a number of Amor's friends. Language wasn't a problem; the music was so loud it made conversation impossible.

Habiba, Nadia and I danced together until Pierre arrived and then Nadia disappeared. Amor took her place, less energetically, his body moving in time to the beat. At intervals, exhausted and hot, we'd return to the table where cigarettes and Pernod revived us. I was unaware of time passing; there was no life outside this shaded, throbbing room. It felt good to be with a crowd of people again. The lights seemed brighter, the drink stronger and the music had more rhythm than the clubs I'd grown bored with in London. My senses had been brought back to life after the emptiness of the previous three weeks.

At the table I lit a cigarette and pulled wet strands of hair away from my neck. I glanced around, looking for a waiter to order another drink. I scanned the unfamiliar faces, picking out Europeans among the crowd, when suddenly my eyes were stopped by a returned look. I knew the face. Ali. He held my gaze just a moment too long for me to pretend I didn't recognise him and, bound by convention, I smiled. He got up from the table where he was sitting with a large group of men and walked towards me. When he reached me he grasped my arms and kissed me heavily on each cheek. I felt the prickles of his moustache and remembered the effect he'd had on me in the summer.

"Back again?" he shouted over the sound of the music.

I nodded. Amor got up and went over towards the bar.

"You didn't go back then?" I asked.

He frowned and turned his head slightly.

"To London," I shouted.

He shrugged and took my arm. I allowed myself to be led outside to the stairs.

"I couldn't hear," he said, indicating that I sit down. He remained standing, facing me. I sat and smoothed my skirt down as near to my knees as it would go.

"You didn't make it back to London," I said. My ears were ringing. The loudness of the music was muted now, but I knew I was still shouting.

"No. I had things to do here."

"I didn't think you'd recognize me."

"Are you still looking for oil?"

I nodded. "Only I'm stuck inside this time, staring down a microscope."

"How's Becky?"

"Fine. Really well. She's back with..." I hesitated, realising it might be inappropriate. "Ciaran. They see each other from time to time."

"And you? Have you come here with anyone?"

"A friend from work. I think he took pity on me. It's my

first night out since I got here three weeks ago. I've tagged along with him and his sisters."

"I hope he will bring you again. How long are you here for?"

"Another month at least. They're drilling like there's no tomorrow." I told him where the lab was and what I was actually working on. I was aware of his eyes wandering over my body as I talked, and was flattered by the attention. He stood over me, lean and tall, listening, his full pink lips sliding backwards and forwards over straight white teeth as he smiled at my stories. He stroked his moustache with his thumb and forefinger and I found myself wanting to kiss those lips, feel again the scratch of his moustache on my face, plunge my tongue deep into his mouth. Stop. I had to stop. I tried to concentrate on what he was saying to me and I stared into his dark, deep-set eyes. He ran slender fingers through his coarse, black hair and stood so close to me, I could smell him, slightly sweet, and feel the warmth from his body.

"I should go back now," I said eventually, trying to stand up. "They'll wonder what's happened to me."

With one hand he held my wrist, putting his other hand under my elbow, helping me up. I swayed slightly and he pulled me to him, clasping an arm firmly round my waist. I turned my head to thank him but there were his lips kissing my cheek. I stretched my head back and closed my eyes, feeling the progress of his lips and tongue over my neck and up, at last to my mouth. I put up no resistance, I wanted this. While his mouth held mine captive, his hands worked their way around my body, squashing my breasts with his palms, squeezing my buttocks, pulling my legs apart. I pulled out his shirt and caressed his back and chest with both hands. Still kissing him, I let my hand wander down and fumble with the button on his jeans. Opened at last, I reached down to feel his penis. I felt it already tight and hard.

"I want you," I whispered, my mouth snatching for air.

He pulled me to him, half-carrying, half-dragging me through a fire-exit door. All was darkness in the corridor but I could hear sighs of other people in the blackness. A patch of wall became our bed as he pushed me against it, lifting me slightly, reaching up my skirt and rubbing his fingers hard, backwards and forwards across the silk material of my knickers. My arms reached out to try and pull at his jeans. He helped me ease them over his buttocks and then he tore at my own underwear. He entered me almost savagely. I caught my breath at the feel of him. My eyes grew accustomed to the dark as he thrust his hips forwards again and again, penetrating deeper with each movement. I looked up to see him watching me. Then his mouth closed again on mine. Locked together, our hips moved in unison until his breathing got quicker and shallower and he moaned out at the point of orgasm. We clung on to each other a minute longer, hot, breath slowing, and then he pulled away from me. Hurriedly, and a little embarrassed, we rearranged our clothing. He took my hand and we stumbled out through a door at the end of the corridor into a kitchen yard. A sharp light burning out from a steaming window hurt my eyes. We dropped to the floor and leant against a huge battered old dustbin. We looked at each other and started laughing. He kissed me again and then took my fingers up to his mouth and started sucking them one by one.

"Stop," I said, "or I'll want you again."

"Not tonight. I have to go. What are you doing tomorrow?"

"Nothing."

"I'll pick you up. You're staying at Sidi bou Said again?"

"Yes."

"Come," he said, getting up and then helping me to my feet.

On shaky legs we walked back through the dark corridor towards the beat of the music. He kissed me on my forehead at the foot of the stairs and then left me standing alone as he ran up the stairs, two at a time.

"What time tomorrow?" I called after him, but he'd already gone.

I went into the toilets before going back to the others,

pulling fingers through my hair and trying to mop up the smudges of mascara around my eyes and the smears of lipstick from my mouth.

"We were just going to give up on you," Amor shouted as I came back to the table. "Habiba wants to go. She's working early tomorrow."

"Sorry. An old friend. I haven't seen him for a long time." My face burned with the lie.

In the car a silence fell over the four of us. Nadia sat in the back with me and gazed out of the window. I hoped she was thinking about Pierre, but Habiba and Amor's silence accused me. I was sure they knew exactly what I'd done and started to feel ashamed - Amor had got to know John quite well in the week we spent together after Christmas.

"Who was your friend?" he asked eventually.

"Just someone I was at college with."

He said nothing more until he pulled the car into the hotel car park. I reached for the door handle.

"The men your friend was with are not good men. Be careful."

"What do you mean?"

"I've heard they are terrorists. Some are PLO, some, I think, from other places. They're dangerous."

I said nothing but sat in the car a minute longer trying to absorb what Amor had said. I didn't know what to do with the information and got out.

"Thanks. And thanks for the lift."

I smiled briefly at the receptionist as I picked up my key.

"Mademoiselle Marshall," she called after me as I hurried towards the corridor, wanting to sort my thoughts out in the quiet of my room. I didn't turn round but she called again.

"What?"

"There was a telephone call for you tonight, from London. He didn't leave his name but said he would call again tomorrow."

I stood there for a full minute before pulling myself off to my room, heavily and slowly. Amor's warning I could almost brush aside - after all it was only hearsay - but a 'phone call from John forced me to face what I'd done.

20

I didn't know what to do. The clock in the bedroom showed the time was one twenty-three. It would be a couple of hours earlier in London. Perhaps I should ring him and get it over and done with. Alcohol made me bold.

There was no delay in getting through. I heard his voice as clear as if he was in the next room.

"Claire! Thank God. I thought you'd never ring. How are you?"

How could I tell him? How could I explain how I was? If I'd spoken to him before I'd gone out that evening I could have said how rotten everything was and how lonely I'd become, but that wasn't true any more. Now, I wanted to stay out here. I was going to see Ali again tomorrow and the thought filled me with guilty pleasure.

"It's really boring. There's nothing to do but work and the blokes in the lab don't speak English. I can't wait to get home."

"Is it hot?"

"Pretty warm. How about you? How's the business going?"

"God, it's good to hear you. When are you coming home?"

"I'm not sure. I've still got so much to do. I don't think I'm even half-way through. Have you kitted out the workshop yet?" I wanted to get the subject away from me and onto him. It felt safer.

"I've another meeting with the bank next week. They want to see plans and projections."

"Give them the best ones, won't you?" I thought back to our evenings together poring over figures. A wave of sadness swept over me. I'd lost something in that dark corridor.

"How is everyone?" I didn't really want to know.

"Eamon's still in hospital."

"Any progress?"

"No. Sean's going over for the weekend. Siobhan's got herself a job with the council. Parks and Recreation, as a gardener. She starts Monday. I saw Matt last night. Said he was going to try and get in touch. He wants to go and see you over there."

"But I'm working." I didn't want Matt judging me.

"He'll look after himself and Dom might come too. Jesus, I miss you. I wish I could come with them. Just hearing your voice makes me feel better. To know you care. You do, don't you?"

"Of course. Don't be silly." I thought he'd be able to detect the falseness in my voice, but he didn't.

"I love you, Claire. I'll sleep better tonight. The bed's empty without you."

"I'd better go, it's gone half-past-one over here, I'm knackered. What time did you ring?"

"What?"

"What time did you ring me?"

"I didn't."

"But the receptionist said there was a call from London. I thought-"

"Could have been Matt. I gave him the number of the hotel."

Shit! There had been no need to ring John, to have covered up, lied. It was Matt who'd telephoned. My mind became tangled in thoughts of predestination. Perhaps it was inevitable that John and I would speak to each other that night. Should I confess? Was that inevitable too?

"John."

"Yes?"

I hesitated. I couldn't be sure. "I'll ring you again. Let you know when I'm coming home. Love you."

Distant. John was a long way from where I was and yet close, too close. I thought I could cut him off as easily as putting down the telephone receiver. After all, it was only temporary, this thing between me and Ali, just a bit of fun. It wasn't going to develop into anything deeper. It couldn't, not with me in London and him in Tunis. Thoughts swirled around my head, contradictory and uncomfortable. However I tried to justify my actions or discount them as unimportant, I couldn't escape from the fact that what I'd done was wrong and would tear John apart if he knew. But I knew too, that I would see Ali again, as much and as often as I could.

I couldn't sleep and ran a deep bath. Lying in the warm, silky water I allowed myself to think about what Amor had said. I remembered Becky telling me how angry he'd become when Israel invaded Lebanon and I already knew that he had a cousin in the PLO. It seemed likely that he would be involved as well, but rather than scare me away, I found the prospect of Ali being mixed up with a liberation movement exciting.

I was woken from a fitful sleep by the long, single ring of the telephone by my bed. A line of sunlight sliced through the curtains across the room. My head ached. I reached for the receiver.

"Yes?"

"A Monsieur Fadi is here to see you."

"Who?"

She repeated the name. It wasn't a name I knew and then it dawned on me that it might be Ali. I dressed as quickly as I could.

"Hello," I said, my head clearing slightly at the sight of him. "I didn't know what time you were coming. I've only just got up."

He put his hand out. "Come. I've borrowed my friend's car. We'll go north."

Outside the day was warm and bright. It felt like a beginning. The car he'd borrowed was a dusty old Peugeot, a dying bunch of jasmine hanging from the rear view mirror. I discovered later it was there to mask the smell of petrol which filled the car. The engine was eventually shaken into life after several fruitless turns of the ignition key. Ali looked at me from time to time, smiling. I wondered how far north we'd get.

"I hope you weren't late last night," I said, fishing for information about where he'd had to go.

"No. It was okay."

"Are you working at all?"

He shook his head, keeping his eyes on the road.

I gave up and relaxed into my seat. When we were out of the city he put his hand on my thigh, massaging it, pulling up the material of my dress. He looked across and smiled at me. I moved closer to him and kissed his ear and neck, while my hands undid the buttons on his shirt.

"Keep your eye on the road," I warned.

But we were turning off the main road, up a track. Red dust churned up by the car followed us like a wild spirit. He stopped suddenly and pulled me to him. I was trapped between the steering wheel and his body as he pushed me to the floor. I felt his hands on my head, down my neck to my back and round to my breasts. I undid his jeans. He slid himself forward and I pulled out his penis, standing up hard and straight, and took it into my mouth. I heard him gasp as I moved my mouth and tongue up and down, teasing all the pleasure I could from it. His own excitement aroused me so much that when he came, I freed myself and pulled him over into the back seat with me. There he pulled off my dress and knickers and ran his fingers and tongue all over me. I moaned with the pleasure of his touch as he pushed my thighs apart with firm hands before dropping his head and, with deft movements of his tongue, brought me to orgasm.

We lay together, hot and panting, contorted by the smallness of the back seat.

"It's never been as good as this with anyone before," I said. "I want you again and again."

He laughed softly and pulled himself up. I wanted him to talk to me but although he smiled, he said nothing.

We arrived in Bizerta in the early evening, battered and sore. We'd stopped a couple more times on the journey and made love. Once in the car, hampered by the hand-brake and gear-lever, and further north we turned off the road where some ruined buildings crumbled among trees. Here we lay on the rough floor. He pulled off my dress and we kissed. Our hands stroked each other, palms hard against skin, we touched and learnt about the other's body. Then he thrust his penis into me again and ground and twisted his body against mine. I wanted to envelop his whole body within me, to become fully one with him. After we'd done, we lay together a long time, saying nothing. I rested my head in the curve between his head and shoulder, and looked up through narrow green leaves into the empty blue sky. I couldn't get enough of him.

Much of the hotel was closed for the winter. Floors were being polished, walls whitewashed and lifts mended, in preparation for the summer guests. It felt like arriving at a party too early. The main restaurant was closed but the Beach Café would provide all we'd need.

We slept before dinner. Our room overlooked the sea and when I woke I went out onto the balcony to watch the full moon trembling on the black water. Bougainvillaea climbed the lower walls of the hotel, the blooms a silvery grey in the moonlight. I could hear the waves wash over the glistening sand. It all seemed so unreal. What was I doing in this place with this man I barely knew? Surely, somewhere in a parallel universe my other, real life was carrying on as before. I heard a cough from inside. Ali was awake.

"We should go down and get something to eat, before the Germans have it all," I said, referring to the party of elderly tourists who were also staying in this ghost place.

It was cold in the café. A breeze was blowing in from the sea through bamboo blinds. I shivered, having brought nothing other than the dress I was wearing. We ate soup, fish couscous and baqlawa. We didn't talk at all as we ate, but afterwards, when tiny cups of hot, sweet black coffee were brought to our table, I asked him about his cousin's family.

"They killed them all. My cousin's wife and five children murdered. Even the youngest, just four years old, they killed him too."

I didn't know what to say.

"Our time will come," he said.

"What do you mean?"

"Arafat came to Amman afterwards, I was visiting my parents and went to see him. He said we should be ready to lose fifty thousand lives in the struggle for Palestine. I gave up my life that night. Nothing matters to me any more except the liberation of my homeland."

"You are a terrorist then."

"Who said so?"

"Just someone. They said you might be involved in an armed struggle."

"I am a soldier, I have to fight. We come from Nablus. My father's family have lived there for generations. We had to leave in '67, forced out. We left with nothing more than the clothes we stood up in. I can remember my father crying - I'd never seen him cry before. He'd lived in that house all his life. Couldn't believe they would take it from him. We fled to Amman where my mother's family were. The Israelis have made dangerous enemies - we are a people with nothing to lose."

The following day we got up late, aching from the exertions of the night before, and wandered along the beach, feeling the warm sand between our toes. It was good to feel the heat of the North African sun on my skin. Until that weekend I'd only got to feel it through the windows of the lab. His hand caught my fingers as we strolled along and when I turned to smile at him I was surprised, just for an instant, that it was his face and not John's that I saw. It made me think back to a similar walk less than two months previously when John had talked of his plans for the future. I couldn't see the future now; everything seemed uncertain.

"I really ought to go back tonight," I said.

"What time do you have to be at work?"

"About eight. You could always stay with me in Sidi bou Said."

"We'll spend the afternoon here, then leave."

We got back about nine o'clock, and I could hear the telephone ringing inside as I unlocked my hotel room door.

"I have a call. A moment please."

Ali came in and closed the door behind him. I sat on the bed and kicked my sandals off.

"Hi, Claire?"

"Matt. How are you?"

"I've been trying to get in touch with you for the last three days. Where've you been? I thought you weren't doing any fieldwork this trip."

"I'm not. I've been stuck here for the last three weeks and got offered the chance to go north for the weekend, so I did." Ali had lifted my legs onto the bed and was sucking my toes.

"I'm booking a flight out to you on the twenty-eighth. Two weeks. Can you book me into your hotel?"

"I'm not going to be around much. I've got to get these bloody cores done." A week ago I'd have been only too happy for Matt to come out, but now I just wanted to be with Ali. His hands slid their way up my legs, pushing up over my belly, to my breasts. He lay on his stomach beside me, kissing my neck, nibbling my ear. I couldn't concentrate.

"Don't worry, I'll look after myself."

"Is Dom coming too?" Ali was undoing the tiny buttons down the front of my dress.

"No. Too much work. He doesn't want to get behind."

"I won't be much fun and I haven't even got a car this time."

"I could always hire one for a few days. What's the matter, don't you want me to come?"

"Yes, course I do. I just hope you won't be too bored,

160

that's all." Ali had opened my dress and his mouth was following the path his hand had taken down over my breasts. I gasped as his teeth gently chewed my nipple. His hand continued to work its way down over my belly, pushing and squeezing it, down further until I felt his fingers inside me.

"You still there?"

"Mmm."

"I'll get a taxi to the hotel then. On the twenty-eighth, okay? Claire?"

"Yes."

"Sure you're all right?"

"Oh yes."

21

I wasn't in love with Ali - I kept telling myself that. It was just a little madness, a reaction against the loneliness of Tunisia. How could I love Ali? We hardly spoke to each other, our time together being taken up with sex. We could have no future as a couple. My life lay back in London, Ali's in his armed struggle. We both knew that when I went back to England we wouldn't see each other again. That knowledge, that certainty, gave an edge to our relationship, a frantic quality which meant we had to hurry, making the most of the hours spent together. And time together was short. We never went away again. I wished we'd stayed an extra couple of days in the peace of Bizerta, where we were calm in each other's company. Staying on wouldn't have delayed my contract much but it would have given us more time together and we needed time.

Once we were back in Sidi we were both locked into our routines. My day was spent at the lab isolated from both my old and new realities, while Ali vanished until eleven o'clock at night, at the earliest. I never asked how he spent his time, but assumed that he sat plotting the overthrow of the Zionist state from the other side of those lines of iron railings. Some nights he'd come in exhausted, then I fancied he'd spent the day doing some kind of military training, but didn't ask. I knew he wouldn't have told me.

The days dragged on interminably and the nights flashed past too quickly. I slept very little during those first couple of weeks and suffered for it. There were days I could barely keep my eyes open, especially in the afternoons, staring down the microscope into the face of the earth's secrets. Cretaceous, Turonian - names, divisions of ages past. Trying to place myself and my problems in the history of the earth, I was overwhelmed by my insignificance. Ali, John, whoever - the earth didn't care, we were all mere travellers clutching onto fragments of her surface, fighting over them and claiming them for our own. We needed to belong but She didn't. She simply was and would be.

With each slide, each snapshot of a minute part of the earth's formation, I grew more weary. They were all the same and all different. I was losing confidence in my skills and had trouble deciding which parts of which cores I wanted cut into thin sections. I was slipping behind schedule. The men in suits wanted a report on their desk in Texas by the middle of March. They wanted confirmation that their investment in this distant land would soon pay off. I had to sort myself out.

One evening towards the end of February, when I came in from work, the receptionist handed me a message with my key. Wandering down the corridor to my room I unfolded the piece of paper.

"Telephone message from Matthew Marshall, London, England, 1310 hours. Change of plan, now arriving 5th March, for two weeks. Please change booking accordingly and book single room. John trying to get flight for 13th March to stay for one week. Will telephone later with details."

I read it twice in disbelief. Inside my room I slid to the floor and wept. Everything was beyond me, outside my control. I didn't know how to deal with Matt coming over, how to put John off, how to finish the cores and pull some sort of report together in less than three weeks, how to leave Ali or face John after what I'd done.

At last, empty and worn out, I dragged myself up off the floor. Of all the troubles piling up, one stood out above the rest - John. I had to stop him coming over. I looked at my watch. Matt would still be at work, I hoped I had his office number.

"You got my message then?" he said.

"Yes."

"Is it okay? You didn't sound too keen last time I spoke to you."

163

"You've got to stop John coming over." I felt my voice crack. I didn't want to start crying on the telephone.

"Why?"

"Don't ask, please. Just do it."

"How? Why can't you ring him and tell him yourself? It's going to sound a bit weird coming from me."

"Say I tried to 'phone him but he wasn't there. Please Matt, it's important. I'll tell you everything when you get here."

"What shall I say to him?"

I paused. "Tell him I've got to go down to Sfax that week, to do some fieldwork and present the report. Tell him I've booked a flight back on the 18th. It's not worth him coming over."

"Have you?"

"What?"

"Booked a flight."

"Not yet, but that's when I'm likely to be back, unless anything happens."

"Sounds like something has."

"Dom's not coming then?" I wasn't going to tell Matt about Ali over the 'phone.

"No. That's another story."

"See you on the fifth."

Talking to Matt calmed me a little, but hysteria hovered close as I sat on the bed deciding how best to tackle my other problems. I needed more sleep and to spend more time at the lab if I was to get through all the cores. Up until then I had spent my evenings reading in my room, waiting for Ali, now I would have to stay later at the lab. Perhaps I could also afford to be a little less detailed in my analysis of the slides.

To most of my problems there were solutions, but I didn't know how I would deal with leaving Ali or how I would react to seeing John again. I couldn't plan the future.

I bathed and made myself up, as I did every night before Ali arrived. I made sure he couldn't see I'd been crying; he didn't need that. Our relationship was too short to be complicated by emotion. I lay on the bed and slept lightly until I heard his soft knocking on the door.

"I woke you," he said, pulling away after greeting me with a long, deep kiss.

"Just a nap. I'm so tired."

He lifted me up, and carried me back to the bed, then sat by my side watching me.

"You'll be able to sleep tomorrow."

"Why?"

"I have to go away for a few days."

"Where?"

He just smiled and shook his head.

"You will come back, won't you?"

"Yes. Don't worry."

I reached up to kiss him, pulling him close to me. I couldn't bear the thought of doing without him. He pulled his jacket off and threw it to the floor. There was a loud thud. I jumped.

"What was that?" I asked.

He moved his body on top of mine, kissing my mouth and face, drawing his knee up slowly between my legs.

Some time in the darkness of the night I got up. Ali was sleeping, his breath deep and slow. I reached down to feel among his clothes which were tossed in a heap. Underneath lay his jacket which I pulled into the bathroom. Before I shut the door I listened; Ali's breathing remained unchanged, I knew he slept on. I switched the light on and pulled the gun from his large inside pocket. I had to see it close up. Touch it.

It was heavy, so heavy I nearly dropped it. Cold, black, scratched and battered from use. A weapon with a history. I turned it over in my hands, feeling the rough texture of its handle between my palms, contrasting with the smoothness of the pistol's barrel. As my forefinger rested snugly into the trigger's gentle curve I wondered if it was loaded. Different from the toy guns of childhood, the trigger peeped out from inside the gun's handle like a flat, black tongue protruding between iron lips.

In my hands I held such power. A single shot through the head would solve my problems. No, the excitement of life, complicated though it was, gripped me. Holding the gun in my right hand, I lifted it so that I could line up the front and rear sights. I squinted and closed my left eye. Before me the bathroom wallpaper was transformed into a hundred vicious enemies. My thumb stroked the hammer gently. Slowly, deliberately, I pretended to shoot the enemies, one at a time, allowing the gun to recoil a little with each silent shot. Sitting on the bathroom floor, I worked my way round in a semi-circle until most of the enemies lay dead. The open bathroom door halted my carnage.

I gasped and my heart thumped as I saw Ali standing in the doorway, his stern expression fixed like stone.

"Just practising," I said, getting up and handing him the weapon.

He didn't smile.

"I wanted to know what it felt like. Is it loaded?" Nervousness made me babble.

Still he said nothing, merely looking down at the pistol before picking up his jacket and stuffing it back inside his pocket.

"Go to bed," he said without looking at me.

"Ali?" I wanted him to look at me.

He glanced at me briefly over his shoulder as he walked back into the bedroom.

I turned off the bathroom light and into the blackness asked, "Have you ever used it? Ever killed anyone?"

I heard him sigh in answer, somewhere in the abyss.

In the morning I brought the breakfast tray into the bedroom. I was dressed, ready to go. My taxi would be arriving in ten minutes. Ali was stirring. I had to talk to him before I left, to make sure he wasn't still angry with me. I took a cup of coffee over to the bed.

"Ali, wake up. I've got to go in a minute."

He opened an eye and shut it again.

"Look, I've brought you some coffee. It's on the side here."

No response. "How long are you going away for?"

This time both eyes opened a little and he frowned as he peered up at me.

"When will you be back?" I asked again.

He shrugged.

"I'm really sorry about last night. I didn't mean anything by it. I was just curious. I'm frightened that because you're angry, you won't come back. Say you will, please?"

His face cracked a little into a smile. "Doesn't matter," he said.

He reached out and picked up his coffee. He took a long sip before replacing it on the bedside table and dropping his head back on the pillow. The telephone rang.

"Mademoiselle Marshall, your taxi is here."

I put the receiver down. Close to tears and panicking, I wanted reassurance that he would come back.

"I've got to go." I was pleading.

His hand stroked my cheek, touched my chin. I grabbed it with both of mine and pushed it to my mouth kissing and biting it roughly. Then, with his other arm he pulled me down on top of him. We kissed - the touch of his lips, his tongue inside my mouth - I couldn't bear to pull away, but the taxi was waiting. I got up.

"Three, four, five days. I don't know," he said. "You be here, waiting."

"I will. I promise."

22

I didn't see Ali again for a week. It was a barren week, like those first three weeks, but worse this time because I was tormented by the anxiety that he wouldn't come back. I worked fourteen hours a day catching up on lost time and trying to blot out the image of his face in the bathroom doorway. On the day he finally returned I'd started to draw up an outline of my report. I'd made good progress.

I arrived back from the lab about half-past-nine, the curtains in my room were drawn back. I could see nothing through the window, just the mirror image of my room, then I heard a knocking on the glass. I jumped. Fear and hope took hold of me but still I could see nothing as I walked towards the window. Then I saw the flash of teeth and fumbled with the key in the lock, cursing my clumsiness, before pulling the balcony door open.

"Ali!" I fell on him, kissing his face and clinging on to his neck.

He pulled my arms down and held them by my side.

"Where were you?" he asked, unsmiling. He had several days stubble over his cheeks and a cut and large bruise over his right eyebrow.

"Working."

"You said you'd be here."

He made me nervous. "What happened?" I asked, trying to raise my hand to touch his wound, but his hand held my wrist with a grip of steel. We looked each other in the eye for a full minute before his face broke into a wide grin, and then he laughed loudly, pleased with himself that he had unnerved me so much.

"Bastard!" I said, releasing my hands and gently punching his arm. "You really got me going then. Come in."

He was dusty and dirty and smelt of the desert. He fell heavily on the bed and then pulled off his shirt to reveal more cuts and bruises on his chest.

"What on earth have you been doing?"

"Playing games. Come here."

I let him take me, use me. I was entirely subservient to him; whatever he wanted me to do, I did. My pleasure could only result from his own.

"I've thought about you a lot these last days," he said as we lay together afterwards. He was stroking my body with rough hands, stopping occasionally and twirling one of my nipples between his thumb and forefinger which were rough as sandpaper. "I did not think you would matter so much to me."

I was silent, frightened to speak. He'd never admitted any feelings for me before.

"Are you pleased?"

"I don't know," I lied.

"And me. How do you like me?"

I turned to look at him. Our faces close together, I didn't trust myself to be cool enough in my response. I hesitated.

"I like you. I think I like you a bit too much."

He squeezed me to him, delighted.

I ran a bath and ordered sandwiches and coffee to be brought to the room. We made love again, this time in the bath, sloshing about and giggling in the hot, soapy water. There was a lightness, a light-headedness about him that night. The smallest thing would set him off laughing, a heavy rhythmic chuckle from deep in his lungs. I lost count of the number of times we made love, but my body ached in the morning as I pulled my clothes on. It felt good.

"What time will you come back?" he asked as I kissed him goodbye.

"Depends what time you're planning to get here."

"I shall be here all day."

"Why don't you come and meet me for lunch, about half-past-twelve? On the beach next to the lab."

"Perhaps."

I spent the morning watching the clock, allowing myself to see what the time was after each slide. At ten past eleven exactly I finished describing the last one. That and the excitement of Ali coming back was almost too much. Amor popped his head round the door. I didn't care about the timing of his visits any more.

"I've just finished the last of the slides. Can I get you a coffee? We can celebrate together."

"I thought you'd fallen behind."

"I caught up."

I poured boiling water onto brown granules which suffused the clear liquid with an earthy brown colour. I'd brought my own instant coffee with me from England; Amor sipped from the mug and grimaced.

"You English! How can you drink this stuff?"

Every day he complained and every day he drank it. I ignored his complaint.

"Come over here and see," I said. "I need to get this lot typed up. The slide descriptions."

"Of course. I'll take them with me now."

"No. Not yet. A couple of days. I still need them to finish off the report. Here's the outline."

He studied it for a few minutes and then nodded.

"Good. It looks very good. They'll be pleased."

"My brother's coming over from England tomorrow. If I can get the report finished this week, I'll stay on with him for a few days. Show him the sights."

"And your boyfriend?"

Flustered, I said, "John's not coming over this time."

"I thought you were seeing someone here."

"He's just a friend." I hoped he didn't realise the friend was Ali. It seemed impolite somehow, after his warning.

170

"We'll have to find something else to bring you back, soon."

"I don't want to leave. Maybe I'll find an excuse to come over and do some more fieldwork on the project Richard and I are doing."

Amor stayed at the lab with me for a long time. When he left I grabbed my sandwiches and went out to sit on the beach to wait for Ali. I'd let him eat them, I was too excited. Waiting and watching the horizon, I compared my happiness with the misery I'd felt during those first weeks. In the warmth of the sun, I thought about the time Ali and I had spent. We probably only had a couple more weeks together at most and the thought of leaving him filled me with dread. My feelings for him were developing into something stronger than the sheer excitement I'd enjoyed at the beginning. I didn't know him well; we hadn't had the time to find out much about each other's lives, but I knew, from the way he looked at me a moment too long when we left the hotel in the morning or squeezed my hand when he woke early in the morning, that given time, we could really care for each other.

By half-past-one he still hadn't arrived. I walked slowly back to the lab. I could see the beach from my desk. The afternoon dragged as I tried to construct a pithy introduction to my report. This was the part of the project I was really looking forward to, the culmination of all those drab hours chained to the microscope. It was spoiled by Ali's absence.

At five o'clock I ordered a taxi to take me back to the hotel but he wasn't there either. I searched the room for a note, some explanation, but there was none. I checked with Reception for messages. Nothing. I didn't know what to do. I had no address or telephone number for him. Perhaps he would turn up as usual at eleven-thirty; I tried not to worry too much until then.

He'd left his watch on the bedside table. He'd taken it off the previous night, before we'd had the bath. The tiny digital read-out was blank, it needed new batteries. That must have been why he'd left it behind.

I couldn't eat and spent the evening struggling with the report. The minutes ticked by too slowly and too quickly, for although the evening dragged, half-past-eleven came round too quickly with still no sign of him. At about one o'clock I finally went to bed, unable to imagine what might have delayed him. I slept a shallow, dream-troubled sleep and woke alone. Where was he? Miserably, I got ready for work, ignoring the breakfast brought to my room, but grateful for the routine.

The 'phone rang to tell me the taxi had arrived. I picked up my paperwork, stuffed it into my briefcase and left the room.

"What are you doing here? Where's the taxi?"

"Today I am your taxi."

It was Amor. He looked grave as he reached for my arm and hurried me out to the car.

"What's going on?" I wondered if he was playing some sort of practical joke on me.

"Get in."

I sank into the seat and Amor slammed the car door behind me. He climbed into the driver's seat next to me. As he stared out of the windscreen the look on his face made me realise this was no joke.

"Your friend, the one you met at the club?"

I nodded. An icy feeling slid over my limbs.

He hesitated, searching for the right words, but couldn't find them.

"He is dead."

Winded, I gasped for breath. "How? What do you mean?" I shook my head trying to comprehend his words. "No. You're wrong. How do you know?"

"Habiba has seen his body at the hospital."

"She doesn't know him."

"He was there two days ago. She recognized him as your friend. They talked about you."

I was already shaking my head. "He wasn't at the hospital two days ago, I'd know." But before I'd finished the sentence I thought of the bruises on his body. His cut eye. I was silent a moment, trying to piece things together. "What's supposed to have happened?"

"He was knocked down by a truck yesterday. He died last night."

I closed my eyes and heard the dense thud of a body hitting the bonnet of a Peugeot pick-up truck. I saw it thrown up into the air, defying gravity, before falling, leaden, back onto the road. A picture of the cat that summer night an age ago, flashed through my head.

"No. It must be someone else." It couldn't be Ali. He was going to die in the struggle for freedom, lay down his life for Palestine. Tears outside my control slid down my cheeks. "He's my friend, you know."

"I know." His voice was gentle.

"I'm sure it's not him. I'd know. We're so close."

"Do you want to go to the hospital? Habiba is there. Then you can be sure."

I didn't know what I wanted and sat there in silence putting off a decision.

Amor turned on the engine. "I think it's best," he said.

We pulled out of the car-park and drove towards Tunis. I was paralysed now, unable to know or feel anything. With each red light, each smoky traffic jam, I relaxed a little, putting off the moment when I'd know for sure. Through unfamiliar streets we went, past shops, workmen, people going about their daily business. I was outside it all.

Suddenly I realized we had stopped. Amor was helping me out of the car, guiding me through battered green metal doors. My legs weren't working properly. Habiba appeared and took my other arm, talking rapidly to her brother in hushed Arabic. We were devoured by a groaning lift which carried us slowly down to the basement. We emerged into a dark corridor littered with broken trolleys, walking frames and wheelchairs. Somewhere in the distance I saw a bent figure sweeping the floor, the swish of his broom rasped my consciousness. Then the dirty cream door which Habiba pushed open. I followed her in. It wouldn't be him.

173

No sheet covered his body, no cloth hid his face. I stumbled and bit my knuckle as hard as I could to stop myself from screaming out. The man's body was broken, distorted, his face swollen and misshapen with eyes sealed shut. His skin seemed too pale, but discoloured in places by the blooms of purple and yellow bruises. Above his right eyebrow the evidence of an earlier injury. Gingerly, I touched his puffy cheek with the tips of my fingers, half-expecting to heal him, to bring life back to the corpse, but there was no response, just a terrible chill. I leaned over to kiss his mouth and saw the trace of dried blood at one corner. I pulled back, unable to do it. This had once been Ali, but he'd gone.

I turned away, sinking my teeth deep into the back of my hand. I closed my eyes to shut it all out and stop the tears. My legs gave way. Amor put his arm firmly round my shoulders and helped me to my feet. Slowly we made our way out of that terrible room, back into the lift, up and outside into daylight.

I was put in the car, still unable to open my eyes, unable to look upon this world without Ali. Fingers stuffed two large capsules into my mouth. I felt the rim of a plastic bottle of water at my lips.

"Drink." Habiba's voice.

I obeyed, feeling the tablets travel uncomfortably down my throat. I didn't care what they were, I just hoped they might kill me. I put my head in my hands and opened my eyes, but there, in my palms, I saw the corpse, mottled and hopeless.

The engine rocked into life and Amor pulled out onto the road. My eyelids were heavy and swollen, my mind drifting. Somewhere Amor stopped the car and got out. Then he was back again handing me a glass bottle filled with tiny tablets. I noticed the green cross of the pharmacy and wondered what they were.

Back at the hotel Amor's arm supported me again as I tottered back to my room, a different person from the one who'd left that morning. I couldn't focus properly and the furniture seemed to float about the room. All I wanted to do was sleep. Amor helped me to the bed.

"My brother..." I started to say, but lost the energy needed to finish the sentence.

"Sleep. I'll come back later."

The only emotion I could feel was an immense sadness somewhere in the distance, waiting. Waves of total exhaustion washed over me and I lost consciousness. When I opened my eyes it was nearly half past four. The sun was trying to penetrate through the thin brown curtains and, just for a moment, I couldn't remember where I was or what had happened. Then it all came crashing in; the shock, his battered face, my loss. Two tablets sat by the clock next to a bottle of Safia. I put them in my mouth, unscrewed the top of the bottle and swallowed. Then, with great difficulty, I pulled myself from the bed and tried to find the bottle Amor had got from the pharmacy. All those little green pills would reunite me with Ali.

I wandered around, holding onto the furniture for support. In the bathroom I knocked pots off shelves in my search for the drugs, but without success. Angry and frustrated, I stumbled back to the bed and lay there trying to piece everything together. I picked up his watch which still lay by the bed and put it to my mouth. I kissed it and detected, very faintly, Ali's smell. I breathed in deeply, savouring the memories the smell brought with it. I clutched it to me as I rolled into unconsciousness again.

When I woke, night had fallen and the table-lamp on top of the television was switched on. Through blurred eyes I saw Matt. He was reading.

"Matt." The sound of my thick voice alarmed me.

"I'm here," he said. "Don't worry."

I wanted to cry, but no tears came. My body felt heavy, I could barely fill my lungs with air. Matt put his arms around me but I couldn't bear any more pressure. I pushed him away and held his hand.

"Amor's told me all about it. It's okay. I know what happened."

"You couldn't know. No one could."

He sat with me silently for a long time, then said, "Amor's

booked us on a flight back to London tomorrow."

"I can't go back."

"You have to."

"The report." I clutched at straws.

"Amor says he'll finish it. He's already told them in Texas you've been taken ill and had to go home. Everything'll be all right."

I didn't have the energy to argue, but the thought of leaving Tunisia, the hotel, this room, was more than I could bear. Matt gave me two more tranquillizers and the pain wandered a little further out of reach. I was aware of him packing my things. Bottles rattled in the bathroom, bundles of clothes were pulled from drawers and stuffed into my suitcase. He opened the wardrobe and I caught sight of the dress I'd worn to Bizerta. Clean and fresh, pale pink and blue, with tiny pearl buttons running down the front of it. Inanimate, it was safe from memories, safe from loss.

"Don't pack that. I'll wear it tomorrow."

"It's too cold for London, you'll freeze."

"I don't care."

23

I knew he was going to die - he'd told me often enough. But it was to have been an heroic death, set at some indeterminate time in the future. I would have left Tunisia long before then. That way I would never know how or when. Perhaps the snatch of a news-item on the radio, as I made myself a sandwich one lunchtime back in London, reporting how Palestinian guerrillas had been shot dead by Israeli soldiers as they mounted a daring raid into Israel from the West Bank. That way he would die nobly on Palestinian soil, not anonymously along a public road in a foreign country. Ali's life would never be used in the liberation of Palestine, Arafat would have to forgo that one. Perhaps in the tactical bloodshed that was planned, no one would notice.

But knowing how and when he died threw up so many questions, the answers to which I'd never know. Was I in his mind, distracting him, as he stepped out into the road? Was he conscious after the impact? Did he suffer terrible pain? Did he call out for me before he died? All these things worried me, nagged at me through the pain. But, above all, I knew that if I hadn't suggested we meet for lunch, he would still be alive.

Early next morning Matt dressed and washed me and brushed my hair. I sat helpless, staring at my face in the mirror as he drew the brush through my hair, over and over. Soothing. We didn't speak, the silence broken only by the gentle sound of the hairbrush. Deep in my pocket, in time to Matt's brushing, my thumb stroked the inside of Ali's watchstrap, smooth, yielding plastic that had hugged his wrist. I could just manage this level of activity but knew we had to go, fly back to London that morning and I knew that when I left this room, so heavily laden with memories of Ali, my loss would be absolute.

Our sullen peace was broken by a gentle knocking at the door. Amor was taking us to the airport. I wanted to ask him for the answers to my questions, the details, the practicalities of Ali's death, but the effort of articulating such questions was beyond me. I was limited to mumbling only sorry and thank you.

As we left the hotel I clutched the talisman in my pocket as tightly as I could. Protection against madness. Outside, I put on sunglasses. My eyes couldn't stand the sting of the sharp Mediterranean sun. I was dimly aware of guilt lurking just beyond reach of consciousness. Matt had come for a holiday. Too late I patted him on the shoulder to get his attention, tell him to stay, apologise, but when he turned the words collapsed in my mouth and I just shook my head. It was then I realized that the journey from Tunisia to England, from the present back into the past, would demand more strength from me than I had.

I thought Amor held me tightly in his arms inside the airport terminal before kissing me goodbye and that he watched us walk through to passport control, but Matt says he dropped us off outside the building, stopping only briefly to find us a luggage trolley before hurrying off to work. It must be a false memory.

We hung suspended above and beneath the blue, as the aeroplane headed off towards Europe. I saw the Alps below us and worried over their insignificance from thirty thousand feet. Perspective diminished them and I grew afraid that time would diminish my grief. In two, five, ten years would I look back on this time as no more than a sharp ripple briefly dislocating the pattern of my life? Part of me hoped I would. That way I knew I would pick up the fragments of my life and keep going. It would mean that I'd want to. But I knew my life could never be the same again. Loss had damaged me.

It wasn't until we started our descent towards Heathrow that Matt told me John would be there to meet us. I shuddered. I hadn't thought of him for days.

"Does he know?" I asked.

"What?"

"About me? Ali?"

"I've told him that a friend of yours was killed. I didn't say who he was or what he meant to - that's up to you."

"Couldn't I go back with you? Back to your place? Please, Matt?"

He squeezed my arm. "It's too late, he'll be there. I know it's hard, but it's best you go back with him. Believe me."

Just before we landed I took two more tranquillizers, to muffle my growing fear of seeing John again.

Through shaded glasses I watched my feet move forwards through time and space. Left, right, left, right, closer to John, closer to the past. I hovered uneasily between two worlds, resisting my return to this one. And then I saw him watching us walk through into the arrivals lounge. He looked agitated.

He hurried up to the trolley, which I was leaning on for support, and bent his head towards me. I couldn't respond to him and stayed staring at the floor. I sensed Matt leaning across, touching his arm, reassuring him.

Matt pulled the trolley away and John put his arm round me. We walked towards the car park.

"I'm so sorry. What can I do?" There was sadness in his voice. Sadness for me.

"She's tired," Matt said quietly to John, trying to explain my silence. "She needs to sleep."

"What happened?" John asked Matt and I tensed, afraid of what Matt might say.

"This friend was run over. It's best that she tells you about it herself."

John squeezed me to him and kissed my cheek.

I sat low in the back seat of the car, on the way home, so John couldn't watch me in the rear-view mirror. I couldn't imagine life with him again; nothing would ever be as it had been. Soon my eyelids closed and a drugged sleep took me over.

We were back at the flat. I tried to climb out of the car and stumbled over the front seat, scraping my knee on the passenger seat lever. The pain brought tears to my eyes and I looked up into the face of Ali helping me out of the car, but his face dissolved into John's. He led me through to the bedroom and sat me on the bed where I remained, catatonic. He went to fetch my luggage from the car and Matt knelt down in front of me.

"I'm going home now, Claire. I'll give you a ring tonight, okay?"

"What?"

"I'll ring you later."

I pulled off my sunglasses and dropped them on the floor. "I keep thinking of him lying there without me. Without anyone. Was he conscious? Why didn't he let me know, somehow? We were so close I thought I'd know if something happened. I was probably asleep when he died."

The front door slammed shut. Matt put a finger to my lips and dropped four more tablets into my hand.

"That should keep you going until tomorrow."

I stared at them sitting there in the palm of my hand for some time, listening to the low rumble of Matt and John's voices next door, before hurling them in a fury against the wall. I wanted my pain sharp and deep. I wanted to feel it slice through me so that I knew just how bad I felt and cope with it, if I could. I'd had enough of this cloaked agony sneaking into my consciousness and taking me by surprise, robbing me of the energy I needed to face it.

"Fuck it!" I shouted at the top of my voice, trying to tear through the heaviness that smothered me.

John's alarmed face appeared in front of me. "Tell me what I can do."

I looked into his eyes, for the first time since coming back. They were troubled and hurt. "Oh, John." My chest started to heave, the mourning had begun and, like a tidal wave, grief took over. In that tiny city flat I screamed out my sorrow. Face drenched by tears and throat raw with crying, I would not stop. With each gasp for air I felt John's arms tighten around me. I frightened him.

180

Later, much later, I heard him say, "If only I could do something to help."

He kissed my head and cheek very lightly and I took his face in my hands and returned the kiss, my tongue reaching into his mouth. Surprised, he pulled back a little and looked at me. I pulled him back to me. If I closed my eyes tight I could imagine it was Ali. I kissed him again, harder, deeper, my hands moving down his back, pulling his shirt up. I wanted to rip it off him, but didn't have the strength. His hands caressed me tentatively, slipping slowly up and down my legs, up, across my back and then gently massaging my neck as he kissed me. Too gentle.

He pulled off his shirt and began to undo the buttons of my dress. My eyes were shut tight.

"Tear," I whispered.

"What?"

"Tear it off. I need you to be rough."

His hands became more forceful but I could feel the fear in his fingertips. Fear of hurting me, making me cry again. Behind closed lids I conjured up Ali's face, but it was John's touch I felt.

Afterwards I turned away from him and curled up, staring out of the narrow bedroom window at the bulbous, grey clouds. I heard him get up and put his clothes on.

"Can I get you something?" He'd come round and was squatting in front of me. His shirt hung open and I touched his bare chest.

"No."

He stroked my cheek, still nervous. "Do you want to talk about it?"

More friend than lover squatting there, I needed his support and, confused by grief, thought I had nothing more to lose. I told him everything. I told him about my loneliness during those first weeks, meeting Ali at the club and finding a friend in him, Amor's warning, the shortness of our time together, my guilt and the day I waited for him but he never came. I stopped, my voice giving way before my mind did. John had remained immobile throughout, squatting, facing me with his back to the wall. He'd made no comment, asked no questions, no points of clarification, just listened. It was some time after I'd finished that he got up and left the room without a word and I, relieved to have unburdened myself to him, drifted off into a dreamless sleep.

24

I gave in to myself totally in the days that followed, placing myself securely at the centre of my universe. I was the only person I could depend on. I stayed in bed most of the time, lost in a black fog of swirling memories and dreams of the brief days Ali and I had shared. The one question that returned to me time after time was, why me? If we'd never bumped into each other at Dave and Sarah's party, we'd never have become involved. He would still be alive and I would be home with John, working things out between us. I barely noticed John except in so far as he was or wasn't there to attend to my needs - run a bath, make some coffee, fetch my cigarettes. He wasn't around much and when he was he said very little, never commenting on what I'd told him. Ali's name wasn't mentioned. Neither did he touch, kiss me or stroke my cheek the way he used to. I appreciated the physical space he gave me, grateful for his sensitivity.

About a week after I got back I got dressed for the first time and went out to the supermarket to buy some milk. I was confused by the bustle and noise of people around me and collapsed in tears at the till, pulling Tunisian dinars out of my purse, searching for English money. I fled empty-handed, vowing never to shop there again. It would be too embarrassing. That day marked a milestone though, because after that I got out of bed and dressed every morning after John left the flat. I'd make myself coffee and sit on the sofa endlessly smoking cigarettes, waiting for the pain to go. On good days I'd turn the television on and watch the images until late into the night when, unable to distinguish between fantasy and reality, I'd roll into bed.

It was Richard's telephone call, three weeks after I got back, that finally dragged me into the world of the living. Usually I let the telephone ring, but that day felt strong enough to answer it.

"Claire! It's Richard. How are you?"

"Okay, thanks." My voice was croaky from nicotine and under-use.

"Good, good. I don't want to put any pressure on you, but just wondered when you might be well enough to come back to work?"

I was completely taken aback by this remark. I hadn't even thought about returning to work, only just managing to cope with my current level of inactivity.

"Work?"

"I wondered what the doctor said. How long before you're feeling better. What is it you've got, exactly?"

"Glandular fever." The speed with which I answered surprised me.

"Ah, right, it can take a long time. Amor was a bit vague about it when I spoke to him last week."

"The doctor said it depended on how I felt, when I went back to work."

"Of course. We miss you. Amor says he tied up your report and sent it to the States. They seem pleased with what you did. I'm beginning to pull ours together. We've still got quite a few thin sections to work on and I'd appreciate your comments - it's all the same horizon. They're expecting our conclusions in about six weeks."

Life was carrying on. Things were getting finished, presented, acted upon. There was a world out there with a space for me in it. Somewhere in the gloom of my mind a door opened. Work would distract me and I was ready for it.

"Can I ring you after the weekend, see how I am then?"

"Of course, but remember there's absolutely no pressure."

"Perhaps I could come in for a few hours first of all. Gradually build up to a whole day." I was talking to myself, rather than to Richard.

"Whatever. But if you just want to pop in, say hello, it'd be lovely to see you."

"Thanks, Richard."

I put the 'phone down and remained sitting in the chair thinking about Amor, witness to my distress. So he was still there in the office in Tunis, making trips over to the lab now and then. He wouldn't need to go every day now that I'd gone. He'd finished the report, sent it off, had my thin section descriptions typed up. Just thinking about him carrying on with life over there reassured me. I wanted to see him, talk to him, be part of his world again. It was these thoughts that made me decide to go back to the Poly, take out the slides I hadn't looked at, and continue where I'd left off. I could always come home if it all got too much.

Siobhan came round that night. She was the first real visitor I'd seen. I'd ignored the 'phone and doorbell when I was on my own and John had fended off Becky, Sarah and other friends who'd called, having heard rumours that I'd come back from North Africa ill. I wanted to feel strong enough before seeing them. It would be difficult to explain what had happened, especially to Becky. Matt sometimes popped in on his way home from work, I recognized his knock. He never stayed long nor talked about himself but there was a heaviness about him. Something had happened in his life but I didn't have the will to ask him about it.

Siobhan looked different, with her long black hair pulled back into a single plait, revealing the colour in her cheeks. She was surprised to see me up and dressed; I wondered what John had told her.

"You're looking well," she said.

"Am I?" I lit a cigarette.

"Better than I thought you'd look."

"I might go back to work next week." Putting my thoughts into words gave them substance. The more often I said it the more likely it was that I would go back.

"Already? John gave me the impression you'd be off for weeks yet."

"How's your job going?"

"Great. It's really great, I love it. The people are so friendly and there's loads to do. My supervisor's already talking about the possibility of me doing day release in September. Horticulture. Seems too good to be true."

She checked herself, suddenly aware that her gushing happiness was inconsiderate in my presence. I pulled her down to my level.

"How's Eamon?"

"They've moved him. It's a long-stay place. They say he's in a waking coma. It'd break your heart to see him. He's like an empty shell."

"Is Sean still going backwards and forwards?"

"Didn't John tell you?"

"What?" He'd told me nothing, but I'd asked nothing.

"He's gone back. Couldn't stand it here. I miss him."

"But I thought...John's been out a lot with him recently. They've been drinking together."

She shook her head. "He left when you were away."

John had hardly spent a night in since I'd been back. Working late, I assumed, in his new workshop, then out drinking with Sean. He smelt of alcohol so often these days.

We sat a moment in silence. My mind was already wandering off the subject but Siobhan said, "John drinks a lot when he's upset. He can really put it away without it showing. The last couple of years we were together he spent nearly every night down the pub. I never saw him. That's why I got involved with Steve."

"Upset? What about?"

"Being back on the building sites. Then you coming home so ill and everything."

"What do you mean, back on the building sites? What about the workshop and his business?"

She looked at me and frowned. "You don't know? The bank wouldn't lend him the money and he'd dropped out of college. There wasn't anything else he could do. I can't believe he hasn't said anything. He was really low about it when you were away."

Conversation faltered; Siobhan was afraid that she'd said too much, while I thought back over the past weeks. Self-obsessed and blind to the disappointments in John's life, I'd lost myself in grief, unable and unwilling to offer him any comfort. I thought I was justified in wallowing in my sadness, assuming that everyone else's life was carrying on as before. I was wrong.

"I ought to go," Siobhan said. Her manner was relaxed and confident. I knew instinctively that she'd met someone, too late for it to matter to me, but I was glad for her. "You and John must come round for a meal again soon. I'll talk to him about it."

I had to find John. I didn't want to believe what Siobhan had told me. If only he'd told me about the bank, his disappointment at being back on the building sites, perhaps it would have moved me to do something. Perhaps. I dismissed the thought that John's problems might go deeper than the bank refusing him a loan as I sat in front of the mirror putting on make-up. It had been so long since I'd bothered.

It was the end of March and the night felt cold. I'd only been out once since coming back and my legs were shaky as I started to walk down the Liverpool Road towards the Angel. There were pubs along there that I'd never noticed before. Pubs overlooked by the young people of Islington; pubs whose sole purpose it was to fill empty bellies with alcohol.

I found him in the sixth or seventh pub I tried. He was leaning on the bar, cigarette and pint glass in hand, his face flushed, staring blankly into the middle distance. The bar was dark, its only brightness coming from behind the counter. A handful of men and one old woman sat on rickety chairs around the walls. A couple of old men played dominoes on one of the small formica-topped tables which were scattered over the uncarpeted floor. Thick smoke hung in the air like a bygone London smog.

"John?"

His eyes flicked towards the voice, but not expecting me there, didn't know me.

"John."

Suddenly he came to life. "What are you doing here?" He was frowning.

"Looking for you."

His hand reached out to me but as though remembering something he dropped it again. "What's been going on?" I asked. "Siobhan's been round and told me all about the bank not lending you money. Why didn't you tell me?"

"Let me get you a drink. George!" He knew the barman. "Another pint and a glass of white wine."

I went and stood close to him while we waited for the drinks.

"So you're the reason he's in here every night till closing time, are you?" the barman asked and winked at me as he waited for the Guinness to ooze into the glass.

"Am I?" I looked at John.

He smiled wearily at George and said nothing. We took a couple of chairs over to a table hidden away in a dark corner under the frosted windows. I shivered, it was draughty there. I sipped the wine.

"Well?" I tried to nudge him to speak, but he was preoccupied.

"Hmmm?"

"Am I the reason you're in here every night?"

He looked into his glass and nodded. "Pathetic, isn't it?"

"Why didn't you tell me about the business?"

"What difference would it have made? You had your own problems."

"But we're a couple. We should support each other."

"A couple? Even when you're screwing other people?"

Winded by his words, I didn't know how to fight back. I was shocked by the venom in his voice. "It wasn't like that."

"No?"

"I tried to explain it to you, all of it, so you'd understand.

What happened between me and Ali had nothing to do with you and me. It was just one of those things - wrong place, wrong time. You've got to believe that. You do still love me, don't you?" For the first time I wasn't sure.

"Not like you to ask that, Claire."

We sat in silence for some time. The windows rattled every time a lorry went past. John drained his glass.

"I cannot bear to touch you," he said, at last. "You made me make love to you before that man's body was even cold. Disgusting. How could you? What happened to you over there?"

His bitterness frightened me, I couldn't answer him. I remained sitting until I felt sure I had enough energy to get up from the table and walk out into the street. I hoped he would follow me. He didn't. I walked along familiar streets, listening for the sound of footsteps running after me, past empty playgrounds, closed shops, deserted schools. People hurried past, anxious to get home or to meet friends and lovers at prearranged places, but John never appeared. Down the Caledonian Road, past the King's Cross street-walkers and up the Euston Road. The noise of the traffic, of chaotic life all around, soothed me. It helped blot out the cruelty of John's words. Opposite Friends House my legs gave up on me; I couldn't walk any further. In surrender I hailed a cab and it was only when the taxi-driver asked where I wanted to go that I realised I might not have a home with John any more. My belongings were there though, and that was reason enough to go back.

He was already home when I got in, washing up in the kitchen. I stood in the doorway watching him for a while. I loved him. He didn't look up.

"I'm sorry, John. I'm sorry I hurt you so much. Don't you think I've been punished enough?"

He raised his head from his work and addressed the blank kitchen window. "I'm not punishing you. I can't help the way I feel."

I took a deep breath and leant on the door-frame to steady myself. "Do you want me to move out?"

The silence that followed was too long. At last he turned to face me, his arms hung down dripping tears of soapy water on to the dirty floor.

"I don't know what I want any more. I want the last few weeks never to have happened. We were so happy at Christmas, what happened?" I could feel his bewilderment. I'd wrenched the ground from under him.

"I shouldn't have told you. I thought I was doing the right thing."

He nodded, glanced at the floor, then back at me. "There should have been nothing to tell."

"Can't we try again?" My words came out in a whisper.

I held out my arms to him but he didn't move. Fighting my fear of rejection, I walked towards him. He stood there motionless as I put my arms around him and rested my head on his chest. There was no response. Unsure, I held him tighter and squeezed my eyes shut. I thought I heard his breath quicken and then felt his arms bring themselves loosely round my body, one hand, still wet, rested in the small of my back. I didn't dare look at him in case I frightened him away.

We stood like that for some time until he said, "I'll go."

"What?" I thought he'd forgiven me.

"You can stay here, have the flat. I'll move out tomorrow."

"Where will you go?" I tried to sound calm.

"Home."

25

The digital clock glowed in the corner of the room. Three forty-three. I hadn't slept and wouldn't, knowing that soon he would be gone. I had to be awake for these last hours, watching him and remembering the good times, grappling with the fear of a relationship ending. Unlike me, John slept deeply. He'd made his decision and was at peace with it, sure at last. But for me the world I'd started to piece back together only that day had disintegrated again. I remembered Becky's distress when Ciaran left, the words I'd said to John, and now here he was, leaving.

In those dark hours I watched him sleep on while I twisted and turned, sighing loudly in the hope of waking him, so that I could tell him how much I regretted my mistake, perhaps persuade him to stay.

"John."

His breath faltered briefly before falling back into its regular rhythm.

"John, listen. Please, John." I spoke louder and shook him. "I'm sorry John, isn't there anything I can do?"

He turned over, resisting me. I was sure he was awake.

"Isn't there anything I can do to make you stay?" I paused, listening.

Silence.

"Won't you forgive me? Give me another chance. What we had is worth working for. Stay. Just for a month to see how it goes. Till the end of April, then, if you still want to go, I won't stop you. John?"

There was no answer. Perhaps he'd think about it. I said no more, hoping he'd change his mind.

Our bedroom faced east and the spring sun pushed its way in through the faded green curtains. Morning too soon. John got up and dressed quickly without looking at me. When he'd finished he pulled a suitcase out from under the bed and left the room. I got up and, in a panic, opened the wardrobe. His clothes were gone; he'd been planning to leave me for a while. I slumped on the floor a moment, feeling totally powerless, and then, frightened that he might leave without saying goodbye, went into the living room. He was kneeling on the floor with his back to me, pulling records from a pile. He didn't turn round.

"You're definitely going then?" I clung to the hope that he might still change his mind.

"I've a taxi coming any minute."

My heart pounded. It was happening.

"Please stay. Please. I don't think I could live without you."

Still he busied himself with the records, his shoulders hunched. He made no reply.

The sun reflected off a photograph he'd taken of me during our Christmas in Wales. My face was pink and I was smiling, ignorant of what was to come. I'd been flattered when he'd had the photo enlarged and framed, then hung it on the wall. He was leaving it behind.

"Talk to me, John. You can't go like this. Can't we at least be friends?"

He turned to look at me. His face was drawn, and I saw for the first time that he despised me.

"Friends? Do you treat them any better than your lovers?" He spat out the words. I had no control over him any more.

"Please stay. I'm sorry." I said the words quietly hoping my vulnerability would move him.

"Sorry? Sorry? You rip me apart and think that by saying sorry everything will be all right again. Jesus! You're more stupid than I thought. You never gave a shit and in a couple of weeks you'll have found someone else to screw up."

Outside, I heard a car hooting. He put the records he'd

taken into a plastic bag and stood up. I followed him out to the front door.

"Where will you be?"

"As if you cared."

He pulled open the door and picked up his suitcase, the cold air rushed in, I shivered. On the other side of the threshold he turned and looked at me again. His face had changed, there was pain in his eyes. He dropped his case and held on to my face with his hands.

"I'm sorry," he said, his eyes wandering over my face.

I fought back tears. I'd used them too often in our relationship. And then he was gone, off to where the taxi waited.

It was finished. I had to block out this new pain as best I could, but it seemed almost impossible. The flat echoed with John's absence. Groceries scribbled on a shopping list in the kitchen in his handwriting, the empty mug he'd drunk his tea from that morning left on the coffee table and, in the bedroom, the hollow in the pillow where he'd slept. Now he was gone and it was my fault. I had to put it behind me and start again.

No one telephoned that weekend or knocked at my door. No one wanted to see me during those long solitary hours. I wondered how long it would take to get used to being alone.

I hadn't been sure up until the moment I left the flat on Monday morning, whether I'd actually be able to go through with going back to work, but Richard was delighted to see me, almost unable to disguise his relief at the prospect of getting the report completed within the next few weeks.

"You're sure you feel up to it?" he kept asking. He couldn't afford for me to have a relapse.

"Honestly. If I get too tired I'll go home. I'll see how it goes."

It felt strange to be back there, in that familiar building, among familiar faces, when my own life had undergone such radical upheaval. I thought everything would be changed.

Rather than tiring me I found the work, tedious though it

was, a release from thinking about John. Looking down the microscope, my world became the slide I looked at, examining it for signs that conditions had been ripe for the creation of oil. I could concentrate on the information trapped beneath the lens. It was only when place-names cropped up that I felt a pang, reminding me of my time in Tunisia with Ali or John. In distracted moments I got confused, wondering with which of them I'd been to a particular locality; or who it was I'd discussed this part of the formation with. It was always John.

I hated going back to the flat and stayed on at the Poly as late as I could.

Towards the end of the first week I rang Becky and asked her to come round. I was so lonely.

"Ciaran's over at the moment," she said.

"He can come too."

"I'll see what he's doing."

She arrived alone just as it was getting dark. The clocks had gone forward; summer wasn't far away.

"Are you better?" she asked as I uncorked the wine she'd brought.

"Getting there, slowly." I had begun to believe the myth that I'd been physically ill.

"What have you had? John was so vague, I got the impression it was life-threatening."

"He probably hoped it was."

"What do you mean?"

"Bereavement. I was suffering from bereavement. I fell in love with someone in Tunisia. I fell in love and the bastard died."

Becky's eyes were wide. "What happened?" She checked herself, "Or don't you want to talk about it?"

"I want to talk. The only person I've told is John."

"You told him? God. How did he take it? Pretty well, knowing John."

"No. He left."

"Oh Claire. When?"

"Last Saturday."

She reached out for my hand. "Are you okay?"

I shook my head.

I told her everything that had happened in Tunisia. She said nothing, just sat there listening. At last I stopped, my tale almost told. I hadn't told her who I'd become involved with and wasn't sure if I would, but then she asked me his name. I had to make the decision whether or not to lie. I didn't know how upset she'd be. Telling the truth had done me no favours, but I told her anyway.

"Ali."

"Ali? Not my Ali?" she said with the certainty that it couldn't be him.

I nodded. "Ali." Not her Ali.

She poured herself more wine and held the glass suspended in mid-air in front of her a long time, before sitting back in her chair, frowning.

"You and Ali....He's dead..."

I nodded, but she wasn't watching me.

"What a waste. God, I feel awful. Poor Ali." Again she paused. "I always thought he'd die fighting. Not yet."

She lit a cigarette. I watched her remembering Ali, their time together and let the silence be. I wasn't jealous. Eventually she brought herself back to the present, "You've no more surprises? I don't think I could take anything else tonight."

There was a knock at the door.

"That'll be Ciaran," she said, stubbing out her cigarette. "I've got to go to the loo. Get myself together." She hurried out.

It wasn't Ciaran, but Matt. I hadn't been in touch with him for over a week and yet it was tonight, with Becky there and Ciaran expected, that he chose to drop in.

"Becky's here," I whispered to him at the front door, hoping he'd get the message and leave.

"Is Ciaran with her?"

"No. You'd better go, you know what she's like."

He was trying to look beyond me, as if he didn't believe Ciaran wasn't there.

"Just for five minutes. Let me in for five minutes then John and I can go for a drink."

"She won't give you his number if that's what you want. You know that. Anyway, John's not here. He left."

Instantly I had Matt's full attention. "When?"

"Saturday. I told him about me and Ali when we came back, but things came to a head last Friday and he left. I think he's gone back to Derry."

"Why didn't you let me know?"

"I don't know. I hate telling people. It makes it worse."

"Yeah, I know. That was almost the hardest part about Dom going."

"When?"

"February. Him and his bloody conscience."

"You should have said."

"You'd got enough on your plate. My problems paled into insignifcance."

I heard the bathroom door open. Becky would be waiting.

"Come on, then. You'd better behave."

I grabbed a couple more glasses from the kitchen, but was in time to see the expression on Becky's face freeze when she saw it was Matt and not Ciaran who'd been at the door.

"Hi, Becky. How's tricks?"

"Okay. I thought you were Ciaran."

"Is he coming here tonight?" He looked meaningfully at me. "You never told me that, Claire. I haven't seen him for ages. How is he?"

Reluctant as she was to give Matt any information at all about Ciaran, he drew it from her gently, until her guarded tone changed to one of pride. She talked of his popularity among the young men he worked with at the youth project in Belfast. It sounded as if she was learning to share him.

"Have you met any of them?" I asked, grateful that the spotlight was off me.

"Yes. Two of them are staying with us at the moment. They're only sixteen and they think London's great. Makes you appreciate the things we take for granted - Soho, Covent Garden, Oxford Street and all that. No army, no road-blocks or stop-and-search."

"Depends what colour you are," I said but she ignored me.

"They think it's great. They've never known anything but the Troubles. It's a real holiday for them."

Talk of Ireland made me wonder what John was doing at that moment.

There was a knock on the door. Becky looked across at Matt, disappointed he was still there.

"Ciaran! You've changed!" I said, when I opened the door. He wore round, gold-rimmed glasses and had had his red curls lopped off. Now his hair was short, spiky on top, and a fine, neat beard covered his chin. The donkey jacket had been replaced by a leather flying- jacket but he still wore jeans and Doc Martens. He hugged me.

"You haven't."

"Becky's been telling us all about your new life. Finally found your vocation?"

His smile remained fixed on his face, but he didn't reply.

"Finished with politics?"

"What do you think?"

I shook my head.

"I'm lower key about it now though. There's other ways to work for change."

"Go on through," I gestured towards the closed sitting-room door.

"Ciaran!" Matt was on his feet, arms outstretched, Becky watching. I wondered how he would react.

"Shit! How the hell are you?" He went over to Matt and they hugged each other.

"I owe you some money," Ciaran said, pulling away.

"The only reason I'm here, mate."

"I've thirty-four pence on me, will that do you?"

"That and the shirt off your back."

"You should be so lucky!"

The two of them laughed.

"Hi, Ciaran." Becky tried to intervene. Ciaran reached for her hand but his eyes never left Matt's face. It was still there, the spark between them. Time and distance hadn't dimmed it. I sensed the beginnings of a sulk from Becky and felt I was in a time-warp, transported back eighteen months. The time in between might never have happened.

"Look," said Matt, "I only popped in for five minutes. I've got to go, but give us a ring. Come and see me, we can catch up."

"You're still at the old place?"

"Still there. See you, Becky."

I walked with him to the front door.

"Looks good, doesn't he. I like the short hair."

"Oh get out, you great big troublemaker. Come and see me over the weekend. I don't want to be on my own again."

Back in the sitting room, Becky was on Ciaran's knee, being petted and stroked by him. He'd slipped and was making up for it.

"So what about you. Where's John?"

"Gone." The third time that night.

"Sure, I thought you'd be married with kids by now."

Becky said, "He only moved out on Saturday."

"Ah, Claire, I'm sorry."

"Can't trust these bloody Ulstermen, can you?"

"And you've been ill, Becky tells me?"

I couldn't be bothered to go through all that again, "Sort of," I said. "Why are you over this time?"

"We've two young lads, got into a spot of bother. They've never seen London, seemed a good time to bring them."

"Spot of bother?"

"Don't ask. You know what kids that age are like. Pour me a glass of wine. I want to make a toast."

I did as I was told.

"To the future."

"The future!" Becky and I said in unison, more to humour Ciaran than with any real hope.

It was close to midnight when they left. Forgiven for Matt, Becky squeezed my hand as she left. "If you get lonely, give us a ring. Ciaran's going back next Thursday, we could get together again then."

I nodded. "Take care, and Ciaran, dodge those bullets. Those men on the telly say Belfast's a dangerous place."

"They would, too. I'll look out for a suitable young man for yourself, when I go back."

"Don't bother. No more foreign men. In fact, no more men."

Watching them walk down the little alleyway hand-in-hand, chatting and laughing, I realised that the evening had emphasized my loneliness rather than alleviated it. Closing the front door, I looked into the sitting-room. Empty bottles, glasses and full ashtrays lay about. I'd moved the furniture around after John left, in a vain attempt to exorcise the ghost of our relationship from the flat. It hadn't worked. I went in, lit a cigarette and sat down. All was quiet except for the variable hum of the television in the upstairs flat. Alone and lonely, I wanted John back.

I wondered what he was doing at that moment. Perhaps he and Sean were drunk together, toasting the future like we'd done. I took my diary over to the desk and sat down. I turned to the address page and pulled the telephone towards me. I lifted the receiver, heard the low purr of the dialling tone, put my finger in the dial and pulled it round slowly. As I released the dial I listened to the mechanism roll back into place. It was midnight, I'd had too much to drink and didn't even know for sure whether he was living at his mother's. I put the receiver down and stared for a long time at the wall.

"I'm so sorry, Claire, for everything I said. I didn't mean it, but I was so hurt. I know you've suffered too. Forgive me." I heard John's voice, deep and clear.

"Come home."

"I will. There's nothing here without you. I love you."

199

I told myself to go to bed. Late nights and alcohol distort the mind.

26

John was always there, always in my mind. I told myself that his presence would diminish with time in the same way as my grief for Ali was beginning to recede, but if anything it seemed to get stronger. There were some good days but mostly they were bad days when everything was a struggle from the moment I got up in the morning. However bad I felt, I forced myself to go to work every day; there was nothing to stay at home for.

Matt and I made a point of meeting each other at least once a week, both of us single and lonely. We often went to a pub in Covent Garden, near Matt's office. I liked the hubbub around there, a welcome contrast from my quiet lab. Matt knew a lot of the regulars and sometimes joined in the discussions about the vagaries of their more eccentric or irritable clients. The first time I met him there he suggested that we sit at one of the tables outside on the terrace so that we could talk.

"You look like shit," he said.

"Thanks. You say the sweetest things."

"Cigarette?"

"I've given up."

He raised his eyebrows and then lit one for himself. "How's it going?"

"Not good. I hate living alone."

"Me too. It was okay for a bit after Dom left, I wanted to be on my own. Now I hate going back there at night."

"What happened between you two?"

"You know most of it. He just got more and more screwed up about our relationship until the night he told me that he was thinking of becoming a priest."

"What?"

"Seriously. He wants to be a priest. I went bananas. It was just escapism - couldn't cope with an adult relationship so thought he'd try celibacy instead." Matt shook his head. "He had no idea of other people's feelings. How his actions affected them. Like that time he told me he'd got a girlfriend, it was such a stupid thing to do. He knew how I felt about him. He knew I'd have waited. I'm still not sure whether he was naive or just plain stupid. Anyway, the whole thing was a bloody mess from start to finish, I'm glad it's over."

"Honestly?"

"Yes. It's taken a while but I know it's for the best."

"Wish I could say that."

"John's only been gone a couple of weeks. Give it time."

"I never thought I'd miss him so much."

"If you could turn the clock back, would you do things differently?"

"You know I would."

Just how differently, I couldn't say. At what point would I have said no? When I met Ali in the club in Tunis, or when Richard asked me if I wanted to go back to look at the cores, or before all that, a year ago, when he'd asked me to be his field assistant? In retrospect John's reaction then seemed to foreshadow everything that followed.

"Maybe living life backwards is the answer," I said.

"No. That'd be too easy. How's work?"

"I spoke to Amor yesterday. It felt really strange. He's well. Habiba might be coming over in the summer. He says he'll probably come with her, for a holiday."

"Did he mention Ali?"

I shook my head. What would there have been to say? "I rang to see if there was any work. Richard and I will have finished soon and I've got nothing lined up after that."

"Can't Richard get you a job?"

"No. He's got himself another contract in Abu Dhabi this summer. He doesn't need me."

"Could Amor help?"

"There's nothing at the moment. I'm looking for a job. I don't fancy mud-logging but there's nothing else around."

"I didn't think they took women on rigs."

"Neither did I, but Peter came into the Poly last week and said that some Scandinavian companies employ women, although the only ones he's come across are about fifty and built like tanks."

"I suppose they have to be. Another drink?"

"Thanks. Lemonade this time."

I watched the people wander around without hurrying. The pale yellow evening, cool but summery, encouraged promenading. The ubiquitous music of buses and taxis was overlain by the murmur of people chatting, heels sliding and clumping over the paving stones and shouts of the street-entertainers demanding an audience. I felt entirely alone sitting there without Matt. As isolated as any time in Tunisia, when I could blame my solitude on the language. Here there was no such excuse; I deserved my loneliness.

"It was good to see Ciaran again," Matt said as he thumped the glasses down on the table.

"At my place or since?"

"How did you know?" He was smiling.

"Pretty bloody obvious."

"He came to the flat last Sunday. Told me all about life in Belfast, his youthwork and stuff."

"And how he feels about Becky?"

"What do you mean?"

"He doesn't love her, does he?"

Matt looked at his drink as he lifted it to his lips and drank.

"Well?" I persisted.

He put the glass down and wiped his mouth. "No."

"So why did he come back?"

"It's complicated. He needs a place in London sometimes and Becky's quite happy with that. He doesn't like using her but he's got no choice."

"She's only happy because she thinks he's come back to her. You know he's told her he loves her?"

Matt just shrugged.

"What about you? Is he okay now about you being gay?"

"He's come to terms with it."

"You're not? You and - No don't tell me, I don't want to know. I couldn't look Becky in the face."

He cleared his throat. "So, will you have finished your report by Whitsun?"

"Yeah."

"Fancy coming to France for a few days?"

"Seriously?"

"We could take the car. Stock up on duty frees and stuff."

Something to look forward to. We spent the rest of the evening making plans and reminiscing about the childhood holidays we'd had camping abroad. One memory led to another; the time Matt was bitten by a fish when he was swimming in a lake in Germany, tumblers full of dark red wine served to us high up in the Alps at a little bar on the Italian side of the Simplon Pass and the view over Florence from our campsite on a hill above the city.

"Remember watching the World Cup at that campsite at Igolstadt?"

"Come on England, bally old England!" A picture of the British army officer on enemy soil shouting for his team, burned in my mind. He wore white shorts and long white socks. I don't know whether the handlebar moustache was real or if I added it as the years went by.

"We were trying to pretend we were German."

"Until England won. Then we danced round like the best of them."

I was tired and left the pub just before ten. I took a taxi back, too exhausted to struggle with the tubes. Outside the empty flat I fumbled for my keys. I could hear the telephone ringing inside.

"I'm coming home."
"You forgive me?"
"Everything. And you? Do you forgive me?"
"I hurt you. There's nothing for me to forgive."
"I love you."

By the time I got in the telephone had stopped. I picked up the receiver but all I heard was the dialling tone.

In the weeks that followed I applied for jobs advertised in the trade papers, national newspapers as well as sending off my CV to the London offices of several oil companies, but all I received was rejection and silence. Mornings were always a disappointment, waiting for the post. The letter I wanted never arrived. An all-pervasive depression took over from the acute pain I'd felt at the loss of John. I thought of Ali less these days and of John more. I wondered whether he'd already found somebody else. A woman who'd really value him and have enough space in her life for someone other than herself. I wanted to be that woman.

He would be seeing a lot of Sean, they'd go drinking together, and he'd be working - perhaps he'd even have another try at starting his own business. His mother would be glad to have him back after so long away, back in the home of his childhood, a refugee no more.

Sometimes I imagined him coming back to me, gentle, yearning, always without recrimination. A man I constructed in my mind, made of memories and hopes but without substance. When I got too carried away I had to stop and tell myself that he was gone from my life, just as completely as Ali was gone, and I would try again to put him out of my mind.

Siobhan dropped in occasionally. I had a little fantasy that John had asked her to keep an eye on me, but experience didn't bear this out. She hardly ever spoke about him and when I did ask whether she knew how he was, she was vague. The only information I got was that he and Sean were working most of the time - casual, temporary work, there was nothing permanent. Once she told me that the two of them were thinking about going to the States if they could get the fare. I stopped asking questions after that; the fear of him going so far away depressed me too much.

Hilary Stokes invited me over for a meal on the Sunday evening after I'd finished work at the Poly. It seemed fitting to mark the sending off of the report in some way and I was grateful to her. They lived way out, somewhere along the Great Northern Electric Line.

"If you come to Gordon Hill, Richard will pick you up," she told me over the 'phone.

"What time?"

"About seven. You'll be able to see the children before they go to bed."

It would have been churlish to mention that I'd be quite happy not seeing them.

Sliding out between the backstreets of north London I felt like a child on a school outing. I'd become trapped in Islington, travelling only from the flat to the Poly and back again, with occasional visits to meet Matt in town. Looking out of the carriage I felt a sense of escape, catching sight of the sweep of Alexandra Park as we coasted past. Outside Wood Green, the sun reflected off the innumerable rails lying in wait, to take people out of London to towns and cities in the north.

The evening was hot when I got out of the train at Gordon Hill. Dogged by weariness, I climbed the staircase towards the exit. At the top of the stairs I stopped breathless, my back and face wet with sweat. I didn't feel well. I hadn't felt well for weeks and knew I should go to the doctor. I needed someone's sympathy. Having caught my breath, I started the long walk up the wooden corridor to the ticket office where, I hoped, Richard waited with the car. He was there holding on to a double buggy stuffed with two red-faced children, struggling to get out.

"Train on time. Great. I thought we'd walk, it's such a

lovely evening and with any luck these two monsters might drop off on the way home."

I smiled weakly at the two cross faces. "You must be Jennifer," I said to the larger child, dressed in a pink cotton nightie. "And you're David, are you?"

At the sound of his name, the infant screwed up his face and began to mizzle.

"He doesn't like the heat," said Richard apologetically.

"You won't be taking the family with you to Abu Dhabi, then?" I asked as we walked out of the station. I wished he'd slow down.

"In August? No fear. I've promised Hilary a holiday in Jersey when I get back. Two weeks. She missed out last year and it's not fair. Besides, with another one on the way we probably won't be able to afford another holiday for some time."

"Another?"

"Bit of an accident really, but we're thrilled. Three children under three, poor old Hilly's really going to have her work cut out." We walked on, more slowly now. "Abu Dhabi will probably be my last contract for a bit. I'm going to have to be home as much as possible. By the way, Amor rang on Friday after you left. They're pleased with the report and are sending the rest of the money over. He said there might be some cores from off-shore to analyse in a month or so, if you're interested."

"Yes. I've had no luck looking for work."

"It's specially hard for you, of course, being a woman. Don't suppose it'll really change, not in the oil industry."

His complacency irritated me. He'd picked up speed again and I had to hurry to keep up with him through the quiet streets, lined with yellow-brick council houses.

By the time we reached the house David was asleep and Richard skilfully transferred him from buggy to cot without waking him. Jennifer, on the other hand, had dozed lightly on the journey back and was now ready to play.

"I gather congratulations are in order," I said to Hilary as she handed me a glass of orange juice.

"I hope I'll have come round to the idea by December. That's when it's due." She was clearly much less enthusiastic than her husband about the new arrival. "Jenny, put that down. Go and ask Daddy to get you a drink and biscuit. He's in the kitchen."

Fortified by food, the child entertained us for a full hour before Hilary suggested to Richard that he put her to bed so that we could eat. Even with her gone, her presence filled the room as Richard regaled me with stories of her exceptional talents. Hilary remained largely silent, chipping in only to curb his more excessive exaggerations. When we'd finished eating Richard cleared away and did the washing up. Hilary and I went and sat in the living room.

"It's quite a revelation to see this side of Richard," I told Hilary. "He talked about you and the kids a lot in Tunisia, but I couldn't imagine him being so domesticated. We see a different side to him at college."

"He's going to have to get even better at it come December. Mind you, it's hard enough to cope now. I'm so tired all the time."

"Me too," I said, giving a short laugh and that's when it hit me. All the exhaustion, the nausea, the heaviness - I was pregnant. As Hilary talked at length about the different symptoms she felt with each pregnancy I groped in my mind, trying to remember the last time I'd had a period. Certainly not since I'd come back from Tunisia, not that I remembered.

"Are you all right?" Hilary caught my attention.

"Fine, honestly."

"Sure?"

I weakened, desperate to tell somebody. "I think I might be pregnant."

"Oh God. I hope nothing I've said has put you off. Me and my big mouth, don't take any notice, I'm such a moaner."

"No. You don't understand. I don't want a baby."

27

Hilary gave me a spare pregnancy test she had, so that I'd know for certain. The hour I spent waiting for the results of the test seemed eternal. If I'd been more experienced in these matters I'd have known that the dark circle which formed after less than fifteen minutes didn't alter, except for growing a little darker and thicker as time went on. It was positive, the chemicals said so.

"Is it urgent?" asked the receptionist.

"Yes," I snapped, wondering whether I'd already be too late for an abortion.

"Ten-forty this morning with Dr Slaney."

He was running half an hour late. Thirty minutes spent flicking through tattered women's magazines. It was hard to avoid motherhood - "My Miracle Baby", "Toddler Gemma's Courage", "Home Birth - Yes or No? Your Comments". I tried to lose myself in knitting patterns, make-up tips, last season's fashions and "Thirty Exciting Ways To Spruce Up Your Home From As Little As £5!", without success. Just as my confidence was ebbing away my name was called.

"Sit down. What can I do for you?" The doctor didn't look up from my notes.

"I'm pregnant."

He peered at me over the top of his half moon glasses and without smiling said, "Congratulations. What was the date of your last period?"

"I don't know."

"Roughly. Last month? March?"

"I can't remember."

He sighed and started scribbling on my notes. I wished I'd

made an appointment to see his wife. She was much easier to talk to.

"I'll make an appointment for you to have a scan. Bart's. It's where you'll have the baby."

"I'm not sure I want the baby."

"No need to make any hasty decisions. After the scan we'll know how many weeks you are. That could affect things. I'll need to take some blood."

He bustled about collecting containers and stickers, humming briskly to himself. I wished I knew him better so that I could have talked it through with him, but I'd hardly visited a doctor since I'd come to London. After a good deal of tapping and squeezing he managed to penetrate a vein rich enough to fill his test-tubes with my blood.

"Come and see me after your scan. We'll sort out your antenatal care then."

"Or whatever," I reminded him.

"Mr Nelson." His mind was already on his next patient.

I sat on the low wall outside the surgery, feeling the sun warming my bare arms and legs. I needed help but didn't know who to go to.

"I'm pregnant, John. It's Ali's child."
Silence.
"John, I'm pregnant. I don't know what to do."
Silence.
"I was pregnant, but I'm not any more. I didn't want to hurt you any more."
Silence.
"John?"

Alone, but not alone. Responsibility hovered close. I really didn't need this, not now. I hoped my father's understanding of his patients' needs was better than Dr Slaney's. I remembered his medical books which Matt and I had sniggered over as children.

We'd pored over the diagrams of the male and female reproductive organs, seminal vesicles, testes, Fallopian tubes, uterus, alien words and labels given to hidden, secret parts of the body. A different chapter, and drawings and photographs showed the tiny embryo developing into a foetus, misshapen but recognisably human and then a perfectly formed infant. I remembered the biology lesson with the film of a woman giving birth. The blood and pain were an unwanted revelation; one of my friends passed out at the sight of it. And there were the other words too that I heard my father use, linked to pregnancy and birth - miscarriage, toxaemia, haemorrhage and stillbirth. I stood at the threshold of another world. I didn't welcome it.

Strangely, the first person I told was Hilary Stokes. She rang me to find out the result of the test.

"Don't tell Richard," I said.

"I already have, I'm afraid. He knew you were worried. He'll be really pleased for you."

"Hilary, I'm not sure I want the baby."

"Oh. Have you and the baby's father separated for good then?"

"It's all very complicated."

"Would you like to come over? Talk to someone? You could stay for a couple of days, if you wanted."

I thought of little Jennifer doing roly-polys round the floor, demanding food, a story or a game - I wasn't up to it.

"Thanks, it's kind but I'll be okay, honestly. I'm off to France on Friday and I've loads to do before then."

"If you change your mind, let me know. I don't like to think of you on your own faced with such an important decision."

She sounded like a big sister. I wish I'd known her better so I could have talked it through with her. I would have trusted her advice.

The hospital telephoned me with an appointment for a scan on the morning of the day we were going to France. I rang

211

Matt to see if we could get a later ferry.

"Yeah, no problem. Why?"

"I've got to go to the hospital for a scan."

"A what? What for?"

I took a deep breath, "I'm pregnant, Matt."

"Shit!"

"I don't know whether I'm going to go through with it."

"Oh." There was a long pause and then he asked "Do you know whose it is?"

"Ali's."

"So you've not told John."

"I haven't been in touch with him since he left."

"Shall I come with you? Then we can drive straight down to the ferry."

"Thanks."

Matt held my hand as I lay on the high bed, stomach exposed. The technician assumed he was my partner.

"Your first?" she asked him.

He froze.

"Yes," I said. "Actually he's my brother, not the baby's father."

"This will feel cold." She smeared clear, icy gel over my abdomen and then pushed the ultrasound probe over the slippery surface. Her eyes were fixed on the monochrome screen as she turned one of the dials with her free hand. "There. See? Lovely and clear. Look, that's his back, let's have a little measure of that... See his heart pumping, just there... Looks like he's got his thumb in his mouth."

She continued with the running commentary as my eyes watched the ghostly silhouette pulsating within the monitor. I couldn't see the detail she could see, not even when she pointed it out to me, but I nodded to humour her. I looked at Matt but he was lost in the view, he was squeezing my hand very tight. It had all become real at last, in that small, dark airless room. There could be no question any more.

"Fifteen weeks. That would make you due towards the end of November. About the twenty-fifth."

She'd removed the probe and was wiping the gel away from my belly with rough white tissue.

"There. Careful." She helped me from the bed.

Matt removed his gaze from the empty screen. "Amazing," he said, shaking his head.

Ali's child. He was dead but a part of him lived on. I wondered if I'd see his face in the features of this unknown child in the years to come.

"I will have the baby," I said, certain of my decision, as we drove down the M2 towards Dover.

"I'm glad. It'd be hard to get rid of it after seeing it like that."

"Looks like I'm lumbered."

"Well, you'd nothing better planned for the next eighteen years. Are you going to tell John?"

"No."

"I think you should. Just think how he'd feel if he found out from someone else."

"Like who?"

"Siobhan. You're bound to bump into her."

I thought back to the previous evening, when I'd met her and Barry in the supermarket. It was the first time I'd seen him and he looked too much like John for comfort. Only when he opened his mouth and spoke with a north London accent did I relax. They'd been together for about four months. Siobhan was wondering whether to let him move in.

"She still pops in sometimes."

"Why?"

"We sort of became friends, I suppose. I'm sure if I asked her not to tell John she wouldn't."

"I still think you should tell him. And what about Mum? When are you going to tell her?"

"Oh God! It's me who's got to go through all this. It's my

baby. Why should I have to tell everybody else?" It would all take so much effort, the explaining, hiding, justifying my actions, but I knew it had to be done.

It wasn't until we were on the ferry that we bumped into Ciaran. He was in the bar, carrying three drinks over to an empty table.

"Hi, Ciaran!" Matt shouted. "Guess what? Claire's pregnant!"

"Shhhh." I felt my cheeks burn. "What the hell's he doing here?"

He guided me over to the table where Ciaran was. Hands free, Ciaran put his arms around me and hugged me.

"Congratulations! Who's the lucky fella?"

"Oh, for God's sake." I pulled away from him.

"Well, I am pleased for you. Just imagine. You, having a baby."

"Stranger things have happened," I snapped. "Like finding you on this ferry."

"Ah." He looked at Matt. "I forgot to say it, didn't I? About the coincidence meeting you here, but if you will tell me news like that, what do you expect?"

"The fact you had three drinks in your hand was a bit of a giveaway," said Matt.

They laughed together. I was on the outside.

"I'm off lager. Can you get me a lemonade?"

"For you, Mommy, anything."

Ciaran squeezed round the table and made his way back to the bar.

"You bastard! How long have you been planning this?"

Matt looked sheepish. "I met him a couple of days ago and told him we were going to France this weekend. He asked if he could come too. What could I say?"

"No."

"I knew you'd be angry, that's why I didn't tell you before."

"And Becky couldn't make it, I suppose."

"She doesn't know."

"You two are the bloody limit."

Ciaran handed me a glass. "A baby, eh? I can't believe it. If it's a boy will you call him after me?" he asked.

"Will I, bollocks!"

Against all my expectations we had a lovely time together, the three of us. For the first time in weeks I didn't feel so tired or sick and Matt and Ciaran ran round after me attending to all my needs. I made the most of it. We drove through Normandy and eastern Brittany, the countryside burgeoning with early summer. We paddled in the thick, cold sea, built castles out of grey sand on windy beaches and sat out on bar-terraces when it was warm enough.

We went to Mont-Saint-Michel on our last day. Mass was being said in the huge abbey and I stayed to watch. Ciaran sat with me. I was mesmerized by the timeless ritual of it. A priest stood behind a stone altar, wearing plain vestments and droning out incantations in French. The congregation were familiar with their lines, answering the priest's requests for forgiveness or blessing from the all-powerful God. Just as I got settled, either sitting, kneeling or standing, a little storm broke out and we all had to change positions. There was no peace there, no space for reflecting on life either here or in the hereafter until Communion, and only then did the constant direction of the congregation stop as the priest placed white discs onto the tongues of the faithful. Finally, the priest blessed us and instructed us all to go in peace. I looked across at Ciaran and was surprised to find his eyes tightly shut as he crossed himself, deep in prayer.

I put my arm through his as we left the church to look for Matt.

"Do you believe all that?" I asked him.

"Some of it. It's hard to throw it over when you've been weaned on it."

"It all seems so irrelevant though, the Catholic Church's

outdated rules. No divorce, no birth control, celibate priests and no homosexuality either."

"I take what I need from it. I'm the one answerable to God."

"And what about peace? 'Go in peace' - tell that to the IRA."

He stopped and turned to face me. "What do you know about peace? Peace doesn't mean taking all the shit they throw at you; keeping quiet while those bastards lift your family and friends from their homes day after day, just for speaking out, or being stopped and searched every five minutes as you try to go about your business. It's not keeping quiet about the torture and humiliation that's part and parcel of daily life in Belfast. You have to fight back because there's no such thing as peace when you're living under the boot of an occupying army." He looked me in the eye. "Your fucking army!"

When he finished he was trembling. The words he said were familiar but the way in which he said them was different. There was a new passion in his voice and, for the first time, he accused me. He made me nervous. I sat down on a low stone wall and looked out at the sea.

"You're involved, aren't you?" As soon as I said it I knew it was a mistake. I didn't want to know his answer.

I heard him sigh. "Everybody's involved, even those who are silent and do nothing. Especially those who do nothing."

"The youthwork's just a cover?"

"Some of the young men who come to us are so brave, it puts me to shame. They've nothing to lose and want to play their part. At last, after centuries, they know the time has come. It's exciting to be living in these times."

We both fell silent. I thought of Ali's fight to go home, back to the land of his family, his ancestors. For Ciaran the goal must be less tangible. The authorities must see him as a foreigner in Belfast, yet he was Irish. Who had the greater claim to the cities, fields and hills in the north-east of that island, Ciaran or John? I wasn't sure any more.

216

28

In the train, on the way home to Wales, I wondered if I should tell Matt about Ciaran. But tell him what, exactly? All I knew was that he was vaguely mixed up with some sort of Republican group. I couldn't be sure it was the IRA, and even if it was I didn't know whether he was just a card-carrying member or on active service. I couldn't imagine Ciaran taking a real hands-on approach, with the attendant risks of being arrested or shot at. He was more the politician, always talking, planning, directing other people in front-line resistance. I wondered if Becky knew or whether I was the only one, distanced enough to have been given such privileged information. Telling Becky could be misconstrued as interfering, but I felt I had to warn Matt.

By the time I reached Reading I'd put the whole business out of my mind. There was nothing I could do while I was at home, where a more immediate difficulty had to be faced - telling my parents I was pregnant. The closer we got to Llandrindod, the more apprehensive I became. I was an independent adult now, responsible to myself for my actions and yet when I saw my parents I reverted to the role of child and craved their approval.

My mother came to collect me from the station; the sight of her made me nervous, wondering how she would react. The afternoon was hot and hazy. Gasping for air, I wound the car window down and squinted at the hills rising low from either side of the river.

"How was France?" My mother had to shout to make herself heard. "You certainly look as though you had a good break. I haven't seen you looking so well for a long time."

"It was great."

"Did John go too?"

"No."

"Poor thing, did he have to work?"

"No."

She fell silent for a while and then asked, "How is Matthew? I do worry about him - his unorthodox lifestyle and so on. He seemed so unhappy when Dom moved out. Even I thought it was a shame. He seemed such a nice boy."

"And that made it all right, did it?" I was hot and irritable.

"You know what I mean. Is he sort of - with - anyone at the moment?"

"Depends what you mean by *with*."

"Oh, Claire, don't be so difficult."

"Sorry. I don't know. Besides, I don't think it would be for me to say, even if I did."

"You two are the limit. I can get no real information about you from Matthew and none from you about him. I'd hoped your loyalty to each other might be overshadowed by your loyalty to your mother."

I laughed with her, relieved to know that Matt would have told her nothing about what had gone on in Tunisia.

Unusually, my father was at home when we got in. He'd made a pot of tea. The afternoon sun tilted in through the windows, lighting up the cool kitchen. Outside I could see the trees hugging the sides of the river, their leaves still pale in the early summer.

"So, what news from the big smoke?" he asked.

I felt my heart pounding and took a deep breath. This was the moment.

"I'm pregnant."

My announcement was greeted by a stunned silence. I could feel my parents' eyes on me, searching for a reason why I'd done it. I cleared my throat, avoided their gaze and tried to lead their reaction somewhere positive. "I'm really pleased. It couldn't have come at a better time. I've finished the contract and haven't had any luck getting a job."

"But you're so young." My mother found her voice.

"You've got a good degree, your life opening up ahead of you. Why? Did you plan it? After all you've said and your career so important to you."

I needed support, a shoulder to cry on, not objections.

"Does this mean you and John will get married? Is he divorced yet?"

"We're not together any more." I spoke slowly, wanting to stay in control and hide my sorrow.

"So whose baby is it?"

I hesitated. I couldn't go into all that. "John's. I haven't told him though. He left before I found out about it."

"But you must tell him," my father said. "It's his baby too, Claire. His responsibility. He has a right to know."

"There'd be no point. We were getting on so badly when he left, it's not as if we'd get back together or anything."

"He always seemed so easy-going," my mother said, almost to herself.

"I'm not talking about you getting back together, just about letting him know that he's got a child."

"Maybe, when it's born. Anything could happen between now and November."

"Is that when you're due? However will you cope on your own?" My mother sounded very concerned.

"I'll manage somehow."

She looked at me and saw that I was close to tears. She came and sat on the arm of my chair and put an arm around my shoulders. "Oh darling, don't worry. It'll be all right. You know we're always here if you need us. You could come home to have the baby, then we could look after you properly."

I shook my head. "Thanks, though."

I spent nearly a month in Wales, enjoying the easy life at home with my parents and having no reason to go back to London. After the initial hiatus and quick acceptance of my news, things settled down in the cottage and my mother and I grew close, united by the common bond of pregnancy. I compared my symptoms and changing emotions with the ones she'd experienced more than twenty years previously. She told me about the miscarriage she'd had between my brother and me.

"It's hard to get over something like that. I think it was worse then, everyone kept saying 'You'll be able to have another one, why are you so upset?' Your father wasn't much better. I think he'd cringe at some of the things he said then. It's all treated much more sympathetically now."

"Why didn't you tell me about it before?"

"Life goes on. You came along and I was so pleased to have a daughter. I was busy with you and Matthew and your father out all hours, I didn't really have time to brood. I didn't hide it from you, it just didn't seem relevant."

We had days out shopping, wandering around Mothercare in Shrewsbury and Hereford, making lists and buying maternity clothes.

For the first time since childhood, I didn't want to leave her when I finally had to go back to London. I'd so enjoyed her companionship and knew I'd feel its lack in London, but I had to go back. I'd 'phoned Richard who told me the cores would be arriving from Sfax very soon. I needed the work.

"Will you come and stay when the baby's born?"

"Of course. Now look after yourself and keep in touch. Let us know how it's all progressing. We must see you before November. Maybe you can persuade Matthew to bring you up for a couple of days when you've finished this contract."

The cores kept me busy for over two months. I'm sure Amor was behind the quantity of rocks sent over, aware that I needed the work and money, but whenever I asked him, he always denied it. Habiba hadn't come to London in the summer but hoped to come in the autumn and he planned to come with her for a holiday. I told him about the baby, hopeful that his trip to London and the birth might coincide.

The days during that hot summer were long and empty. The corridors of the Poly echoed only to the footsteps of cleaners, caretakers and a handful of technicians. I grew bigger, daily it seemed, as lumbering up to the lab became more of an effort and bending down to peer through the microscope, increasingly uncomfortable. It was a lonely existence. I saw so few people, avoiding Becky in case she asked me awkward questions about Ciaran, and I know Matt was avoiding me. I'd tried to warn him about Ciaran when I got back to London but he wouldn't listen, insisting my accusations were too vague. When he tried to pin me down to exactly what Ciaran had admitted, I couldn't answer him. I thought of Amor's warning to me about Ali. I hadn't wanted the information he gave me and didn't know what to do with it anyway, and the same was true for Matt. I couldn't judge him.

It was a Sunday morning in late September when I dragged my bulk over to Camden Lock. I'd just received the last of my payment from Austin and wanted to buy myself something special. I was examining beads, bracelets and earrings, trying on soft gold rings, worn with age, when I felt a hand on my shoulder. I turned my head.

"Sean!"

"I thought it was you." He held out his arms, causing browsers to tut and squeeze grudgingly past him.

I turned to hug him, catching the surprise in his eyes as I did so. After a minute he held me at arm's length, looking me up and down.

"Saints preserve us, just look at you! You look marvellous. When's the happy day?"

"A couple of months."

"Can I take you for a drink? To celebrate."

"Is John with you?"

"I left him at home, sleeping off the whiskey I brought over."

I sat uncomfortably on a plastic chair, the sun in my eyes, with Sean facing me, perched on a low wall. We clashed our glasses together.

"Here's to the baby!" he said.

"The baby."

"Siobhan never said a word about your being pregnant."

"She doesn't know. I haven't seen her for months."

"No. She practically lives at Barry's these days."

"I thought he was going to move in with her."

"They're looking to buy somewhere together. I think there's wedding bells in the air. She and John are finally divorced."

I squinted away tears and looked at a point a few feet above Sean's head. So, they'd got divorced at last, for reasons that had nothing to do with me.

Sean put his hand on my knee. I wasn't disguising my pain very well. "But tell me about you and the baby. Who's the lucky man?"

"There isn't one."

"It's not John's, is it?"

I shook my head. "I wish it was. Did he tell you why we split up?"

"Not a word."

"It's all so complicated. I don't know where to begin."

"It's none of my business. Don't tell me if you don't want to."

I did want to and to let him know the extent of my remorse, so that he could tell John, but I was too ashamed.

We sat in silence for a bit. I watched the sun's reflection shimmer on the surface of my drink, aware of Sean's unspoken concern.

"John seems to have sorted himself out a bit, now he's back in London."

"When did he come back?"

"End of June. Couldn't settle in Derry. Said he felt more English than Irish. He's living in a squat down in Clapham."

He'd been back in London all that time and I hadn't known. Perhaps he'd tried to get in touch with me while I was in Wales. I shouldn't have stayed away so long.

"Who's he living with?"

"Some of the fellas he works with. It's a bit of a comedown from Barnsbury - you can imagine."

I screwed up my courage and threw dignity to the wind, "Is he with anyone?"

Sean hesitated. "Nothing serious."

The scene shattered into shards around me.

"Who?"

"The sister of one of the fellas in the house. They go to the pictures together, Claire. It's no more than that. They're like a couple of kids really."

"Does he ever talk about me?"

He held his arms out and raised his shoulders, unsure of what I wanted to hear.

"I'm sorry, I know I shouldn't ask, but I need to know."

He looked into his empty glass. "No. He's never mentioned your name since the night he turned up in Derry and even then all he said was, 'Me and Claire have split up'. Wouldn't say why and still won't talk about you. I don't know what happened between you and him Claire, but he's still hurt."

Like a scrap thrown to a starving dog, I fell on Sean's last words. Was there a chance for me?

"Don't tell him I'm pregnant."

"He's my best friend, Claire."

"He'd just hate me more, I know he would."

Sean shook his head. "I don't think so."

We spent the rest of the day together. I think he was reluctant to leave me, aware of how much I still missed John. I tried to read between the lines of everything he said, listening hard for any new information he might let slip about John. There wasn't much. The girl was called Alison. She was nineteen, lived at home and worked in a shop in the West End.

At about six he got up to leave. We'd been sitting in Regent's Park, soaking up the last of the summer sun.

"I'm taking the train back tonight. I have to get my stuff

from John's."

"When are you coming over again?"

"Don't know. Couple of months, maybe. I've some work at the moment."

"Come and see me. I may have had the baby by then."

He kissed me on the cheek. "Take care."

I watched him hurry away until I couldn't distinguish his shape from that of the other people walking through the park. Sitting there in the softening light I wondered what he would tell John.

"Sean, where've you been all day?"
"I met Claire."
Silence.
"How is she?"
"She wants you back. She's missing you badly."
"You're sure?"
"Certain. She loves you John."
Silence.
"Perhaps I'll give her a ring. Drop round and see her."

The baby gave my bladder a sharp kick, reminding me that my little scenario was rubbish, but for the next few days my heart leapt every time the telephone rang or someone knocked on my door. It was never John.

29

Heartburn and itching - two torments I feared I'd be stuck with for the rest of my life - along with a grossly distended belly. If there was a baby inside me it would never be born. It was already five days late and I would have to accept that it would stay inside forever. When I went to the doctor he tutted over my blood pressure and threatened to have me admitted the next time I came to see him, but, to my surprise, he never had the chance.

Amid much screaming, shouting and swearing, my son was born on the afternoon of December 1st, all eight-and-a-half pounds of him. It was the closest I'd ever been to a miracle. I was euphoric after the agony of labour, holding the tiny, fleshy child and pressing his bemused face to my lips. He smelt of the earth, of puppies' breath and tears all mixed up together. My gift, my responsibility. I wouldn't let him down.

"Have you got a name for him, Mum?" A nurse had taken him away to weigh, measure and label him while a medical student sat between my legs, sewing me back together again.

"No." My voice was hoarse from all my complaining.

"Baby Marshall then, till Mum decides what to call you." She secured plastic labels to his wrist and leg. He was mine, there could be no mistake.

We were wheeled down to a ward full of more women and babies. They took my black-haired, wrinkly baby and put him in a perspex fish-tank on wheels by my bed. I couldn't take my eyes off him. His long fingers, each one crowned with a sharp pink nail, curled into a fist and moved up to his open mouth which was rooting for food. Not really hungry, his eyes soon closed and he fell asleep. In a moment of pride I believed this motherhood thing was easy.

I wheeled the 'phone to the bed so I could broadcast my news without being separated from him.

"And you're all right?" Matt asked from his office in the West End.

"Just knackered."

"Can I come and see him?"

"Of course! Seems to be open visiting here till about nine o'clock. Could you pop into the flat and pick up my sponge bag? I forgot it. You've got a key."

When I told my mother she started sniffing and passed the telephone receiver to my father who wasn't much more coherent. They said they'd come down the following day.

I lay on my bed pretending to sleep, but watching every movement the baby made. I wanted him to wake up, missing him already, but he'd had a busy day; being born is exhausting.

It had been dark for some time when I saw the ward sister pointing out my bed to Matt. He was carrying an enormous bunch of flowers and several carrier bags. He hurried towards us, then turned and beckoned to someone behind him.

"Let me look. Can't I pick him up? God, he's amazing, so tiny. I've already seen you, little mate," Matt spoke to the sleeping infant, " when you were hardly more than a twinkle in your mum's eye. I've brought the camera, to get some shots of you both. When's he going to wake up?"

"Amor! Brilliant timing."

He stood at the bottom of my bed, also holding flowers, his smile radiating warmth.

"A son. Can I see?"

"If you can get Matt out the way. Here, let Amor have a look."

"I found him outside your flat making the place look untidy, so dragged him along here."

"It's good to see you."

Amor transferred his attention from the baby to me and leant over to give me a kiss. I suddenly felt aware of what a mess I must look, but remembered that the last time he'd seen me I'd looked much worse.

"I thought babies cried all the time," Matt said. "Isn't he going to wake up?"

We all gazed at the transparent cot willing him to wake, but when it became evident that he wasn't going to stir the two men sat on my bed and I started opening the presents they'd brought. Matt went off in search of some vases.

"When did you arrive? Is Habiba with you?"

He shook his head. "Yesterday, just for a holiday. Habiba's not coming now. Nadia left home in the summer. She's living in Grenoble with Pierre. You remember Pierre?"

I nodded.

"My mother is very upset. Habiba needs to be with her."

"Doesn't seem fair. She was so looking forward to coming to Great Ormond Street."

Matt returned with two vases. "I'm trying to persuade Amor to stay the night so we can get really pissed," he said. "Wet the baby's head properly. Then he can stay sober for the rest of his holiday."

"Your brother!"

"I wish I could come with you. It's not fair."

"I'll see what I can smuggle in next time. How long are you likely to be in?"

"Depends. Mum and Dad are coming tomorrow. If Mum stays and the hospital's happy that everything's all right at home, they could let me out in a couple of days."

When the sister asked the visitors to leave, the baby still hadn't woken so I lifted him up, kissed his head and handed him to Matt. He stirred and gave a faint cough, his fingers dancing in the air. Matt held him carefully, afraid to move. He started to cry and Matt's arms went rigid.

"What did I do?"

"Nothing. He's probably hungry."

"He's beautiful." He handed the bundle to Amor.

Amor was more confident with the baby, obviously having

227

had more experience. He kissed him on his forehead and held him up in front of him so he could take a good look at this brand new human being.

"Well done," he said giving him back to me.

"What are you going to call him?" Matt asked.

"I haven't decided yet."

"Hurry up, I can't keep calling him *the baby*."

I felt exhausted when they left, exhausted but unable to sleep. One of the nurses came to help me feed him and, afterwards, change his nappy. It was like playing with a doll, all his needs new and exciting. I hated leaving him when I needed to go to the toilet or to wash and refused all offers of putting him in the nursery when he grew fretful in the long, dark hours of the night. It was during those hours, rocking him gently to and fro, that I decided to call him Amor. He'd been so good to me in Tunisia and his arrival in England when the baby was born seemed like fate. It was a way of saying thank you, as well as acknowledging the baby's Arab ancestry.

I'd had hardly any sleep when the grey daylight crept sluggishly into the ward, and resented being woken by the baby roaring at the top of his lungs. I tried to feed him but he was too upset to latch on. Dark green meconium leaked from his nappy onto my clean, starched bed linen and, with my hands full of baby, I didn't know what to do. A Filipino nursing auxiliary put her head round the curtain and asked if I needed help.

"Yes, please."

She took him from me and rocked him, speaking softly to him in a foreign language.

"I change his nappy then I change your bed, okay?"

"Thank you."

I followed her out of the darkened ward to the dim yellow room where the babies were washed and changed. I sat on a chair, watching her expert hands clean my baby. I could hear the build-up of the rush-hour traffic outside, while in corridors not far distant I heard the welcome chink, chink of cutlery on crockery. I was starving.

The baby settled as she tied the ribbons at the back of his cotton nightie. Then she showed me how to swaddle him, wrap him tight in the cotton blanket, to make him believe he was still safe inside the womb. He was calm but awake when she handed him back to me.

"When you had him?"

"Yesterday."

"Beautiful."

I knew she must have said it about all the babies she dealt with but I believed her that my baby was especially beautiful.

"He like his dad?"

I wished she hadn't asked. A question demands an answer. I'd been looking so hard from the moment he was handed to me, but could see no resemblance. It's impossible to tell whom a newborn baby resembles. I tried again to fit a face into his features but simply saw the face of my son, dark-haired and squashy-lipped, tiny blue eyes, clear but unseeing.

"I don't know."

She tickled him under his chin and smiled before she left the room, leaving me staring into the baby's face, still looking for traces of his father. The seeds of doubt were sown.

Amor Matthew Marshall is the name I registered him under, in a huge official building in the heart of the City of London. We call him Amatt, to distinguish between little Amor and big Amor, who's been around a lot during his holiday. I opted for a short birth certificate, giving minimum details about this new British Citizen.

My mother stayed to help me. It's been good to have her around but I've been surprised how well I'm managing. What I find really hard are the long nights when Amatt wakes at one or two in the morning and then won't settle again until about six. Sometimes my mother stays up with me, other nights she sleeps through, leaving Amatt and me to face those bleak hours alone together. I turn on the heating, make myself tea, listen to the radio, its airwaves jammed and crackling in those hours, and stare at the wall, dazed by exhaustion. Some nights I get obsessed about finding out who Amatt's father really is, feeling I should know which culture he belongs to - Celtic or Arabic. When the morning seeps in though, I wonder if it matters.

My mother sometimes comments on how much an expression of Amatt's reminds her of John, but then she'd see a resemblance where there is none, since she thinks John is his father. I think she exaggerates what she sees too, in the hope I'll tell John about the baby. I sometimes think I see John in Amatt's features, sometimes a look, half-remembered, which reminds me of Ali, but most of all I see Matt. On this my mother and I agree.

"He's just like Matthew as a baby," she says.

"How on earth can you remember?"

"He's so familiar."

The health visitor pops in from time to time, to weigh Amatt and make sure he's being looked after properly. She's younger than me and doesn't have children herself.

Amor's pleased that I called the baby after him. He's not said much but I can tell it means a lot to him. Every time he comes, he brings a little gift for Amatt.

It's hard to believe it was only a couple of days ago that Matt and I went out for a meal with him. The night before he was due to fly home. I wasn't keen on going, it would be the first time I'd left Amatt, but my mother assured me she could cope and pushed the three of us out to enjoy ourselves.

We went to an Italian restaurant in Camden Passage, so that I could be home in ten minutes if there were any problems. We were lucky to get a table. It was December 16th and most of the tables were taken up with various groups holding their Christmas parties. We had to shout to make ourselves heard over other people's merriment, even being drawn in occasionally to the party closest to us when they pulled their crackers and threw streamers.

"Christmas isn't like this at home," Amor said.

"I know. John and I didn't know what to do with ourselves last year. Mind you, you know how to celebrate New Year. Remember the meal at Sidi bou Zid?"

"I do. Austin paid."

"Earl and his expense account!"

"You know he's gone over to Shell?"

"I thought he was a company man, born and bred."

"Jeff is, not Earl. Jeff's taken Earl's place in Texas now. He still comes over to Tunisia sometimes. He wants me to go to Texas for a while."

"What do you think about that?"

"Of course, I want to go. I worked hard to get a job with an American company. I want a green card."

"What about your mother?"

"Habiba is with her. She doesn't expect me to stay at home, that's my sister's place."

Matt sucked air in sharply through his teeth. "If you want to leave this restaurant alive, I shouldn't come out with any more comments like that, mate. Not with Claire sitting next to you."

"What time's your flight?" I asked Amor.

"Not until nine. I have to check out of the hotel before midday. I've got some shopping to do."

"You can leave your stuff at my office," Matt said. "Save you lugging it around with you."

As soon as we finished our coffee I wanted to go home, anxious about Amatt. It seemed such a long time since I'd left him.

Outside Amor hailed a taxi.

"When are you coming to Tunis again, Claire?"

"I don't know. I'll have to get some money together before then."

"I'll see if I can find anything for you to do. Help you out. And bring my baby with you."

"I'm not going to leave him behind."

We kissed each other, cheek to cheek, before he got into the cab which joined the line of traffic waiting at the lights at the Angel.

30

"Claire!" My mother called out. "It's Matthew on the telephone. He wonders if you've heard anything from Amor?"

"No, why?"

"Apparently he still hasn't picked up his suitcase."

I came out of the bathroom, rubbing my wet hair and glanced at the clock. Half-past seven.

"He's cutting it a bit fine."

She handed me the receiver.

"What time did he say he'd come?" I asked Matt.

"About five. I've got to go, I'm supposed to be meeting Ciaran in Highgate in ten minutes. I don't know what to do."

"Can't you leave a note and bring his stuff here?"

"I'll have to. See you in a bit."

Matt didn't turn up till quarter to nine.

"I thought he must have picked his stuff up," I said, taking Amor's suitcase from Matt at the front door.

"Central London's seized up. There's been a bomb or something. Traffic isn't moving. He must have got stuck."

"I hope that's all. He said he was going shopping."

"He'll be all right. See you later."

It didn't feel right. I had an empty feeling in my stomach and picked up Amatt for comfort.

"Claire, are you all right?"

"Turn the news on, Mum. There's been a bomb."

The siren-like music of the Nine O'Clock News blared out, followed by the chime heralding the main news items.

"A car bomb has exploded outside Harrods, killing six and injuring many more. The IRA have claimed responsibility, confirming fears that a Christmas bombing campaign is underway. The Prime Minister has condemned the atrocity as a barbaric and cowardly act..."

I watched the pictures of ambulances, shattered windows and walking wounded wrapped in blankets, and scanned the faces on the screen for Amor's. It wasn't there.

"He must be all right," I kept muttering.

My mother noted the emergency telephone number which was given out after the news item, but the lines were constantly engaged.

"I wish there was something we could do," I said.

"I'll make some tea. Try that number again."

As I reached for the telephone, it rang.

"Hello?"

"Can I speak to Claire Marshall?"

"Speaking."

"It's Habiba - Amor's sister. There's been a bomb-"

"I know." I hoped she wasn't going to ask me to find out if Amor was all right.

"Officials from the Embassy were here this afternoon. Amor has been injured. He's in the hospital. Tomorrow, my mother and I fly to London."

"Oh God, is he badly hurt?"

Throughout the conversation, as we arranged practical details and she told me what she knew, Habiba remained stiff and formal. Apparently his legs took the worst of the blast but she also mentioned chest injuries and lacerations from flying glass.

Before I put the 'phone down I asked her how she felt.

Her voice changed. "I'm so frightened. He's in Intensive Care. He might not live. We've lost Nadia, it will kill my mother if she loses Amor too."

A couple of hours ago, just before midnight, there was a knock at the door. My mother had already gone to bed, but I couldn't sleep even though Amatt was quiet. I'd rung the hospital but they wouldn't give me any information about Amor.

233

"We're on our way home. I just wondered if he's turned up?" It was Matt, hands thrust into his jacket pockets, collar turned up against the winter chill.

"You bastard!" I screamed at the figure hovering beside Matt. It was Ciaran. "Get away from here. I never want to see you again. You and your fucking politics. Six people dead - does that make you happy? Does it? God knows how many injured and most of them, just tourists. Innocent. They've got nothing to do with the situation in Northern Ireland but you blew them up just the same."

Ciaran stood there expressionless, watching me spit out my fury. His eyes were fixed, reminding me of the way Ali had looked the night he found me in the bathroom with his gun. Freedom fighters, terrorists - labels to describe and contain the monsters we've created.

"No, Matt, Amor hasn't turned up. He's lying in the hospital fighting for his life, his legs blown away by Ciaran's bomb."

"It's not my bomb. I'm not responsible. If you're looking for someone to blame try your government." Ciaran's voice was hard and low. "Hurts, doesn't it, when someone close to you gets caught up in the violence. Welcome to the real world, Claire. It happens all the time in Belfast. Now you know how it feels."

"He's got nothing to do with the conflict. He's just a tourist. Hurt me - yes - maybe I am responsible, but why Amor? He's done nothing to you."

"It's not personal, it's strategic. To put tourists off. I'm sorry about your friend."

"Fuck off! I'm sick of your bloody rhetoric. You've got an answer for everything."

I looked at Matt, "Are you coming in or what?"

He looked at Ciaran and wavered.

"It's okay. I'll get a cab or something," Ciaran said, then turned and walked away.

I went inside and Matt followed. We slumped into chairs.

After some time Matt said, "I don't suppose I'll ever see

him again."

"I tried to warn you."

"You still don't know if he's ever done anything. You were the one who said he was all talk."

"An apologist for murderers."

"Just like you. Remember?"

I don't know anything any more. A year ago I was so certain. I had an opinion about everything and knew I was right. It's not like that any more, there are no simple answers.

I wonder how I'd feel if Ali had died killing someone else. A Jewish conscript in the Israeli army, an American tourist? Real people with families and friends, not just names in a newspaper report. Perhaps it's best for me that he died the way he did, so I don't have to judge.

If only I could be sure of things again, know who's right and who's wrong. I want someone to blame.

31

Amor's out of Intensive Care, but Habiba says he's still very ill. I can go and see him today. Apart from family, the only people they've let in to see the injured are the press. They stormed through the ward taking photos, and in yesterday's papers the tabloids had "interviews" with the victims, including Amor, but he'd spoken to nobody - the words printed were pure propaganda.

The ward's brightly lit. I can see Amor's bed, Habiba and her mother are sitting close to it.

"Hello."

His face is ashen as I lean to kiss him.

"Only two visitors at a time." The nurse bustles up officiously. "I'd turn a blind eye, only the doctor's due on his rounds."

"We'll go and get a drink," Habiba says and holds her mother's arm. She leads her out of the ward.

I don't know who looks worse, Amor or his mother.

"How do you feel?"

"Better today, but my legs hurt."

I take his hand, the one without the drip. "Can you remember what happened?"

He shakes his head. Dark hairs cover his pillow; shock is making it fall out.

"I was shopping. Looking in the windows... The next thing, people are screaming and I could see lights flashing. Someone was stroking my head, telling me it would be all right. He was crying... The next thing I remember is the hospital, a lot of noise, shouting. Everything hurt but they wouldn't give me anything for the pain, not until they'd taken X-rays and done other tests... They say I'll need operations on my legs."

"Here or in Tunisia?"

"I want to go home." He looks up at me, "Where's my baby?"

"They don't let babies in here. They think they're germ factories. You'll have to get better soon, then you can see him."

I hate hospitals. I don't know what to say. If we were in a restaurant, at work or back at the flat we'd chat easily, but sitting here watching him it's all so artificial. He's in so much pain, dipping in and out of consciousness. He's muttering something in Arabic. I feel like I'm watching him drown - if only there was something I could do to help.

There's a nurse looking at the chart at the bottom of his bed, asking if he wants more painkillers. She smiles at me, her face full of sympathy. She thinks I'm Amor's girlfriend.

Habiba's coming back. It's best if I go now.

"I'll come and see him again in a couple of days. Let me know if there's anything I can do."

She nods and kisses me goodbye.

I wish I'd brought an umbrella. This drizzle's persistent. I'm so tired, I haven't slept properly for nights, wonder if I ever will again. I love Amatt but it's nice to have a bit of a break. Perhaps I'll go home via Oxford Street, there's time to do a bit of Christmas shopping, look at the lights. Christmas bombing campaign. Maybe I'd better just go home, I need to be careful now.

There's someone coming towards me. Hands pushed into the pockets of his donkey jacket, head down against the rain. He hasn't changed at all.

"John."

"I'm glad I caught you. I thought you might have gone." Familiar voice. I want to drown in it.

He's looking at me but I can't speak. I want him to reach out and pull me to him but he's standing just out of reach.

"I need to talk to you. Shall we go for a coffee? There's a place around the corner."

Dancing on thin ice. Be careful not to say the wrong thing. Show him you've changed.

"How's Amor?"

We're walking close to each other.

"Still in a lot of pain. He's out of Intensive Care."

"I couldn't believe it was him, when I saw it in the paper. Will they let me visit?"

"Probably. Ring the hospital first."

My legs are jelly, I've got to sit down. "I'll get a table."

He nods.

I can see him from here. Watch him. He looks just the same. He's reaching into his jeans pocket for change. I gave him that jumper last Christmas; I wonder if his wearing it today means anything? I can feel the geode in my coat pocket, the one he gave me two years ago. I'll put it on the table.

"Have you still got the other piece?" I ask him as he puts the coffee down next to the hollow rock.

He shakes his head. I wish I hadn't asked.

"It's somewhere in the Irish Sea."

"That'll confuse the geologists in millennia to come."

He's smiling. God, it's good to see him smile.

"I went round to the flat this morning, to see about Amor. Your mum was there. She was holding a baby." He pauses, looks at me. "Why did you not tell me?"

What should I say? I daren't hurt him, I know he'll get up and go, but I have to tell him the truth. I look out of the window trying to find the right words. A curtain of rain throws itself against the glass. I can see nothing.

"I'm not sure who Amatt's father is."

Silence. He's concentrating on stirring his coffee. I wish he'd say something.

"Right up until he was born I thought Ali was his father, which is why I didn't tell you. I didn't want to hurt you even more."

"And now?"

"I'm not sure."

"Your mother said he was mine. I thought he was my son. I held him... You don't know whose he is?"

"He's mine. I'm the one who carried him for nine months, I'm the one who gave birth to him and I'm the one who'll spend my life looking after him."

"I'm sorry." He's taking my hand between his. I can feel his warmth. "Has it been hard for you?"

"It's been lonely...If you knew for sure Amatt was your son, would you come back?"

"Do you want me to?"

"I've missed you so much."

He pulls away from me and lights a cigarette. "I've met somebody."

I have Amatt, whatever happens I'll always have Amatt. He's the most important thing in my life. Nothing else matters.

"Alison."

"How did you know?"

"I saw Sean."

"He never said."

"I asked him not to. Is it serious?"

"It's uncomplicated, light. We have fun together. She loves me for what I am, not for what she wants me to be."

That hurts. "Do you love her?"

He's thinking, forehead wrinkled.

I ask again, "Do you love her?"

He closes his eyes and shakes his head. "No. I don't know. I want to. I want to love her the way I used to love you, but I can't. It's not there."

Used to. I will not cry. If I keep my eyes on that clock the tears will fade. It's a dirty clock, dust glued to its face with cooking oil. The hands have stopped at five past five. How many years ago? *I want to love her the way I love you, but I can't.* But that's not what he said.

I pretend to sip my coffee, but can't swallow. In the silence between us I can feel him watching me, my eyes now fixed to the table. What's he thinking?

"What went wrong, Claire? Why did you stop loving me?"

"I didn't. I lost my way and still haven't forgiven myself for that, for what I did, but I never stopped loving you. I still do. I'd give anything to have you back. It wouldn't be like it was before - I've changed so much this last year. Grown up. Things would be different this time, better. I promise."

He stubs his cigarette out onto the foil ashtray and buttons his jacket. Have I said too much or too little?

He scrapes his chair back from the table and stands up. "I have to go."

I pull on my own coat and hurry out of the café, into the rain, before he does. I turn and stop him. "Will I see you again?"

"I don't know, Claire. I've so much to think about. To work out in my own mind... It's good to see you though."

His arms are around me, strong, lifting me, holding me tight. His kisses soft and familiar. Don't let go.

He pulls away, shakes his head and turns, leaving me standing here alone. He's going back the way he came, heading towards the corner.

Please look back.